THE DREAMER'S DREAM

THE YOUNG GUARDIAN BOOK TWO

CHIA GOUNZA VANG

ISBN:

Ingrams: 978-1-953100-61-0

Amazon: 9798875924651

Cover Design: Dreams2Media

Editor: Sharona Wilhelm

For the heroes in my life. My mother, Xao Yang, and mother-in-law Chao Lor Lee, whose bravery and self-sacrifice were a source of inspiration for me. My dedicated considerate mentor, Leykn Schmatz, whose guidance and expertise had played an important role in making my writing dreams a reality. You all had shaped both my personal and professional aspirations.

TRADEMARK ACKNOWLEDGEMENTS

Roll of Thunder, Hear My Cry by Mildred D. Taylor
The Last of the Really Great Whangdoodles by Julie Andrews
Edwards
Shopko
Piggy Wiggly
Bambi
Corduroy by Don Freeman
H.C. Prange Company
ABC Weekend Specials
Alexander and the Terrible, Horrible, No Good, Very Bad Day by
Judith Viorst
Curious George
Star Wars
Disney
Tylenol
Superman
Spiderman
Magna Doodle drawing board
Goodwill

ACKNOWLEDGMENTS

I am incredibly grateful to my mentor, Leykn Schmatz, for consistently supporting my writing. They not only believed in me, but also provided encouragement, read my work, and offered valuable suggestions until we both were satisfied with the book before sending it off to my publisher. I'm fortunate to have such a remarkable mentor. Thank you for all that they have done.

Thank you to my brother, Noah Vang, for reading and sharing his insights. I would also like to express my gratitude to Chong Thao Ly, Chue Cha B Ly, Chong Neng Lee, Phoua X. Lee, Mindi Blake, and all the others who generously shared their experiences with me. Additionally, I want to extend a special thank you to Kathleen Westbrook from the Appleton Public Library for drawing a detailed map of the old library from memory, providing descriptions of the city, and sharing a list of popular children's books in the 1970s.

I am thankful for the invaluable comments and suggestions from the team at Scarsdale Publishing. They have truly shaped this book into its best form.

Finally, a heartfelt thanks to my children and husband for being there for me. Their presence and support have been my main source of motivation, courage, and strength throughout this journey.

Thanks to the Appleton School District for allowing me to use the real school names in Appleton, Wisconsin.

Local places, like parks, street names, and churches are real names of places in Appleton, Wisconsin.

NOTE TO READER

Thank you for choosing to read The Dreamer's Dream, the second book in The Young Guardian series. If you haven't yet had the opportunity to read the first book, The Illiterate Daughter, I highly recommend starting there. By embarking on this initial chapter, you will acquire a comprehensive comprehension of the story, from the war-torn landscapes of Laos to the characters' new life in America.

Chia Gounza Vang

HMONG TERMS

- Daim nyias (dai niyah) - a baby carrier, a black rectangular cloth embroidered with
- colorful textiles and sewed with a green sash at the top
- Hu plig (who plee) - a soul calling ritual
- Khawv koob (kau kong) - an art of magical healing
- Kuam (koua) - a shaman's spiritual tool made of bull horn
- Lwm qaib (lue khai) - a ritual performs at the door of the groom's house to ward off
- any evil spirits before the new bride can enter the home.
- Niam Tij (nia thee) -older sister in-law
- Paj ntaub (Pa ndau) - flowery cloth that describes appliqué, reverse appliqué, batik,
- cross stitch, and embroidery
- Tso plig (jaw plee) - A soul releasing ritual
- Ua neeb (uah neng) – shaman practice

1

America, Saturday May 20, 1978

The plane wheels screeched as our plane touched down on the runway. After my fourth flight, I recognized the sounds of landing and braking. I had memorized the words *Appleton, Wisconsin,* and picked them out of the garbled English announcements that blared through the cabin. We had arrived in our sponsor's city.

When we left the Thai refugee camp one day ago, I felt excitement and relief, but now anxiety twisted my stomach in knots. We had no family members or relatives in America. We arrived as orphans without a clan in a foreign land. I had dreamed of coming to America, but now, the very thought of immigrating to a country where we might not be welcomed or accepted gave me chills.

If I had learned some English, I might be more confident. Besides being illiterate, I was a girl. If I failed to protect and care for my three-year-old nephew Nhia, or my sixty-four-year-old mother, an amputee, I would live in shame. I would disgrace Nhia's father, Pheng, and my brother Toua. They disapproved of my taking Nhia and Mother to America, but I brought them with me anyway to pursue my dreams and hopes for a better life. Now, upon arriving, the confidence I'd felt when I stood up to Pheng and Toua disappeared.

I had a big responsibility ahead. Our new lives could be good or bad depending on whether our sponsor, the Johnson family, was compassionate.

Father, my ancestors, and Lord of Heaven, please make the Johnson family be kind to us, I prayed.

Nhia, in the seat on my right, scowled. His eyes brimmed with tears. He wanted to get out of his seat, and I'd lied to him several times, saying we were almost there.

I pulled him onto my lap, and whispered, "We're really here now."

His scowl disappeared. My mother, in the seat next to his, smiled faintly. Exhaustion lined her face. Strands of white and black hair fell across her lined face. I wouldn't allow our sponsor to see us so drained and untidy.

"Mother, move over to Nhia's seat. I need to fix your hair."

She slid over next to me. I removed the loose barrette and combed her tousled hair with my fingers, then gathered her hair at the back of her head and clipped it with the barrette. Next, I fixed my own hair.

The plane slowed and rolled to a stop. The passengers around us began to stand. I stood, stretched my legs, and sighed with relief. My legs, arms, and back were stiff and sore after the long trip.

As the passengers disembarked, I lifted Nhia to my hip, and Mother retrieved the blue tarpaulin bag from the overhead compartment, which contained the few possessions we'd brought from Thailand. We followed the stream of white people off the plane. The Johnson family would have no problems identifying us.

This airport was smaller than those at our other stops in Japan, Seattle, and Chicago. At the terminal, a few people waited. A young, tall man dressed in a yellow collared short-sleeved shirt and brown, wide-legged pants held up a paper with Mother's name, Choua Lor. The woman next to him wore a beautiful blue shirt-waist dress with a belt. She smiled at us and advanced in our direction with the man at her side. Their friendly expressions lessened my anxiety. They seemed like good people.

"Hi," said the woman.

I recognized the word from watching people on our trip.

"Hi," I replied with my only English word.

She and the man spoke. The unfamiliar words flew over my head. I pushed my frustration down and smiled to show respect. How were we going to understand each other?

The woman cradled a black handbag in one arm. With the other, she pointed to herself. "Mary."

"Miali," I said.

Her thin smile told me that I had said her name incorrectly. She dug in her bag, took out a small piece of wrinkled paper, and wrote, *Mary*.

Thank goodness for the month of education in the refugee camp, where I'd began to learn to read and write. Our native Hmong language is based off the English alphabet, and that helped me recognize her name's spelling. In Hmong, we call the letter m *mos*. I didn't know what it was called in English. Was the English language difficult to learn?

"Mary," the woman repeated.

The handsome young man watched me. Did Americans always stare like they were now, or were they staring because we were different?

Mary wrote *Peter* on the paper and pointed to the man. "Peter."

Maybe he was her son?

"*Piter*," I repeated.

She smiled. Lines creased on her forehead and her eyes crinkled at the edges. Her shoulder-length, shiny brown hair curled away from her face and gave her an attractive appearance. She was my height, so maybe not all Americans were as tall as those I had seen during our journey.

"Nou," I said. Then I pointed to Mother. "Choua."

Peter's round, blue eyes fixed on me. He smiled, showing white, shiny teeth. His long, light brown hair covered his forehead and ears. He was so tall. The top of my head reached only to his chin. My heart fluttered. I could stare at his light complexion all day. In my culture, pale appearance was preferred and considered beautiful. I lowered my gaze to stop my fluttering heart.

Peter took the tarpaulin bag from Mother, and we followed them outside. Surrounded by strange people, Nhia clung to me tightly. The hazardous trek through the jungles of Laos to Thailand had traumatized him so much that he feared people and cried easily.

Outside, the cool air brushed my face, and I squinted at my first look at America from the ground. Countless cars of various colors sat in neat rows on the gray pavement across the road, and green grasses painted the gaps between the buildings and the paved roads. I didn't see rubbish or dirt anywhere. This place was nothing like the dusty and littered refugee camp.

We followed our sponsors across the street and past many cars until they stopped at a blue car. Peter opened the back door for us. Mother got in first. I slid in beside her and put Nhia between us, then they got in up front. While Peter drove, Mary looked over her shoulder and spoke to us. Again, I smiled because it was the only way I knew to communicate. I wanted to talk with her and show her I was smart, but I couldn't. At last, she got tired of my smiles and stopped talking.

Mother rested her head on the door and dozed and Nhia hid his face against my shoulder. I gazed out the window. We stopped at a red light as cars on the other road passed through. When the light turned green, Peter drove forward. Thus, I began to learn about America. The lights controlled the flow of cars.

2

Peter turned off the busy road onto a quiet street with house after house. A man and woman walked arm-in arm on the sidewalk to the left. I marveled that they showed such open affection. In Laos, husband and wife never showed affection in public. He turned down several more quiet streets until he pulled to a stop in front of a light blue, two-story house. Across the street, a man stood in his yard with a long hose, watering his already green grass. He stared as we got out of the car, and I noticed a woman in the house next to his staring out her window at us. Were they not accustomed to seeing new people or was it Nhia, Mother, and I, with our olive-colored skin and dark hair, who were strange to them?

We faced the house in front of us. Like the house where the man was watering the grass—and every other house on the street—green grass grew in the front area, no dust to be seen. I immediately loved this clean place. The nearby houses were also mostly two-stories, and they appeared sturdy and comfortable. The quiet and peaceful surroundings convinced me that we were safe here. I breathed with ease.

Mary grabbed a box of fried chicken and buns from the front

seat, and we followed her and Peter to the left side of the house and up the driveway where a white car sat parked. An old man stared out the front window on the first story, until we were out of sight around the side of the house where we started up stairs leading to the second floor. Were we to share our home with him, Mary, and Peter?

Halfway up the stairs, Peter glanced back at me. Did I look dirty or weird? My yellow twill skirt and white collared shirt couldn't be strange because they were donated to us from the United Nations High Commissioner for Refugees (UNHCR). My cousin told me the clothes were from America, so I brought them from the camp so I could fit in with the Americans. Mother wore a sarong skirt and a floral blouse. Whatever his thoughts, I hoped he would be kind. It would be difficult to live with a family that thought we were strange.

Mary opened the door to reveal a small kitchen. She set the fried chicken and buns on a small wooden table with four chairs. Next, she led us through the open doorway down a short hallway and into a small room that featured a long, brown seat with cushions. Mother flopped down onto the cushion with a long sigh.

"Sofa," Peter said as he set our tarpaulin bag down beside the sofa. He pointed to the soft, gray floor. "Carpet."

He crossed the room to a black and brown boxy machine that sat on a stand in front of a large window overlooking the street, and said, "TV."

Peter turned the knob on the TV and immediately people appeared on the screen and were talking. He turned the knob again and the machine cut off. Peter motioned for me to try. I turned the TV on and off.

On the table next to the TV sat a notebook and a blue pen. A calendar hung on the wall beside a round clock that read three-ten p.m. I knew my numbers from my brother Toua, who taught me basic mathematics.

Mary and Peter took me down the rest of the hallway and

showed me two rooms, each with a bed. Then we went to the last room, the smallest room of all.

"Toilet." Mary pointed to an oval bowl. She turned a metal handle and said, "Faucet." Water spurted into the sink. She turned it off.

Back in the kitchen, Mary opened the tall, yellow-green rectangular box and said, "Refrigerator."

She grabbed a bottle and closed the refrigerator door. She opened the cabinet doors above the counter, took out five tall, green glasses, and set them on the counter. After filling the cups with liquid, she gave us each a cup.

I took a tentative sip and smiled. The apple juice was sweet and refreshing. Nhia quickly finished his cup. He wanted more, but I couldn't ask Mary and didn't want to take more without permission. Thankfully, Mary understood Nhia's body language and refilled his cup. While he drank his juice, she opened the drawers to show us boxes of crackers and other food. Under the sink, I couldn't help but smile when I spied more juice bottles.

Mary gave me a sheet of paper with numbers written on it and motioned for me to follow her. At the green machine hanging on the wall, she said, "Phone," and I paid close attention as she dialed the first three numbers on the paper to demonstrate. Then she pointed to the phone numbers labeled *Home* and *Johnson family*. Below the phone numbers had what I soon learned was our address, 715 ½ N Appleton Street. She handed me the keys that she had used to open the door earlier.

I stiffened in shock. Did she mean this was our house? That they lived somewhere else? I thought about the old man I'd seen in the window downstairs. His home was separate from ours. How was it possible this house was ours? I was equally excited and worried. Would we be alone in this strange new world with no one to guide us? We didn't have a car. How would we travel?

Despite the difficulties, we were fortunate to have a house. We had gone from thatch huts with bamboo walls and elephant grass roofs to a wood and concrete house that had indoor water and electricity. I no longer had to fetch water from the stream or collect firewood as I had in Laos. I had dreamed of this wonderful life.

I wanted to thank Mary and Peter, but I didn't know how to express my gratitude in English. I presented my biggest smile. Mary seemed to understand and smiled back. She opened her arms to hug me. We didn't hug in our culture. But I couldn't be rude and wanted to show appreciation, so I hugged her.

Peter handed me a sheet of paper with his name and the number nineteen, which I took to be his age. I grabbed a pen from the table and wrote *sixteen*. He smiled. On our documents, the interviewer had chosen May 24 for my birthday because we didn't know my real birthday, which meant I would turn seventeen soon. In Laos, we didn't have calendars, so my parents didn't know their children's birthdates, only the seasons in which they were born.

That evening, we ate the fried chicken and buns. The chicken was greasy but tender and juicy. I liked its firm, crisp texture. The buns were soft. I gulped down each bite, barely chewing. We finished the juice bottle. We would soon grow fat on this amazing food. Our culture preferred plump women and girls, and we were skinny as needles.

Mother napped on the sofa, and I turned on the TV. I soon grew bored by the unfamiliar language and turned it off. Nhia and I sat on the carpet, and I told him the usual folktales that I told every night.

I had helped my sister raise Nhia, so I was his second mother. He and I had grown close during our hazardous trek to freedom, especially after Der, Nhia's mother, was shot by Communist soldiers. I would raise him until he was ready to live with his father, Pheng. We hoped and prayed that Pheng could come to America soon. For the time being, I must not fail my sister. I must do everything to support Nhia, who was traumatized and needed love, patience, and caring.

Nhia wanted more apple juice, so we went to the kitchen.

Under the sink sat three bottles of golden liquid. I poured a cup and gave it to Nhia. His eyes gleamed as he took a big gulp. Then his face contorted in disgust, and he burst into tears.

Heaven! What happened? I put the cup in the sink and picked up Nhia. "What's wrong?"

He wailed. I tasted the liquid and grimaced. It was oil, not juice.

A lump rose in my throat. "I'm so sorry."

I hated myself for not checking the bottle's label, but even if I had checked it, how would I know what it said when I couldn't read? I sighed deeply. Our first day in America, and I was already failing Nhia.

Mother appeared in the doorway. "What happened?"

I frowned. "I gave him oil instead of juice. The bottles under the sink are all the same color."

"Not your fault. Why would Mary put oil with juice?"

"Maybe she forgot that we can't read."

Nhia kept crying. I put him down and grabbed another bottle. I opened it, poured a little into a fresh cup, and tasted it. The liquid was sweet. I poured half a cup and gave it to Nhia.

"It's juice this time," I said. "Drink it. It'll wash down the oil."

He emptied the cup and wiped his eyes with the back of his hands. I took Nhia to the bathroom to give him a bath. In the bathtub, I turned on a faucet. Water spurted out, wetting his feet.

"Cold," he wailed.

I turned it off and turned the other faucet on.

"Hot!" Nhia cried.

I twisted the faucet closed and pulled Nhia out of the tub. We hadn't bathed in two days, but without a bucket to mix the water, we would have to wait. Why hadn't Mary given us a bucket? How were we going to take a bath? I began to see how our new life would present many struggles. How were we going to survive in this modern, foreign land?

We went to bed at eight o'clock in the same bed, like we used to in the refugee camp. Mother and I tossed and turned. "I can't sleep," Mother complained. "I think the bed is too soft."

I agreed. I pulled the sheets from the bed and arranged them on the carpet in the living room. I gathered the pillows and blankets, and we lay down. Nhia slept soundly, but Mother and I still tossed and turned. I didn't think our problem was the mattress. We left Thailand on the twentieth and arrived in America on the same date. I didn't understand this, but maybe this strange time difference was why we couldn't sleep? I'd ask Mary to explain this when I could speak English.

3

Mother stood at the window with a slack expression and downturned mouth. She had looked out the window countless times. For four days had passed since we arrived in America, we hadn't stepped outside once. While Nhia and I enjoyed the delicious American food, mother didn't, and she grew thinner. A hollowness gripped my heart.

Today, Wednesday, would be another long, depressing day. On the second and third days of our arrival, our naps made the days bearable, but on the fourth day as we had grown accustomed to the time change and new environment, so we remained wide awake all day.

The day passed so slowly that I worried a devil may have put a curse on the sun. We felt like prisoners in our home. We didn't understand why Peter and Mary hadn't come to visit and bring us rice instead of buns and crackers.

Like mother, I had looked out the window countless times but, today, I forced myself to sit on the couch, instead. The more I looked the more depressed I became. Before coming to America, we took an oath to be good citizens, so we didn't want to break any laws. We couldn't risk deportation to Laos.

I decided to pace from the kitchen to the living room, hoping to stop the hollowness in my chest and get my blood flowing.

Finally, Mother left the window and went to the bathroom. Nhia was watching a puppet show and laughed at their antics. His smile warmed my heart and gave me hope. How nice it was to be a child, to be worry-free in a new country with adults upon whom he could rely.

"Nhia, when Grandma comes to the living room, ask her to watch TV with you," I said.

He nodded. "Yes."

A few minutes later, Mother returned to the living room.

"Auntie and Grandma, come watch TV with me," Nhia said.

Mother and I joined him on the sofa. Nhia's infectious laughter got us to laughing too.

A noise from downstairs snagged my attention.

Mother looked at me, fear in her eyes.

"You hear it too," I said.

I recognized the murmur of voices. I went to the window and looked outside, but no car sat parked in front of our house, and no one was walking along the low-lit sidewalk. We couldn't make out what the people were saying.

"Our neighbors must have company," I told Mother.

She nodded as sadness flashed across her face. "I miss Toua, *nyab*, our friends, and neighbors in the camp."

"Me too."

We longed for company. In the Thai refugee camp, we were always hungry and fearful of deportation back to Laos, but we had been surrounded by family, friends, and neighbors. Now that darkness and longing filled our hearts, I realized I had taken everyone for granted. Without human voices to cheer us and the sun to warm us, the world seemed dead.

Nhia's joy had rubbed off on us a little, but Mother didn't enjoy the show he was watching. She continued to rub her fingers, making me think of our *paj ntaub*, our story cloth, that we left behind. We believed we wouldn't need it, and I thought I would attend school and wouldn't have the time for embroidery. But now I wished very much we had brought it to help pass the time.

I wanted more than anything to attend school, to learn to read and write well. Could someone like me be a writer? If I had known how to care for my family's wounds, maybe I could have saved my father's life when Communists shot him. Der, as well, when she was shot as we raced through the rice field. Could I have saved her if I had of understood medicine? As a doctor, I could help save lives. If I worked hard, maybe I could become a writer and a doctor.

Mother rose and went to the window again. It was her fourth time, and I joined her for the second time today. Cars came and went, and the man who we had seen that first day watered his grass again. We had seen a few people occasionally walking but not today. How could Americans stay inside so much? Didn't they get bored watching TV?

I looked into Mother's sad eyes. "Mother, sit on the chair. I need to fix your hair."

"My hair is fine," she whispered.

"It looks messy, and I can pluck your gray hair." She turned from the window. "There are more grays now than before," I said.

She sat on the chair near the window. I unclipped her hair, combed it with my fingers, and found several gray hairs. I pulled them out, one by one. I had heard a woman in the refugee camp say, *"My hair turned white due to grief and stress."* After losing six children, two husbands, and an arm, Mother was fortunate to have any black hair left. A Communist's bullet tore through her forearm during our trek through Laos, and in Thailand, her arm was amputated below the elbow.

Mother's life had been difficult even before she lost her arm. She had given birth to ten children, and I was the only one still with her. We didn't know if my three half-sisters who had been left to care for their father's family were alive or dead. They hadn't been allowed to come with Mother when she married my father. I hoped they were alive.

I had promised my mother I would take care of her as a son would. As a girl, I doubted my ability, but so far, I had done the best I could to care for her.

"Mother, you don't look well. Are you in pain?" I asked.

She sighed. "No pain. I'm thankful for this house, but I feel like a prisoner." She paused. "Don't worry about me. I'll get used to it."

"We must learn to adjust to this new place and culture."

"I wouldn't have survived without you and Nhia," she murmured.

"We survived our trek through the jungle," I said. "We can easily overcome this new adjustment. Once I learn English and can drive, our lives will be better."

"I am hopeful because I have you and Nhia." Mother spoke barely above a whisper.

I had to find a way to ease her pain and thought of the man watering his grass. I went to the window and saw he was now sitting on a chair in his porch enjoying the fresh air. Why couldn't we do the same? I went to kitchen and tentatively opened the door. Fresh air washed over me, and my heart soared. Maybe we could just sit on the landing.

I hurried to the living room. "Mother, Nhia, come with me."

Nhia, always a good boy, jumped to his feet and hurried to my side. Mother gave me a questioning look. I smiled, wanting this to be a surprise. She rose and I led them to the kitchen. Mother halted and looked at me, eyes wide.

"We can stand just on the landing," I told her. "The air is wonderful."

Nhia pulled free of my hand and ran toward the door. I chased him and caught up with him at the threshold.

"You must be careful," I said. "You don't want to fall."

We stepped outside and I thought I had never felt anything so wonderful as the sun beating down upon my face. Nhia grasped the wood railing and looked out over the yard.

"I want to play," he said.

My heart fell. I should have known a little boy wouldn't be satisfied standing at the top of the stairs.

"We must first ask Mary and Peter if we're allowed," I said. "Then we'll play."

His little brow furrowed in uncertainty, then he said, "All right, Auntie. Can I go back and watch TV?"

I laughed. "Yes."

He went back to the living room, and Mother stepped outside with me. She closed her eyes and turned her face up toward the sun. I did the same and breathed deep of the wonderful fresh air.

The phone shrieked. I jerked my eyes open and spun to face the door as Mother cried out in surprise. Had someone reported us for going outside? Surely, it wasn't wrong just to stand at the top of the stairs? Nhia raced into the room, eyes wide, and I lunged into the kitchen in time to catch him before he ran out the door. Mother hurried inside and I gently eased Nhia to her as the phone rang again.

I crossed to the phone and, with a shaky hand, picked up the receiver. "Hi."

"Hi." I recognized Mary's voice, but I didn't understand anything she said. After a moment, she hung up.

"Who was it?" Mother asked.

"Mary. I don't know what she wants."

I closed the door, and we went to the living room and watched the TV.

At six o'clock, Mother looked out the window again.

"They're here!" she cried.

I hurried to join her. Mary and Peter walked toward the house, each carrying full plastic bags. Finally!

I reached the kitchen and opened the door. Peter and Mary entered and placed several small bags on the kitchen table and a huge black bag on the floor. Mary hugged me. Her rosy scent and warm arms made me breathless. Peter opened his arms to hug me, but I backed away. I hated to be disrespectful, but hugging a man wasn't proper in our culture. He smiled tightly and averted his eyes as I lowered my gaze. Did Peter hate me now? Would he understand I couldn't hug him?

As I crossed to the table, I found oranges, bananas, more bread, a bag of candies, and some used clothes in the bags. Although I was hoping for rice instead of bread, I smiled broadly to show my appreciation. Mary and Peter smiled in understanding and my tension eased.

I motioned for Mary to follow me to the bathroom. I turned on the hot water, touched it with my hand, shook off the water, and frowned. After a few seconds, she seemed to understand. She turned on both faucets at once, felt the water, and gestured for me to put my hand beneath the stream. The temperature was just right. Then she turned a metal knob between the faucets, and water sprayed from the showerhead above our heads. Why hadn't I noticed that knob? The shower operation seemed simple, but without experience, I hadn't understood. I had so much to learn. Common sense to Americans wasn't common sense to me.

We returned to the living room, where Mary and Peter prepared to leave. I needed to tell them that we needed rice. I got the notebook and pen from the carpet where I'd been teaching Nhia and drew tiny ovals for rice and demonstrated eating. Mary and Peter looked confused, then slowly nodded. I hoped they understood me and would bring rice the next time they came.

They smiled at me. I hesitated, I wanted to go to school, but how did I explain that? I ran my fingers through my hair, wondering if this was what it was like to be deaf and unable to communicate.

I grasped Mary's hand and led her to the window. Peter joined us. I frowned deeply to show them I was sad about staying home. Then I demonstrated writing with my pen and paper. I smiled to show them I would be happy if I were allowed to attend school. Mary and Peter exchanged dialogue. Then Mary spoke to me and patted me on the shoulder, which I took to mean she understood. I hoped they would let me go to school soon. I had left my brother and Pheng behind to pursue my education, not to be locked in a house.

4

On the calendar, today was Saturday. I had been marking off each day, and we had been in Appleton for a week. We had felt the sun only the one day we ventured out onto the landing. I should have asked Mary and Peter if it was okay for us to go out onto the steps, but I had been so startled when the phone rang the day we did go outside that the question had fled my brain. In Laos, we worked outside every day as farmers. Being shut inside was torture. I couldn't be a coward. The weather was nice outside, so I opened the door and let the fresh afternoon air come into the kitchen.

Nhia came into the kitchen. "Can I have juice?"

I took out the apple juice from the refrigerator, then poured some into a cup and handed it to him. A child's squeal jerked my attention toward the open door. I went to the door and discerned children's happy cries. I scanned the yards around me but didn't see the children.

Nhia came up beside me. "I want to play."

"I know," I said. "Soon."

The next time we saw Mary and Peter, I would find a way to ask them if we could go outside. I closed the door and returned to the living room with Nhia, where Mother stood by the window and talked to herself, as she so often did these days. Sometimes, she sang sad traditional songs that brought tears to my eyes. The longer we stayed isolated the more our mental health deteriorated. I prayed that Peter and Mary would take us shopping or even just out for a drive, any place to leave this house.

Nhia and I sat on the carpet, and I taught him numbers.

After a few minutes, Mother called from the window, "Several cars have pulled up and Mary, Peter, and other people are coming up. They have more bags."

We hurried to the kitchen, and I opened the door.

Peter reached the door first, carrying a brown paper bag. Another woman I didn't know stood behind him.

"Hi," he said with a smile.

He looked handsome in his light blue shirt and brown shorts that revealed muscular legs.

"Hi," I replied shyly.

Peter pulled a small clear bag out of the brown bag he carried and showed it to Mother and me. I caught my breath seeing rice through the clear bag. I smiled with teary eyes. Mother smiled too. He entered the kitchen, followed by a young woman carrying a box and a man carrying an infant. They were Hmong. My jaw dropped. We weren't alone.

"Hi," the young woman said in Hmong. "I'm Mai Lee. I'm your translator." She gestured to the man. "This is my husband Phia and our one-month-old son, Michael. We gave him an American name."

So, they had assimilated to their new country. Mai was shorter than I, with ear-length, curly hair. Her white blouse, which was tucked in at the waist of her long, black skirt, brightened her olive skin.

"Hello," said Phia. "Nice meeting your family." He was an average-height Hmong man with black hair parted nicely to the side.

Mother flushed with excitement. "I can't believe it! I thought we are the only Hmong family in this city."

"There are a few Hmong families here. You're not alone." Mai handed Mother the box. "It's a rice cooker."

"Thank you," Mother cried. "I've been wanting rice. You know what we need."

Joy, relief, and a sense of security overwhelmed me. Mary and a man about her age joined us. Mai and Mary exchanged dialogue.

Mai pointed to the man and said, "This is Tom, Mary's husband."

"Hi," said Tom.

He seemed nice and was as tall as Peter. Both had light brown hair.

"Hi," I replied.

More people arrived and Nhia clutched my leg tightly as they welcomed us to America. Some of them placed food on the table, and others added to the pile of colorful wrapped boxes on the floor. Nhia began to cry. I picked him up and bounced him on my hip. A man in a black tunic extended a hand toward me. We shook hands. Lines marked between his brows, and his eyes were friendly.

"This is Father Dan," Mai said. "He's the priest at Peter's church, and he's in charge of overseeing the refugee families that the church sponsors. Peter's family volunteered to care for your family."

I realized that Mai could teach me to thank people.

"How do you say 'thank you' in English?" I asked.

"Thank you," Mai said slowly.

I wouldn't remember. "Mother, can you get my notebook for me?" I asked.

Mai and Father Dan spoke as Phia excused himself and his son to the living room. I frowned in confusion. In the old country, a wife always carried her child while her husband conversed, but he had taken charge of their child while she did the talking. Did he not speak English?

Mother returned and handed me the notebook, then I gave it to Mai.

Nhia began to cry again, but I ignored him and said to Mai, "Can you write 'thank you' for me and help me say it?"

Mai wrote *thank you* in English and wrote *teeb khia* in Hmong but then crossed off *khia* and replaced it with *q*.

"This is the letter q in English." She pointed to *teeb q*. "You would say, 'Thank you.'"

"Thank you," I tried.

"Good!" she cried.

Father Dan's eyes sparkled.

"Thank you," I said to him.

He nodded. Nhia held me tighter and wailed. Father Dan slipped away to join the others in the living room. Mary and a few women set the table with the food they had brought.

Nhia embarrassed me, but yelling at him would only make his crying worse, so I took him to the bedroom. Mai followed. We sat on the bed, shushing Nhia until he calmed down.

"What are these people doing here?" I asked.

Mai caressed my shoulder. "They're here to welcome your family. Although your birthday has passed, they want to celebrate it today."

"My birthday?" I gaped. "But we don't celebrate birthdays, and May 24 is just a date the interviewer put on the form. Why celebrate?"

"A birthday is very important to Americans. They celebrate their birthdays every year. I heard you turned seventeen."

I couldn't believe it. These people cared about me and my family.

"Does your husband speak English?" I asked.

"Yes, but not as well as I do." She smiled. "It must seem odd that I'm doing all the talking while he cares for our child. He's a wonderful man and has adjusted quickly. He also helps me cook and does chores."

Someone knocked on the door, and Mai jumped up and opened it. A woman said something to her, and Mai smiled, then turned to me. "They're ready to celebrate your birthday."

"Nhia will cry again," I said.

"Let him cry."

In the kitchen, Mai pointed to a rectangular box covered in white cream with blue writing on top. "That's a cake. The writing says 'Welcome' and 'Happy birthday.'"

A cake? I thought it was just a box. The more I learned, the stupider I felt. Mai opened the box and I gasped. The cake was so beautiful, I couldn't halt the tears. Mai gave me a napkin to wipe my eyes. Mother took the crying Nhia from me, and they disappeared down the hall.

The group began singing. Everyone watched me as if I was a princess. I felt valued and embarrassed at the same time. The pleasant song calmed me. I loved it.

After they finished singing, we ate hotdogs, hamburgers, potato salad, potato chips, and fruit. The Americans seemed to hiss when they spoke to each other. I picked up words such as *yes, no, I, you,* and *okay*. I wondered why they hissed so much with the snake sound.

Mai asked me to cut the cake, but I refused because I didn't know how. She cut it and served me the biggest piece. I chewed slowly with my eyes half closed, enjoying the waves of pleasure the sweet, spongy morsel sent through my body. If not for Peter staring at me, I would have asked for a second piece. He seemed to always be watching me, and my cheeks warmed with embarrassment. What did he expect from a refugee who had never attended school and had just arrived in America?

Mai handed me a white envelope and gestured for me to open it. I pulled out two five dollar bills that looked similar to Thai paper money, except they were green.

"My gift for you," she said. "I figured you would want to buy something."

I smiled. "That's so thoughtful of you. Thank you."

"You're welcome. Mary will take you to the grocery store and laundromat tomorrow after church. They work on weekdays, so you'll see them mostly on the weekends."

Now I understood why they had left us alone for a week—and probably why we had seen so few people on the street. Most Americans must work during the week. My heart grew heavy at the prospect of staying inside every week until Sunday. Being without a car was like being without legs. We were prisoners in our home.

"The other gifts are for your mother and Nhia," Mai said. "They can open theirs later."

I opened my presents to discover new clothes, hair accessories, shampoos, and jewelry. Tears sprang to my eyes, and I quickly dabbed at them with a napkin.

"We have one more present," Mai said. "I think it's very special. Peter's present to you is tutoring you on Tuesday and Thursday every week from five to six, starting next week."

Peter grinned broadly. My heart raced. How could I learn from such a handsome man? Heaven, I would be looking at him the whole time and embarrass myself to death. I couldn't let him see my ignorance.

I looked down at the floor. "It's very nice of him, but I want to go to school."

"School will be over in two weeks, so you'll have to wait until fall," Mai said. "Peter graduates high school this year. He can help you prepare for next year."

School was almost over? I bemoaned the timing of our arrival.

I leaned close to Mai and said in a low voice, "I feel more comfortable with a woman teaching me."

"Peter wants to teach you," Mai said solemnly.

His kindness was extraordinary. How could I overcome my diffidence and ignorance? "I prefer a Hmong, so I can communicate."

She nodded. "True. I'd love to tutor you, but I can't."

Oh heavens, I was imposing upon her. "I understand, you have a baby. How did you learn English?"

"I learned English in Laos, and I've been here for two years. When you talk to the Americans, make eye contact with them to show courtesy. This is their culture."

So, this was why Peter and Mary always looked me in the eye when they spoke. I looked at Peter. "Thank you."

A smile shone in his blue eyes. My heart melted.

Peter spoke. His words were like the wind, flying fast over my head. Couldn't Americans speak more slowly? Mai translated that he couldn't wait to teach me English on Tuesday. He spoke some more. Mai explained that Peter's church paid for our first month's rent and that he had started our application for the Aid to Families with Dependent Children (AFDC) program, a federal government program that provided financial assistance to needy families.

Peter and Mai spoke, and Mai explained that we qualified for $310 a month starting in July. He would take us to sign the necessary forms at the welfare office on Tuesday. Until we received the government assistance in July, we would continue to receive food vouchers from the church. We would then pay our own rent of $110 per month, as well as pay for our food, clothes, and other expenses. We qualified for the program because Nhia and I were underage, and Mother was an amputee. The knowledge of our financial supporters helped me understand and appreciate the people involved in our survival. The Johnson family were taking such good care of us.

Mai pressed a piece of paper with her phone number into my hand. "If you need anything, call me."

"Mai, tell everyone that this is my first birthday celebration and I love it. I feel so special."

Mai translated for me, and the adults moved toward me with open arms to give a hug. A wave of anxiety washed over me, and I took a step back from the group.

Mai sensed my awkwardness. "Hug them. It's their culture for caring. They love and care for you."

The men frightened me. I'd never hugged a man before, not even my father. I must show my appreciation and would try hugging the women.

"I'll hug the women only," I said quietly.

Mai spoke and the men stepped back and I hugged the women. Eventually, everyone left, and only Mai and Phia remained.

"Mai, can we go outside to get some fresh air during the time Peter and Mary aren't here?" I asked.

"Yes. Just don't wander too far. You might get lost."

I sighed in relief. "We'll sit on the stairs outside. Maybe walk on the walkway near the house and go to the backyard."

"Perfect," Mai said. "Now we have to go."

"Come back to visit when you have time," Mother and I called after her and Phia as they descended the stairs with their baby.

"We will," Mai said, and they disappeared around the house.

Mother and I watched out the window as Mai and Phia drove away, wondering when we would see them again. Although we weren't related by blood, as Hmong, our bond was forged through our shared cultural traditions. Mai and Phia's existence in this foreign place gave me a sense of security, and the warm celebration had eased my anxiety.

5

E arly on Tuesday, we woke and dressed in preparation for Peter to take us to an office to sign the paperwork for our government assistance. He arrived at seven-thirty a.m., dressed in navy shorts and a gray T-shirt. His bright eyes and enthusiasm put me at ease, but I wished I could communicate with him.

I made eye contact with him. "Hi."

"Hi," he replied.

He spoke more, but the foreign words flew over my head. I could only smile, and we went to the living room. When Nhia saw Peter, his eyes widened, and he ran to Mother, who sat on the sofa.

"It's all right," I told Nhia. "He's here to help us. He's a good man. We're going outside."

Nhia shook his head. I picked him up, and we followed Peter to his car outside. The cool air kissed my skin, and the fragrant smell of grass filled my nose. How fortunate we were to be in this wonderful place.

Nhia pressed his face against my shoulder. Peter opened the car door for us, and we crowded into the back seat. Nhia wouldn't let go of me, so I kept him on my lap. The car made a vroom sound and Nhia squeezed me tight.

"It's all right," I whispered, and held him close.

We passed more houses and two red lights, then big concrete buildings of various shops loomed before us. Through the huge glass window of a two-story building stood three figures dressed in dull colored clothes. Beyond that, racks of clothes filled the shop. Cars of different colors parked alongside the streets and the stream of cars on the road looked like an army of ants. How I wished I could read the signs, street, and shop names.

We stopped at a three-story, concrete building with high ceilings and many rooms. I carried Nhia and assured him he was safe, but he kept his face buried in my shoulder. The few people we met smiled at us as Peter led us to a room filled with beautiful wall decorations and air that smelled of rain. What a warm, cozy, and comfortable room! What did I need to do to get a job in an office like this? Would I have such an opportunity?

A lady with wavy, brown hair greeted us from behind a shiny wood desk. She and Peter spoke. Then she pulled a sheet of paper from the pile on her desk and pointed to a line and motioned for Mother to sign her name. Mother had signed papers in Thailand, so she knew what to do. She took a long while to sign her name in English, and the letters looked crooked, but the lady didn't seem to mind.

As we were leaving, I said, "Thank you."

The lady smiled. Happiness swelled within my chest. This was a wonderful country with accepting people.

We left the building, and I lifted Nhia into my arms as we headed down the sidewalk toward where Peter's car was parked at the corner. A man and woman approached and stared as they passed. The man said something in a low voice to the woman and Peter frowned. Nhia gripped my neck tighter and I glanced back to find the man looking over his shoulder at us.

Once back in the car, Nhia still clung to me. Peter drove back home by the same route we'd taken. He glanced in the mirror at Nhia, and I realized Peter was being quiet in an effort to lessen Nhia's anxiety. What a kind person.

He dropped us off, and I thanked him. He said some words I didn't understand, then held up five fingers and I realized he was saying he would return that afternoon at five to tutor me. My first lesson would be today! I smiled and showed all my teeth. He smiled back, then left.

In our lonely house, I wrote letters to Pheng and Toua about our new life. I didn't worry them with how lonely we were. In Pheng's letter, I told him Nhia loved American food, playing with his toys, and watching TV. I asked him to come to America quickly so Nhia could have a male role model in his life. I folded the letters and put them in the envelopes I brought with me from Thailand.

As promised, Peter returned at five o'clock. With a smile, he handed me a tote bag full of books.

Tears prickled my eyes. "Thank you."

His eyes danced and he smiled. We sat at the table. He smelled fresh, and my pulse quickened. He was my teacher. I couldn't allow him to distract me. Other handsome men had distracted me before, but I had stayed on course.

Peter pulled a book from the bag. He pointed at each word on the front of the book, and said slowly, "The Little Golden ABC."

The first page had the letters *A* and *a* with paintings of an apple, airplane, and other words that began with *A*. He taught me how to say each letter in the English alphabet. With the pictures, I grasped the letters quickly. He wrote the letters in my notebook from A to Z and sang the alphabet for me. His charming voice pleased me. Then he gestured for me to sing with him. I started to refuse, then stopped. I had led my family to safety through the jungles in Laos. This was just another challenge I had to face. I sang along with Peter. His warm smile when we finished rewarded me beyond words.

He pulled out another book and read the title, *500 Words to Grow On*.

The cover had pictures of dogs, a pumpkin, a bird, a hotdog, and other objects. Each page featured different words with colored pictures: house words, kitchen words, food words, and many others.

I pointed at each picture. Peter said each word, then I repeated it. He waited patiently while I wrote the pronunciation in Hmong to study later. Writing the pronunciations took a lot of time, and I worried they weren't accurate. A family in the refugee camp had a tape recorder, and I wished I had one to record Peter's reading. How to communicate that I needed a tape recorder? I motioned to the paper where I drew a rectangle. Inside the rectangle, I drew a circle with dots for the speaker and a square for the part to insert a cassette.

Peter studied my drawing. Finally, understanding dawned in his eyes, and he said, "Yes."

After we worked on four books, Peter taught me simple sentences, such as, *My name is Nou. I am a girl. I have a mother. I want food.* And *You are welcome.* His handwriting of measured block letters was as beautiful as my father's. How could I print letters as beautiful as theirs?

At last, he checked his watch, the time was seven-ten p.m. I had kept him longer than the six p.m. scheduled time. He wrote *I have to go* and said the words slowly. I wasn't sure if it was my familiarity with his voice or I that was learning English, but I heard less hissing when he spoke.

He wrote *Bye. See you on Thursday* and repeated the written words.

Oh, how I wished he would stay and teach me more, but he had a life.

I motioned for him to follow me to the living room, where I gave him the letters for Pheng and Toua and the five-dollar bill Mai gave me. He took the letters but refused the money. My heart filled with gratitude.

6

On Thursday, June first, our thirteenth day in America, Peter arrived at five p.m. with a brand-new tape recorder. Happiness burst inside me as he removed the tape recorder from the box and inserted a new cassette. Before he began recording, I presented him with my notebook page of the words and sentences I had been practicing.

"Me say," I said.

Peter nodded. "Okay."

"My nā is Nou," I read, and turned to Peter for approval.

"Good job."

He underlined *name* and said, "Nām."

I repeated, "Nām."

He gave me a thumps-up. I had said the word wrong. This was why I needed the tape recorder to listen to his voice.

Next, I read, "Fōō, people, boy, house, vôdər...."

Peter didn't correct me, but I knew I hadn't said most of the words accurately. He smiled and raised his hand toward me with an open palm. With his free hand, he grasped my hand, sending sparks through me, and brought my palm to his open palm. We gently slapped our open palms.

"High five," he said.

"High five," I whispered.

We practiced it again. My heart pounded when our hands made contact. He explained and drew smiling faces to show that this was a celebration. His excitement boosted my self-esteem. If I had magic power, I would stop time to keep him with me forever to teach me.

Peter opened the book, *500 Words To Grow On*, to the "People" page and turned on the recorder. He pointed to *father* and said, "Faathər".

"Faathər," I repeated.

I was beginning to understand the English language and for the first time my dream of going to school to become a writer and doctor seemed possible. We were having so much fun that seven-thirty came too soon.

Peter spoke slowly, "I love teaching you."

"You gu teacher. Thank you."

"You are a good teacher," he corrected.

"You are a good teacher," I repeated.

"Good job. You can also say 'You're a good teacher.'" I frowned, and he explained how some words are put together as *contractions*. He spent another twenty minutes explaining contractions, then left.

Peter surprised me on Friday evening. He brought us hamburgers, French fries, soda, and ice cream. Nhia cried when he saw Peter, so he and Mother ate in the living room while Peter and I sat at the kitchen table.

"How was your day?" Peter asked through a mouthful of hamburger.

"Fun. Busy," I replied.

"Fun? How?"

"Study." I pointed to the recorder among the books and note-books on the kitchen table.

The corners of his mouth turned upwards. "Studying alone isn't fun."

"For me, yes," I said. "Why you here?"

He wrote the word *inspire* in my notebook of new words and illustrated a girl and boy with smiling faces and wrote *teacher* for the boy and *student* for the girl. Then he wrote, *You inspire me. You are cool and amazing,* then read the sentences.

I smiled. "Thank you."

Once we finished our food, Peter recorded himself reading the book *Frog and Toad Are Friends*. The story, *A Swim* brought back memories of our hazardous trek from Laos to Thailand. I cringed at the horrifying images that swirled in my head.

Peter paused the recorder. "Are you okay?"

I shook my head and grabbed my notebook. I sketched stick people trapped in a jungle surrounded by enemies with guns, then I wrote *hungry* and *hurt* next to the stick people. I drew two wavy parallel lines indicating the Mekong River. Peter waited patiently as I told him my story through my crude drawings. I wished I could draw better, but my parents gave me no talents beyond a caring heart and a desire to learn.

By the river, I illustrated plastic ring tubes and wrote *bad,* and below the stick people who waited at the river I wrote *no swim, no canoe, two days, no food, or water.* I drew a stick girl with shoulder length hair, a sad face, and huge raindrop tears.

Tears welled in Peter's eyes. He pulled me close, and for the first time I hugged a man. At last, I pulled back.

"Are you ok?" Peter asked. "Would you like to stop?"

"No. Read, please," I said.

He nodded and began reading again. We finished the remaining books in the tote bag, and I thought how my father and sister Der would be proud of me.

That night, I read *Frog and Toad Are Friends* to Nhia, and he loved it as much as I did. He learned English quickly from watching TV and from my reading to him. Still, I told him Hmong stories, so he would know both languages.

Over the weekend, I taught Mother a few words, but she didn't retain them well. I guessed her old age, stress, and depression hindered her ability to learn.

The tutoring sessions, the TV, and the cassette of Peter's reading improved my English skills tremendously. I called Mai to translate difficult words.

Like Frog and Toad, I felt lucky to have Peter and Mai. My grandmother had blessed me before her last breath, and I believed her blessing had brought the Johnson family into our lives.

7

Toward the end of our tutoring session on Tuesday, Peter said, "My graduation is Thursday, June eighth. I would like you to attend the ceremony. Will you come?"

Graduation and *ceremony* were among my new vocabulary words, and I realized Peter had taught me the words so I would understand his invitation. I felt honored, but fear tightened my belly. A good Hmong girl needed a chaperone to appear in public with a man. Nhia and Mother couldn't come because Nhia would do nothing but cry. Additionally, I was uneducated and fresh from a refugee camp. My awkwardness could embarrass and shame me and the Johnson family. I was curious about the ceremony though, and I didn't want to disappoint Peter after all he and his family had done for us.

He waited patiently for my response, and his big, blue eyes glimmered. What should I do? I stared at the books on the table.

"What's wrong?" he asked.

"Mother not happy I go wi boy."

"Your mother doesn't allow you to go with a boy in public?" he asked.

I nodded.

"Why? Is it your custom?"

"Yes," I said in perfect English.

"In America, it's ok for girls to go out with boys in public. I hope your mom lets you come."

America was my home now. I had to push my shyness aside and convince my mother to let me go.

"Okay. I go."

Peter's mouth quirked. "Thank you. My family will be there."

"What I vear?"

"What do you wear?" He spoke the words slowly so I would understand.

I nodded.

"Let's see what you have."

I led him to our bedroom closet and showed him the four used dresses I owned. Peter examined each one carefully, then removed the yellow dress with a yellow belt, and handed it to me.

"I think you'll look nice in this. Try it on."

I went to the bathroom to change. The dress felt a little tight around my arms and waist. I examined myself in the mirror. The dress fitted perfectly on my thin body. I was surprised how much I liked it.

The half-open bathroom door squeaked. My eyes flew to the image of the opening door in the mirror and Peter, as he stuck his head into the room. He smiled. My pulse accelerated. In Hmong culture, men didn't come invade a girl's privacy. Yet, I had brought him into my bedroom.

His expression softened. "I think you would look nice with your hair down."

Making eye contact with Peter always made me nervous. Those blue eyes, unblemished complexion, and white teeth captivated me. I wondered if attraction was the reason eye contact was considered disrespectful in my culture.

I released my barrette clip and combed my hair with my fingers.

"Wow," he whispered. "You have beautiful silky hair and big, round eyes."

I averted my eyes. It felt weird *and* good having a man stare at me. Was this the American way or was it Peter's way of showing desire?

"With makeup on, you'll be the prettiest girl at the graduation," he said. "I'll have my mom put makeup on you before the ceremony."

I faced him. "What mā up?"

"Māk up," Peter corrected. "Make sure to include the k sound."

"Māk up," I said slowly, looking at him for approval.

"Yes. Good job."

I released a breath. Every new word was a challenge.

"What is a good way to explain makeup?" He held up a finger. "Be right back."

A few minutes later, he returned with a thin book and said, "I found my mom's magazine in my car." He turned to a page with a beautiful woman and pointed to her flawless skin and huge eyes with long eyelashes.

"Makeup makes women more beautiful," Peter said.

The beautiful women weren't natural? What would I look like with makeup?

"I need makeup to go?" I asked.

He shrugged. "No, but you'll love it."

I wanted to try the makeup but had no money. Being illiterate made me feel stupid. But I could live with that because I could learn and grow with wisdom. Being poor, however, made it impossible to live life.

"Do you have shoes to go with the dress?" he asked.

What kind of shoes did I need? I didn't have good shoes or matching shoes. This was more complicated than I thought.

We dug through the shoe box and found a pair of black sandals. I put them on, but they engulfed my feet.

"My mom is about the same height as you. Her shoes might fit you. I'll have her bring a pair or two," he said.

"Okay."

The next day, Mary brought two pairs of shoes, but they were too small.

"We'll go shopping for makeup and shoes," Mary said slowly.

I shook my head. "I have no money."

She patted my shoulder. "Don't worry. Peter gave me money to take you shopping."

I hated the idea of them spending money for luxury items for me. But Peter wanted me to look good for his graduation. And I wanted to please him.

"Okay." I nodded. "Thank you. My mother and Nhia go?"

"Yes."

Mary took us to Shopko, a giant store compared to Piggly Wiggly. When we walked by the toy section, Nhia and Mother stopped to browse. Mary and I continued to the makeup section.

She studied the foundation shades, pulled out a bottle, and held it to my cheek.

"This one matches your olive skin tone. What do you think?"

"I don't know."

"I think it might work. We'll try it."

She put the foundation in the cart, and we continued down the aisle to another section. Mary studied my face, picked up a flat case of pink powder and another case of blue and purple powder and held them to my cheek and eyes. I had no idea what she was doing, but it seemed she knew what would make me beautiful.

"These colors will look good on you." Mary smiled.

I smiled back. "You kind. Thank you."

Mary grabbed more items and dropped them in the cart. It was a good thing she didn't ask my opinion anymore because I had none. I couldn't wait to try the makeup.

We went to the shoe section, and Mary picked a few shiny dress shoes for me to try on. After trying them, we determined I was size seven. Since my dress was yellow, Mary thought that silver shoes would match better than black or red. I settled on a three-strap, open-toe sandal with a low heel.

At the checkout, Mary paid for my items while I paid for Nhia's chocolate bar. I couldn't believe my good luck in spending the afternoon shopping with Mary. This must be what it was like to shop with a sister or a girlfriend.

Graduation day arrived and Mary arrived at three p.m. to help me apply the makeup. When she was done, she took me to the bathroom mirror. The beautiful girl in the mirror looked like a stranger to me. Her hair was parted evenly at both sides of her long face. Gray eyeliner and blue eyeshadow emphasized her round eyes. Her pink cheeks and pink lips brightened her face. I couldn't believe that makeup could transform a person so much.

"You're beautiful," Mary said.

I flushed. "Thank you."

I walked to the living room to show Mother.

Mother's eyes twinkled. "I love your new look."

"Auntie Nou?" Nhia stared at me.

I smoothed his hair. "I can't take you and Grandma with me. You be a good boy for her. I'll be back soon."

"Okay," he whispered.

He was a sweet boy and had his father's slender nose. He would grow up to be a handsome man like Pheng.

Mary took two pictures of me, then took two of me and my family. Outside, she took more pictures of me. We arrived at West High School to find the parking lot half filled with cars. We went to a giant room called a gym. Two sets of bleachers sat on the sides with a stage at the far end and rows of chairs arranged nicely on the floor facing the stage. We sat on the first row of bleachers with other people who were already there. Mary explained that the school system consisted of grades K-6, which was elementary; grades 7-9, which was junior high; and grades 10-12, which was high school.

"A student must have good grades to go onto college," Mary said.

I frowned. "What käli?"

"After high school, a student goes to college, a higher education."

I wanted to go to college. I wanted the highest education available. Would this be possible?

More people arrived and found their seats.

Mary greeted a woman her age and introduced me, "This is Nou Vang. Our church sponsored her family from Thailand. This is her third week in Appleton."

The woman gave me a long stare, then said, "Does she speak English?"

"A little," Mary said.

"Hi. Nice meeting you," the woman said loudly. "How do you like Appleton?"

"Good," I said.

"Welcome to Appleton." She gave me a tight-lipped smile.

I nodded. "Thank you."

As more of Mary's friends arrived, she continued to introduce me. Their loud conversations brought attention to me. I was the only Asian person in a sea of white faces. My stomach clenched with anxiety.

Mary began to wave at someone, and I spotted Peter and Tom in the crowd to our left. Mary waved them over. Peter's blue gown made his eyes seem even bluer, and an orange sash hung over his shoulders. He carried a blue cap with a yellow tassel in his hand. When would it be my turn to wear such a gown?

Peter smiled. "You look gorgeous." He turned to Mary. "Mom, take a picture of us."

Peter put his cap on and gestured for me to stand next to him. He pulled me close, and his clean, fresh scent surrounded me. My pulse quickened.

"Smile," Mary said.

After I posed with Peter, he took pictures of Mary, Tom, and me together. As Peter snapped the last picture, a woman in a cap and gown with long, brown hair the color of a coconut shell stopped beside us.

Her eyes fixed on me. "Peter, who's she?"

"Her name is Nou," he replied. "My family sponsored her family from the refugee camp in Thailand."

Her red lips stretched in an obligatory smile. I lowered my gaze. She was very beautiful. I now understood why Peter wanted me to wear makeup, and I appreciated it. If I hadn't worn makeup, I would have hidden in the bathroom.

"Hi, I'm Susan," she said. "Welcome."

Showing respect, I made eye contact with her.

"Thank you." My voice came out softer than intended.

"Nice meeting you."

Though her words were nice, her eyes betrayed jealousy. I suddenly wished I hadn't come, but I replied in an even voice, "Me too."

Her eyes shifted to Peter.

"Congratulations, Peter. We did it." She smiled broadly.

"Yeah, congratulations to you too," he replied.

"Thanks." She looked across the bleachers, and said, "My grandma's here," then walked away.

"Peter, she's your friend?" I asked.

"Ex-girlfriend," he said. "She's going to college, and I'm not, so we broke up."

Before I could respond, a redhaired girl in a graduation gown stopped beside us. She looked at me from head to toe. My insecurity further tightened the knot in my stomach.

"Peter, you two look so cute together," she said. "Let me get a picture of you."

Instinct urged me to decline, but Peter said, "Okay," and leaned close, as she snapped the picture.

"What's your name?" she asked me.

"Nou."

She tipped her head to one side, a slight smirk on her freckled face. "What did you say?"

"It's foreign," said Peter. "It sounds kind of like the word *you*, replace y with n."

"Oh." Her gaze shifted to Peter and her expression softened. "Congratulations."

"Same."

The girl gave me one last look then turned and disappeared into the crowd.

I mustered my courage, and asked, "Who is she?"

"That's Kate. A classmate." Peter checked his watch. "I have to go. I'll see you all later."

As Peter disappeared into the sea of blue gowns, a redhaired boy walked slowly by, staring at me. I swallowed hard and looked him in the eye until he looked away.

Soon, people crowded into every available space in the gym, and music blared over the speakers to signal the ceremony's start. There were four speakers, two administrators and two students. Their quickly spoken words made little sense to me, but I was sure their speeches were inspirational.

Amid much clapping and cheering, each graduate walked across the stage to receive their diplomas. Mary and Tom shouted when Peter strode across the stage to shake hands with the administrators. I remained quiet because I didn't want to sound weird. The cheering and excitement of the crowd made me breathless. Tears sprang to my eyes. This was my first uplifting educational experience.

Once the ceremony was over, we picked our way to the hallway in search of Peter. I caught sight of him down the hall, posing for pictures with his guy friends. They laughed as Peter made antlers with two fingers above one friend's head. Another friend made his eyes bulge, and the other friend crossed fisted hands over his chest.

I had no idea Peter could be silly. With me, he was gentle and serious and spoke slowly. Now he and his friends spoke so fast I could discern only a few words. Their goofiness was so funny that a laugh burst from my mouth. I clapped a hand over my mouth and looked around. No one paid attention to me amid the raucous noise.

A sea of people squeezed past us as we waited for Peter, their eyes on me. My palms sweated. Finally, the crowd thinned out. Peter's friends greeted me, but their whispers and hisses put me on edge.

When we finally left the building and stepped out into the cool air, my anxiety faded. Mary asked me to go with them to a restaurant to celebrate Peter's graduation. As much as I wanted to celebrate with them, I had to go home to cook for my family. I explained in broken English that my family expected me home and would worry. Peter told his parents he would meet them at the restaurant, and we left.

On the way home, we sat in silence for a while before Peter said, "You look beautiful."

I looked down at my hands folded in my lap against the yellow fabric. I wasn't as beautiful as Susan, but I would take the compliment. She and Peter were a perfect match. I didn't understand why he didn't want to go to college when an illiterate person like me wished to go to college.

"Why you not go college?" I asked.

"I didn't want to, but now...I think I should go."

I turned slightly to face him. "What you want to do?"

"I want to improve myself." He looked at me, a soft smile on his face. "You taught me that."

I blinked. "Me?"

He nodded and faced forward again. "You've been through so much, yet, instead of being angry, you want to better yourself. How could I do any less?"

Pride swelled in me. "Good! You go college, okay?"

"I will." He cleared his throat. "Nou, I...I really like you."

My heart pounded. Sometimes, the way his eyes shone when he looked at me made me wonder if he liked me, but I couldn't be certain because of our cultural differences. I wanted to tell him that he was the most handsome man I had ever met and that I liked him. But I was uneducated and low class. Physically and intellectually, we were totally unmatched. Mary and Tom wouldn't want an uneducated daughter-in-law. Who would?

But I wouldn't be uneducated forever.

"I like you too," I said.

"Yes!" He glanced at me with bright eyes. "Thanks for coming to my graduation. It meant a lot to me."

"You are welcome. I learn a lot."

Peter pulled into our driveway and parked.

I grasped the car door and waved at him. "Goodbye."

"Good night." He smiled. "I don't have school tomorrow, so I'll come around noon, if that's ok."

"Okay." I got out of the car and closed the door.

Peter waved, then drove away.

"Auntie Nou!" Nhia hurried down the stairs as I rounded the side of the house. "I missed you!"

I quickened my pace to meet him at the bottom of the stairs and swung him up into my arms. Mother sat on the top of the stairs. I had been gone only two hours, and they already missed me. When school starts next fall, they would be home all day by themselves, which would be yet another adjustment.

In the bathroom, I studied my reflection. Butterflies skittered across the inside of my stomach at the memory of how Peter found me attractive. If I could attain Susan's level of education, I would have a chance with him. How long would it take me to become fully literate? I washed my face and went to bed, determined to study harder.

8

At noon the following day, Mother called me to the window. "I have never seen those people before," she said.

Three ladies got out of a gray car in front of our house. Had Peter sent someone to visit with us? Two of the women carried covered baking dishes. I stood frozen, uncertain if I should allow strangers into the house. If Peter or Mary were with them, I wouldn't worry, but....

"Look." Mother pointed, as the women headed down the walkway to the front of the house, instead of the left side, where the stairs led to our home. "They must be visiting the older couple downstairs."

I breathed a sigh of relief. "They're bringing food. They're probably family."

Mother nodded. I started to turn away, then caught sight of Peter's car turning onto our road.

"There's Peter," Mother said. "He's always on time."

I hid a smile, and said in an even tone, "He is a good man."

She looked at me, and I quickly turned away.

I grabbed my book bag from the bedroom and reached the

kitchen just as Peter knocked on the door. I dropped the bag on the table and opened the door. Peter smiled and came inside. We sat at the table, and I expected that we would continue to work on the books Mary had given me. Instead, Peter opened my notebook to a fresh page, retrieved a pen from his pocket, and wrote *library*.

He pointed at the new word. "Sound it out."

I studied the letters. "*Lī-be-ry*."

"Nice try," he said. "Say lī brerē."

"Lī-be-rē."

I knew I hadn't said it correctly because he didn't compliment me. I often struggled with the *br* sound in English. My native language had no such sound.

"I'm taking you to the library," he said.

"What's that?"

"A place full of books. You can borrow the books, take them home to read, and return them when you're done. Bringing the books home is called *checking them out*."

I gasped. "Read free?" I couldn't believe such a place existed. "Nhia and my mother go?"

He nodded with enthusiasm.

We all headed for the car and, as usual, Peter opened the car door for us, and we got in the back seat. I was pleased the ride was short. Maybe I could walk here by myself. The library was a two-story concrete building. Just inside the entrance, a set of stairs on the right led to the second floor. Row upon row of bookshelves stretched out before me. I stared in awe. Several tables with four chairs each filled the spaces between the shelves. People sat scattered throughout the area with some reading quietly while a few conversed in whispers. I hoped Nhia didn't cry. I never wanted to leave.

I browsed the bookshelf in awe. What stories lived between the multi-colored book covers? I was where I needed to be. A place full of books. A person had to be smart to read all these books. I had left my brother and Pheng behind for the chance at an education.

When the Communists burned our village in Laos, I risked my life to return to our house for my books because I thought they were the only two books in the world. There had to be thousands of books in this building alone. More than I could ever possibly read.

As I came to the last bookshelf in the imposing room, I realized I had lost Peter, Nhia, and Mother. I retraced my steps and quickened my pace to look for them. I found them at one of the tables near the entrance. I sighed with relief as I realized Peter had stayed with them.

"Where were you?" Mother's lips twitched in panic.

"I'm sorry. I was on the other side of the room," I said in Hmong. "I didn't mean to abandon you." Then to Peter, I said in English, "Sorry, Peter."

The twinkle in his eyes lessened my guilt. "It's okay. I knew you were curious."

I relaxed. Tears glimmered in Nhia's eyes, and I took him from Mother.

"It's all right," I said.

Carrying Nhia on my hip, I pulled a thick book from a nearby bookshelf, unable to resist its dark green cover and gold lettering. Tiny print filled each page. What secrets did this book hold?

"That one is too hard for you," Peter said.

I returned the book to its shelf, and we followed Peter upstairs to the second floor. To the right, stood more rows of bookshelves. Peter led us to the left, to a section where picture books filled the bookshelves against the wall. Between the shelves, hung pictures of black and brown bears, giraffes, sheep, elephants, and dogs. A big round table dominated the center of the section. We were the only people in this section. In the corner, stood a playhouse with a basket of stuffed animals.

"Peter, can Nhia play?" I pointed at the basket.

"Sure."

We sat on the carpet by the basket and Nhia picked up Bambi and smiled. He hugged the deer to his chest. Nhia loved watching the animated film *Bambi*. He grabbed the stuffed elephant and studied it.

"Nhia, you can play with them and take more from the basket. Will you be all right if grandma plays with you?"

He nodded and Mother sat with him. I stood and followed Peter to a nearby shelf where he pulled out two books. I took one. We sat at the table to read. My book was called *Corduroy*. I read it with Peter's help. English wasn't like Hmong where I could blend the consonants, vowels, and tones together. Peter showed me how to sound out the word *palace*, and after several attempts and with his help, I got it but didn't know its meaning. English was difficult.

Half an hour later, people started coming in, and Mother and Nhia joined us at the table. With Peter's assistance, I read to Nhia. A plump woman accompanied by a small girl came to our table and conversed with Peter. He told her that we were Hmong from Laos.

"Hi. Welcome to Appleton," she said.

I knew by her smile and kind eyes she was nice.

"Thank you," I replied.

"Nice meeting you."

I smiled and nodded.

People looked at us as they walked past where we sat at the table. I felt safe and protected with Peter and focused on reading. A few weeks ago, Peter had been a stranger. Now, he was like family.

After an hour, more people crowded the place. Nhia wanted to go home and started crying. We checked out eight books. I still couldn't believe the books were free. My dream of reading was coming true, and I knew I would never again be bored. I had all the time in the world to learn to read, and when I could read well, I would check out even more difficult books.

On our way home, I sat with Peter at the front seat and studied the buildings and streets, so I could walk to the library over the summer.

"I'll walk with you to the library tomorrow," Peter said, as if reading my mind. "The library isn't far from your home."

"Thank you."

That evening, I read all eight picture books we checked out, first to myself and then to Nhia. I felt smarter already.

9

Mother lay on the bed covered with the thick comforter, her drooping eyelids and pale lips worried me. Three days after our trip to the library, she started having headaches. The pain didn't respond to the herbal medicine we brought from Thailand that I had given her. She had lost her appetite the last two days and now complained of a pain that moved from place to place within her body.

"Mother, you need to see the doctor. I'll call Peter to take you."

"No doctor. I'll get better soon. Don't worry."

I worried but didn't know what to do. Illness wasn't like studying where I could take control through hard work.

When Peter arrived for our tutoring session that afternoon, I told him about Mother's illness and took him to the bedroom. The house was warm but Mother still covered herself with the comforter, her face contorted in a grimace of pain.

"How are you doing, Choua?" Peter asked.

Mother looked at me in confusion.

"Peter wants to know how you're doing," I translated.

"I'm weak," she moaned.

"She weak," I told him. "She don't go see doctor. You make her go."

"Choua, I am taking you to the doctor. It's important that you go."

I translated for Mother. She shook her head.

Peter's brow furrowed in concern. "She needs to see a doctor."

I sat on the edge of the bed. "Mother, Peter will take us to the doctor. You must go. You need medicine."

"The doctor can't help me. I'm not sick from an illness." She spoke so softly I had to lean close.

"What is it, then?"

She glanced at Peter. "I'll tell you later."

I huffed in frustration. I wanted to help her, but she wasn't cooperating.

"Do you have pain medication?" asked Peter.

I shook my head. "No money."

"I'll get some for her."

It hurt to rely on the Johnson family and the church for financial support. We wouldn't get our AFDC check until July, which was still two weeks away, but I couldn't allow Mother to be in pain.

I nodded. "Thank you."

He looked down at Mother, who had closed her eyes. "Your mother is stubborn."

"She not like this before."

We went to the door and Peter opened the door.

"Please buy oranges too," I said.

He nodded and left.

I returned to Mother's bedside. "Mother, we've only just begun our good life in America. You must live a long life. Tell me how I can help you." Tears filled my eyes, and I took her hand in mine. "I know I'm not much hope for you because I'm a daughter, but I'm your only child now. I'll do anything to save you."

After a while, Mother said, "You and I can't do anything about my illness."

I cocked my head. "I don't understand. Why can't the doctor help?"

She expelled a heavy breath. "We don't have a man to do the ritual."

"What ritual?"

"Der and your father died during the trek through the jungle. Their souls are wandering and can't reincarnate. We have to perform the *tso plig* to release their souls, but we can't do it without Toua and Uncle Cher Moua."

I had heard of tso plig, a soul releasing ritual. I squeezed her hand. "How do you know Father and Der need a tso plig?"

"Recurring dreams about them and the pain in my body," she replied. "Their spirits have been summoning me to do the ritual. The pain that moves from spot to spot inside me is the spirits pounding my flesh, telling me to do what they need done."

I stared at her. What could I do? My brother lived so far away. In our culture, we depended so much on our family, relatives, clan, and the community for these situations.

"What happens if we don't release their souls?" I asked.

"I won't get better. Anything could happen to me."

My pulse raced. "Mother, you should have told me this earlier. We can't perform the ritual, but maybe we can have Toua and Uncle do it in Thailand?"

Her expression relaxed. "Yes. Why didn't I think of that? I've been losing my mind. Have I become useless already?"

"You're sick and depressed. Once you're better, you will think clearly. I'm here for you." I stroked her hair. "Sending a letter and money to Thailand takes a long time. Also, we won't get our AFDC until July. You can't be sick for that long. We must find a shaman to tell the spirits to wait."

"Where will we find one?" she asked.

I considered our options. "I'll call Mai. Maybe she can help."

If Mother didn't get better, it would be my fault. I had vowed to be like a son, but as a girl, I had limitations. Only a man could conduct cultural practices, which was why Mother was desperate for a son. She did have sons, but they all died.

My half-brother Toua could stand in as a son. After his mother died when he was six months old, our father married my mother. Mother raised Toua as her own. But he hadn't wanted to come to America.

Peter returned half an hour later with oranges and medicine. He set the cup of water on the lamp table, twisted the Tylenol bottle cap open and poured out two tablets.

"Mother, Peter brought medicine," I said. "Take them. You must get better."

She sat up on the bed. Peter gave her the tablets and she took them with water.

"Get better soon," Peter said.

I translated. Mother nodded, then laid back on the bed and pulled the blanket over to her neck. "Don't worry about me. Go study."

I wanted to obey, but I was too worried to concentrate. Peter and I went to the kitchen. I planned to cancel our session and didn't invite him to sit. We stared at each other grim-faced.

"You look worried." Peter's voice was tight with concern. "I'm sure your mother will be okay."

I hoped he was right. "Hard to study and eat. You go home."

"I'll stay for a bit to make sure your mother gets better before I go," he said.

"Thank you." My voice cracked a little as I was unable to mask my emotion.

Peter took my hands in his. "If you need anything, you let me know."

His gentle eyes and earnest voice soothed me. I embraced him. Embarrassment and shame warmed my cheeks. I couldn't believe I had initiated the hug.

Peter released me. "Let's study a bit. It'll take your mind off your worries."

His confidence in me made me feel I could do anything.

An hour later, Mother felt better and ate two oranges and some gruel. Peter went home with instructions to call if I needed him.

The hand on the clock pointed to seven, so I was sure Mai was done cooking dinner or eating. I dialed her phone number.

On the third ring, the phone picked up, and Mai said, "Hello."

"Hi, Mai. This is Nou. Do you have time to talk?"

"Of course."

I explained the tso plig and our circumstance.

"You can't do the ritual without family members' help," Mai said. "It was so hard for us that we decided to convert to Christianity. Now, we no longer need traditional rituals and shaman. We pray to God when we need help."

The idea sounded good. "How do we convert?"

"Attend church and get baptized. You can attend Peter's church or my church if you would like to convert."

It sounded easy enough. "Okay. Thank you. I'll talk to my mother."

I hung up the phone and explained my conversation with Mai to Mother.

"I think we should convert to Christianity. What do you think?" I asked.

Mother shook her head. "If we convert to Christianity, when I die, I won't reunite with your father and my children because I will be in a different world."

I wanted to be with my family. I wanted to be Der's sister again, but Mother's well-being was my priority. If God could heal her until we could perform the tso plig, why wait?

"Mother, it takes a long time for a letter to reach Toua. I don't want you in pain until then. Can we please go to church and see if you get better? We can just try it. We don't have to convert."

No response.

"Please, Mother. It doesn't hurt to try. We should go this Sunday."

She sagged against the pillow. "All right."

I breathed a sigh of relief. "Thank you."

I hurried to the kitchen and dialed the Johnson's number. Mary answered the call and gave the phone to Peter when I asked for him.

"Hello," Peter said.

"Peter, this is Nou."

"Hi, Nou. How's your mother?"

The concern in his voice touched me. "Better. We want to go to church. You take us Sunday?"

"Okay," Peter said excitedly. "You can wear a dress to church. Most women do."

"All right."

"I'll pick you all up Sunday morning at eight."

"Okay. Bye."

"Bye."

We didn't have very nice, good clothes. I went through the closet and found each of us clothes that I thought would be appropriate for church. I hoped medication and attending church would heal Mother. I wouldn't know what else to do if the medication and church didn't work.

10

We rose earlier than usual on Sunday and ate rice and leftover stir-fried vegetables for breakfast. I dressed Mother in a black skirt and a floral blouse and Nhia in a white shirt and black pants. I put on the yellow dress that I wore to Peter's graduation.

Peter arrived at eight. He was clean-shaven in a black suit, a white shirt, and a blue tie. He looked as handsome as a magazine model. My heart drummed when his eyes met mine.

"You're beautiful," he said. "

"Oh. You beautiful too," I said.

He laughed. "Thanks."

We went to the living room for Mother and Nhia. I had told Nhia to be a good boy, so he got off the sofa and hurried to me. I picked him up. Mother didn't look my way and remained seated on the sofa.

"Mother, we're going now," I said.

She turned to me with sad eyes.

"The medicine helps your pain, but I want you to be free of illness. We must try," I insisted.

Slowly, she got off the sofa and we followed Peter to his car.

The parking lot at St. Paul's Catholic Church was almost full when we arrived ten minutes later. The huge white, brick church had a front entrance made of tan stones.

"This church is small compared to others," Peter said.

The building seemed huge to me. Inside the gathering area, a few people socialized. Their friendly smiles and greetings warmed my heart. Mary and Tom were there, waiting for us.

"Welcome." Mary smiled as she hugged me and Mother. "I'm so glad you decided to come."

"You and family are welcome any Sunday," Tom added.

I smiled. "Thank you."

Nhia clung to me as we followed Peter and his parents into the big room. Its high ceiling, colorful painted glass windows, and hanging lights were spectacular. People filled the pews on both sides of the aisle. Straight ahead, Father Dan stood next to the altar in his white outermost garment.

Nhia hid his face in my shoulder. I worried he would cry, so I stroked his head to soothe him. Peter was heading toward the front, but I didn't want to sit in the front or middle row.

"Peter," I whispered. "Sit in back."

Peter glanced back at us and nodded. He led us to the second pew from the back and motioned for us to sit. Mary and Tom sat with us.

A few moments later, Father Dan began speaking, and the room went silent. Nhia began to cry softly. I wasn't sure if he was afraid of Father Dan's voice or of being in the room with so many people. I hushed him and stroked his head, but he wouldn't stop. No one seemed to mind, but Nhia's whimpers embarrassed me. I rose and took him to the lobby. Still, he wouldn't stop. We went outside and walked the neat pathway that connected the church to the street. After a few minutes of walking, he stopped crying.

"Can we go back inside now?" I asked.

"No." He shook his head vehemently.

"The people inside are good people."

"I'm not going in. I'm scared."

I huffed. How could I help him to overcome his fear? I had assured him many times that we were in a safe place with good people and still he was afraid. I swallowed back my frustration. A warm breeze brushed my face as we paced the length of the sidewalk.

Ten or fifteen minutes later, Mother and Peter emerged from the church. I hurried Nhia forward so we could meet them.

"I want to go home," Mother said.

I looked her over. I had given her Tylenol for her pain before we came, and she seemed better. "We've been here only twenty-five minutes. Why so soon?"

"I don't understand anything, and I can't sing. We don't belong here. I'm getting a headache. Have Peter take us home."

Leave church in the middle of worship? I felt ashamed for my family, but I realized we shouldn't have come in the first place. Mother hadn't wanted to come, and in my desperation, I had forced her.

I looked at Peter, whose brows wrinkled in worry.

"Sorry. My mother head hurt," I said. "She go home."

"It's all right. She should see a doctor," Peter said. "I'm worried about her."

"You are nice. She say no doctor."

We walked to his car in silence. He opened the door for Mother and Nhia to climb into the back seat. Then he opened the front passenger door for me.

When he got into the driver's seat, I said, "Peter, I'm sorry you miss church service."

"It's okay." He smiled. "I go to church only when I can. No big deal."

I hoped that Mary, Tom, and the other churchgoers understood why we left. The war had traumatized Mother and Nhia. They needed patience, love, and caring to help them move on. I, too, was traumatized, but Nhia and Mother were my duties. I had no choice but to move forward.

That evening, I called Mai.

"Hello," she said into the phone.

"Hi, Mai. This is Nou. We went to church today."

"Oh. Good."

I fiddled with the pen I held. "My mother didn't like it, so we won't be converting to Christianity."

"Oh. That's all right. Older people are hesitant to change."

"Do you know any shamans in the area?"

"Yes. Auntie Shoua Nu Thao," said Mai. "I can give you her phone number."

I exhaled in relief. A woman shaman was even better. I could talk to her without a man's mediation. Mai gave me her phone number and said Auntie lived with her son in Menasha. She was the first wife of Shoua Nu Thao. Her husband and his other wife lived in Menasha too. Shoua Nu had been a CIA soldier during the Secret War, and his family had been air lifted to the refugee camp in Thailand. They were the first wave of refugees to arrive in America.

After I hung up the phone, I took a deep breath and called Auntie Shoua Nu. Mother entered the kitchen and sat at the table as a man answered the phone after three rings.

"Hello. May I speak to Auntie Shoua Nu," I said.

"Sure. Hold on a minute," he replied.

"Hello," Auntie said a moment later.

"Hi, Auntie. I am Nou Vang. My mother, nephew, and I live in Appleton."

"Hello, Nou," she replied in a strong, loud voice.

Nervous, I twisted a strand of hair around my index finger. "I heard you're a shaman. We need your help because my mother's been sick."

"I'm sorry your mother's sick. I'm not sure I can help."

I must convince her but how?

"Please, Auntie," I begged.

"Tell me her illness."

I explained Mother's recurring dreams of Father and Der and the tso plig.

"Based on what you told me, it is best to do a *ua neeb* for your mother. I'll do it."

The constriction in my chest loosened. "Thank you, Auntie. When can you do the ritual?"

"Tomorrow works for me. My son can give you our address. Pick us up around seven a.m."

Pick them up? I sighed heavily. "Auntie, I...can't drive."

"Ohhh," she said slowly. "No worries. My son will drive."

The son took the phone, and I gave him my address, then hung up.

Mother's expression had turned bright as the sun. Her happiness made me forget the burden we'd put on Auntie and her son.

11

untie Shoua Nu and her son arrived that following day, Saturday morning. Her son carried a wooden bench. Auntie, a short, stout woman, hugged Mother.

"I'm happy to meet you. Thank you for coming." Tears filled Mother's eyes, and for the first time in a long while her voice sounded strong.

"You're welcome. I'm happy to help." Auntie's loud voice echoed in our small kitchen. She studied Mother. "You're bony. You need to eat more."

"I haven't been well."

"You'll be better after the ua neeb."

Auntie embraced me. Time had weathered her features, but she must have been a beautiful woman when she was younger.

She pulled away and looked me over from head to toe. "What a beautiful daughter."

"Not that beautiful," I said, which was the proper response in my culture.

Auntie pointed to the man. "This is Xa, my son. He's single and a good man."

Xa was taller than me and lean. He had thick, ear-length black hair that framed his long, handsome face.

His eyes fixed on me. "Hello. I'm my mother's shamanic assistant."

"I'm Nou. Thank you for helping my family."

"You're welcome. We'll do the ritual in the living room."

Xa still held the wooden bench. I picked up Auntie's black shamanic tool bag, and we went to the living room. Nhia jumped from the sofa where he watched TV and ran to me. He clung to my leg and hid his face in my thigh. I set the tool bag on the carpet and picked him up.

"Don't be afraid," I said. "This man is Uncle Xa. He's here to help grandma get better."

Nhia started crying. I took him to the bedroom.

"Okay, you stay in here and play with your toys," I told him. "I'll play with you when I'm done helping Uncle Xa."

I hurried back to the living room.

Xa asked, "Do you have a small table?"

"No," I said.

He looked around the room. "We'll use your TV table."

"Okay. You set up, and I'll prepare food for you and Auntie."

"My mother and I ate before we came. We'll eat after the ritual."

While Xa set up the shamanic table, Auntie and Mother talked about life in America. Mother told her how lonely and depressed she'd been. Auntie said she was the same way when they came to America and assured Mother that things would get better.

"Auntie, could my mother call you to talk sometime?" I held my breath in anticipation of her agreement.

"Yes. Call me any time. I'd love to talk to her."

I smiled thanks, and we all waited while Xa covered the TV table with joss papers; spirit money sheets. Then he placed two bowls filled with rice on the table. One bowl held an egg and a stick of incense, and the other bowl had three sticks of incense. He added a plate of roasted rice, one bowl of water, and four small cups of water. Then he placed two finger bells on the table and lit the incense. Their smoky fragrance soon filled the room. Finally, Xa set the wooden bench before the table.

Auntie changed from her American clothes to traditional Hmong clothes. She put a red veil over her head and ring bells on her fingers, then sat on the wooden bench. Xa beat the gong gently with a cloth-head mallet while Auntie started the trance. After several minutes, he stopped beating the gong. A few minutes of silence passed, and Auntie stomped her feet on the carpet three times.

Someone pounded on our floor from the home below us. My heart leapt into my throat. The elderly couple downstairs seemed nice, but they must not like the noise. I thought about telling them what we were doing but decided to wait in hopes they wouldn't be further bothered. When Auntie stomped again ten minutes later, no response came from below and my nerves calmed a little.

Nhia called for me from the bedroom, and Mother went to check on him. A knock on the front door startled me. I hurried to open it to find a middle-aged, uniformed police officer standing there. Heaven, what was he doing here? Were we getting arrested? My heart fluttered, and my knees trembled.

I drew in a deep breath. "Hi."

"Hello." His lips curved upward in a friendly smile. "I'm Officer Wilson. Can I come in?"

I wanted to tell him that he shouldn't disturb the shaman because any disruption could harm Auntie, but I didn't know the word *shaman* in English.

"Yes. But my mother sick. My nephew scare."

"Okay. I won't come in then," he said in a steady voice.

"Why you come?" I asked.

"The family downstairs said you're making too much noise. I'm just checking."

Auntie's loud chanting could be heard from the living room. The officer looked past me.

I pressed my palms together. "My aunt help my sick mother. Our culture."

"Okay." He nodded. "Try to keep the noise down."

"Okay."

I closed the door. We had angered our neighbors. Could the police arrest us for doing our rituals?

"Who came?" Xa whispered when I returned to the living room.

"The police."

He clenched his jaw. "Why?"

"We're making too much noise. The couple downstairs called them."

"Americans don't understand our traditions."

"I'll have to apologize to our neighbors."

Xa reached across the chair where he sat near his mother and grabbed my arm. "No. They called the police on you. They aren't good people. You don't need to apologize."

Was he right? Mother was still with Nhia in the bedroom. If she and Nhia had seen the uniformed officer, they would have been terrified.

Xa moved from his chair to the sofa about a seat apart from me. "How old are you?" he whispered.

"Seventeen." I surveyed the carpet. "You?"

"Twenty."

Auntie's loud chanting resounded through the house, making it hard to hear.

"When did your family come to America?" I whispered.

"February 1976. We arrived in Houston, Texas, and moved here to be with my uncle."

"Are you a student?"

"No. I went to high school for a year. I'm working now."

"Do you want to go to the university to continue your education?" I asked.

He shook his head. "No. English is hard."

"Yes. Very hard."

Xa rose and lit more incense. Smoke hung in the air and stung my eyes. I excused myself to check on Mother and Nhia.

Mother looked up as I entered the room. "Nhia's bored and wanted to read, but I can't read."

"I'll read with him," I said. "You join Xa in the living room."

Mother left and I read aloud the books that I'd checked out at my last trip to the library. I wanted to visit the library every day, but Mother's illness prevented it. Since our first visit to the library, I had returned only twice. How I hoped she would get better soon.

Nhia and I remained in the bedroom until Auntie completed the ritual. I reheated the food then put everything on the table. I gave Nhia food in the bedroom.

If my brother was present, he and Xa would eat first. But we had no man, so Auntie insisted that Mother and I eat with Xa and her. We sat on the opposite side of the table from them. In courtesy of our culture, I spooned rice on both Xa and Auntie's plates.

"I want to talk before we eat," said Auntie. "My shamanic guides informed me that your husband and daughter wanted their souls released."

"So, they were trying to tell me in my dreams?" Mother said.

Auntie nodded. "I assured them you would release their souls in a few months."

"Thank you."

Auntie smiled. "You're welcome. You should be better within three days."

Mother blinked and tears slid down her cheeks.

"Don't cry," said Auntie. "From now on, you'll be fine. If you need help, just call me." She picked up her spoon and started eating. Everyone followed suit.

"Auntie Nou!" Nhia called from the bedroom. "Come here!"

"In a minute."

I ate quickly, then excused myself and hurried to Nhia. He stood in the hall with his empty plate.

"Do you want more food?" I asked.

"No."

Nhia returned to the bedroom. I took his plate to the sink, then Xa followed me to the living room. Once out of the women's sight, he stepped close. He smelled of the smoky incense.

"Can I have your phone number?" he asked.

I stepped back to put space between us. "Yes. Your mother and my mother need to contact each other."

His mouth quirked up at one end. "It's for her and also for me."

He seemed like a good man. I supposed it wouldn't hurt to get to know him. I grabbed a notebook and pen and wrote our phone number on a blank page, then handed it to him.

Xa smiled. "Thanks." He began packing his mother's shamanic tools.

Soon after Auntie finished her food and visiting with Mother, she and Xa left.

The discontent of angering the downstairs neighbor nagged at me. We were in a foreign land without a clan or extended family, and we couldn't afford to have enemies. I went downstairs and knocked on the door. The woman we'd seen that one time opened the door. She had short, white hair and seemed to be in her seventies.

"Hi," she said.

"Hi. I am Nou. I live upstairs."

"I'm Linda." Her face remained expressionless, but her voice was pleasant.

"I am sorry. We make loud noise today. My mother sick. We do culture."

She strained her ear like she had trouble with my accent. "What were you doing?"

How could I explain the shamanic ritual to her in English? I shook my arms up and down as I took small jumps to demonstrate the ritual.

She nodded. "I understand."

I worried she would ask more questions that I wouldn't know how to answer, so said, "Bye."

"Nice meeting you. If you ever get bored and want to talk, you can always come down. My husband and I love company."

Happiness overwhelmed me. "Thank you," I blurted in my best English. "You very nice. Next time."

She smiled as she closed the door, and I knew I had made the right decision to talk to her.

12

Mother's laughter in the kitchen with Auntie on the phone resounded in the living room. She and Auntie talked every day, and she looked out the window less and smiled more. Her health had improved since the ritual a week ago. The downside to our relationship with Auntie was Xa. He called me every other day and wanted to talk endlessly. But I couldn't be rude, so I went out of my way to irritate him by pestering him into explaining English words to me. He hated translating English words, so our phone calls became brief.

Nhia walked in the living room and handed me the *daim nyias*, the baby carrier, a black rectangular cloth embroidered with colorful textiles and sewed with a green sash at the top.

"Auntie, I want to go back to the library. I want to play with the stuffed animal again."

I took the daim nyias. "I have to carry you again?"

He nodded.

Yesterday, Thursday, Peter walked Nhia and I to the library, which had become Nhia's and my favorite place. The fifteen-minute walk was worth it, especially since they had air conditioning.

Nhia and I went to the kitchen. Mother was still on the phone.

I mouthed to her, *Nhia and I are going to the library. Do you want to go with us?*

"Grandma, I want to play with the stuffed animals." Nhia grabbed Mother's hand. "Come with us."

Mother nodded and said into the phone, "I'll talk to you later. Bye." She hung up the phone and turned to us. "Is it safe to go without Peter?"

I thought a moment. This would be our first time going without Peter. "We'll be fine. We can't depend on him for everything. We'll burn him out quickly if we're not careful."

I stuffed the daim nyias into my backpack, along with the books I needed to return. I wouldn't carry Nhia until he was tired from walking.

When we reached the bottom of the stairs, Nhia squealed as he ran ahead of Mother and me. We followed Appleton Street for four blocks, then turned left on College Avenue. We wound our way through the people entering and exiting the department store, H.C. Prange Company. Clusters of old and new cars lined College Avenue. One more block and we turned right on Oneida Street then passed the tall Zuelke Building before arriving at the library.

At the circulation desk, Mrs. Whitman, a tall, thin woman in her late forties with ear-length, brown hair smiled at us. "Hello," she said.

"Hi, Mrs. Whitman."

She looked at Mother. "Is this lady your mother?"

"Yes."

"Well, nice meeting you all. Enjoy your time here."

"Thank you," I said.

I dropped off the books, and we went upstairs to the children's section. After playing with the stuffed animals, Nhia and I each pulled a few books from the shelves. He sat on my lap while I read to him at a table. Mother watched with half-closed eyes.

Nhia and I were absorbed in our books when sharp laughter

drew my attention to three boys a little younger than me, who stood between the shelves. I instantly recognized the redheaded boy from Peter's graduation. The boys pointed at Mother, whose head had fallen forward in sleep. I nudged her, and she opened her eyes. The boys laughed again. The librarian hushed them, and they disappeared behind the shelves.

Mother's face flushed. "Are you ready to go home?"

I wasn't, but she seemed uncomfortable. I quickly put away the books and took some to check out.

Once outside, Nhia refused to walk. I pulled the colorful baby carrier from my backpack, squatted and Nhia got on my back. Then I secured him across my back with the baby carrier. As we started home, I noticed the three boys who had laughed at us walking down Franklin Street.

We hurried forward to avoid them, but they followed. Laughter echoed behind us, and a voice repeatedly shouted a word I didn't know but rhymed with the word *librarian*. We picked up our pace.

"Who carries a baby like that?" one shouted.

So, he bullied us for carrying a child with a cloth carrier? Humiliation flooded me, weakening my legs. I blew out a breath and reminded myself that it shouldn't matter how we carried a child. There were many ways to carry a baby. It didn't have to be the American way.

The redhaired boy caught up with me and laughed in my face. Nhia wailed.

Mother's expression tightened. "What do the boys want?"

If they had been Hmong boys, she would have scolded them. But Hmong boys would never bully an adult.

"I don't know." Anger and fear boiled inside me.

The redheaded boy stepped in front of me.

My face grew hot. "Go away!" I shouted.

"Go away," he mocked with a disgusted expression, and laughed again.

Mother's cheeks reddened. "What a cruel boy!"

He scowled. "What are you saying, cripple woman?"

How dare he call my mother a cripple! I grabbed Mother's hand and pulled her away. Nhia was still crying as he bounced against my back.

"What are you doing in my country, bitch?" the redhead called.

I knew the bad word from TV. Tears burned my eyes. For the first time since we'd arrived in America, I felt like we weren't welcome.

"Answer me!" He laughed. "You stupid or something?"

I had tried my best to avoid trouble, but my patience was stretched thin and the fire inside me threatened to explode. I spun to face the boys when the blond-haired boy pointed to a building across the street.

"Let's go. There's a lady over there staring at us," he said.

They raced down the street and turned the next corner out of sight. I scanned the building across the street. A tall woman stared out a window from inside the building. Her mere presence had stopped the boys. Despite being an inexperienced teenager, I understood what had happened. She was an American. She belonged here. She had power. We weren't Americans. We didn't belong. We had no power.

I took several deep breaths to slow my racing heart. Did the boys know why we came to America? Would they have empathy if they knew? When Peter called that night, I didn't tell him about the boys. He shouldn't have to escort me to the library. I should be able to go any day I wanted. I prayed the boys would leave us alone. My family just wanted peace and a chance to live a happy life.

13

On Saturday morning, Nhia and I sat comfortably on the sofa watching the *ABC Weekend Specials* show while Mother rested in the bedroom. A knock came at the door. Who would visit so early? Peter usually called ahead or told me the day before. I rose and looked out the living room window. Xa's white car sat parked on the street.

Frowning, I went to the kitchen and opened the door. "Hi," I said.

"Hello." Xa stepped inside, and I was forced to retreat two paces.

I closed the door behind him. "What are you doing here so early?" This wasn't a proper question to ask a guest, but I considered it impolite to show up at seven a.m. without calling first.

"I...I want to spend the day with you."

I stiffened. Did he intend to spend the entire day with me? I wanted to read.

I forced a smile. "Next time, call before you come."

He nodded and started toward the living room.

"Nhia's watching the TV, so if you don't mind, we can talk in the kitchen," I said. "I don't want him to cry."

Xa faced me. "You have so much patience with Nhia. Do you ever spank him?"

I stared. What kind of man was Xa? Why did he think I should spank Nhia?

"When I was little, my mother spanked me and I hated it, so I don't spank him. I loved my sister, which means I love Nhia more than if he was my own child."

"He's such a crybaby," Xa said.

I shook my head. "No. He only cries at strangers. Why didn't you bring your mother? My mother would love to visit with her."

"A man doesn't take his mother along when he goes to talk to a girl."

I pursed my lips. "We aren't officially courting. You're here to visit us. Your mother can come along."

"Okay. Next time." He sat at the chair and rested his arms on the kitchen table. "I hope you don't mind that I'm here to have breakfast with you."

At least he was honest—sort of. I suspected he was here to check out my cooking skills, like traditional men in our culture. I would prove to him that I had them, that I was a diligent worker with good manners. But that didn't mean I was interested in him.

"I don't mind," I said, then started cooking.

A few minutes later, Mother came to the kitchen and greeted him.

"Auntie, I'm so happy you are healthy again," he said.

"Thank you to you and your mother for helping me get better."

Xa stood and wrapped an arm around her shoulder. "You're welcome, Auntie. My mother and I are happy to help your family. Please allow me to help you like I'm your son. You can ask me to do anything."

Mother's lips stretched wide, showing the smile I hadn't seen in a long time.

"Very thoughtful of you. Next time bring your mother along."

"Sure. I didn't bring her because I'll be here for a while. I want to take your family shopping."

"I'd love that. It's so boring staying home every day."

I didn't want to burden Xa. Plus, I didn't want him thinking he was our man. "You don't have to take us shopping," I said. "Peter takes us every weekend."

Xa frowned. "Who's Peter?"

"He's our sponsor's son," I said.

Xa puffed out his chest. "I'll take care of your family from now on. We don't trust the Americans."

The incident with the redhead might have made me agree, but Peter's family wasn't like that.

I gave him a cold stare. "I trust my sponsor's family."

Xa joined me at the sink and watched me wash the green onions. "Believe me. I've been in America longer than you and know more than you."

Xa was Hmong like me, but we had met only a week ago. He didn't need to be concerned about us, and he definitely didn't need to act like he was our man.

Nhia came to the kitchen and whirled back to the living room in tears.

"Xa, come with me to the living room," Mother said. "I'll introduce you to Nhia. The more Nhia sees you and knows he's safe, the less he'd be afraid of you. This is only the second time he's seen you."

Xa followed her into the living room.

After breakfast, Xa helped us into his white, two door car. Mother asked Xa about his job.

He puffed out his chest again. "I work at a packaging company and get paid $2.50 an hour. I pack diapers and other things. It's good work."

The work might be good, but it seemed easy and boring.

We bought food at Piggy Wiggly with the food vouchers we received from the church. In a week, we would receive our AFDC money from the government for the month of July. I would be so relieved not to have to rely so much on Peter, his family, and church.

We arrived home an hour later. Xa sat at the kitchen table as I put away our groceries. Then I put my books on the table for Xa to teach me English. I sat opposite him and pulled out *Alexander and the Terrible, Horrible, No Good, Very Bad Day.*

On the first page, I pointed to the word *skateboard.* "Do you know this word?"

After a few seconds, he said, "I don't know. Like I said, I didn't do well at school. Learning English has been difficult for me." A flicker of shame crossed his face.

"It's okay. You know more than I do. Is the difficulty in learning English why you didn't go to college?"

He nodded as he rolled up his pant legs. His legs were covered with scars. I drew in a sharp breath.

"Shrapnel wounds," he said. "I became a soldier at fifteen. A year later, I almost died." His voice was tight as if he were on the verge of tears. "I lost some of my friends in an explosion. Luckily, I survived." He hesitated. "Once in a while I still have nightmares."

My heart ached for him. "I'm sorry. I have nightmares too, but I have my mother and Nhia to comfort me."

"My mother usually does the ua neeb for me when I have bad moods and nightmares."

I smiled. "You're lucky."

"If you need anything, call me and my mother." He met my gaze. "You know, I need a wife to take care of me and my mother, and you need a husband to take care of you, your mother, and Nhia. I think we're perfect for each other."

He grasped my hand. An image of Peter flashed in my head.

I pulled free of his grasp. "Please don't touch me."

His eyes narrowed. "I just wanted to feel your hand. Why can't I?"

His aggressive approach didn't please me, but I valued respect, so I held my tongue and I frowned.

He studied me a few seconds, then stood. "I should go home."

I nodded. "Goodbye. Thank you for taking us shopping."

He went to the living room to speak with Mother. He repeated his offer of help, and Mother complimented him on what a good son he was.

He returned to the kitchen and on the way to the door, he said, "Bye. I'll call you later."

"Okay," I replied.

I closed the door behind him and leaned against the wood. Xa was different from the few men I had known. Had fighting in the war made him more assertive? He was handsome, and the fact that he wanted to take care of my family should make me happy. Instead, my stomach churned with anxiety.

14

The following Sunday, I opened all the windows, yet our house still felt as hot as fire. We thought it would be cooler outside and sat on the stairs, but the hot sun beat down on us like a demon. We went back inside. Mother and I sat by the living room window and fanned ourselves with papers like we used to in the refugee camp.

Peter arrived at noon after church wearing a white T-shirt and blue tight shorts.

"It's hot in here," he said, as he walked into the kitchen. "I'll bring a fan next time. It's gonna be hot for a while."

"Yes. A fan please." I wiped beads of sweat off my nape. My pink T-shirt clung to my back in sweat. "You want water?"

He nodded and followed me to the sink. I grabbed a cup, poured water from a plastic jar, and handed it to him.

He gulped a mouthful, then set the cup on the counter. "It's eighty-five degrees outside. I want to take you swimming."

Excitement zipped up my spine. My experience crossing the Mekong River had taught me the importance of learning to swim.

I resisted the urge to hug him. "Yes! I want to swim!"

Peter smiled. "You spoke perfect English."

"Thank you. Mother and Nhia go, too, please?"

Peter hesitated. "Sure. Nhia might like to play in the park. Bring a towel."

We had read about the park in our books. Nhia would love to play there.

I went to the living room where Nhia played and watched TV while Mother sat on the couch. "Peter is taking us to the park. Let's get ready."

Nhia put his toys in the box. Then I grabbed my towel from the bedroom, and we headed out to Peter's car.

He pulled into the Shopko parking lot, and I asked, "Why we here?"

"To buy you a swimsuit."

"Peter, that is too much," I said.

He shook his head. "It's no big deal. You'll use the swimsuit a lot."

I hesitated, but he got out of the car and came around to my side of the door. He opened my door, and I got out. Mother and Nhia slid out from the back seat, and I took Nhia's hand as we started across the parking lot.

The store's cool air welcomed us with an *ah* as we entered. Peter led us to the women's section, where he selected three pieces from a clothing rack and handed them to me. Then we went to a fitting room while Mother and Nhia looked for candy.

"Try them on," he said. "Pick the one you like best."

I stepped inside a small, rectangular room, pulled the door closed behind me, and faced the tall mirror hanging on the wall. I studied the two-piece, navy-colored suit and couldn't imagine wearing it in public with my belly button showing. The suit was more like underwear than swimwear. I hung it on a hook and studied the two-piece, brown-colored suit. It was the same as the first. I decided to try the one-piece floral swimsuit. This one covered more of my skin, but I hated how the tight fabric showed every curve. I felt naked. I couldn't believe people wore this in public. If Mother saw me wearing this, she would be ashamed of me.

After I changed back into my jeans and shirt, I returned to where Peter sat in a worn chair outside the fitting room.

He stood. "Which one do you like?"

"None. I can't be naked outside."

"You won't be naked. If you're going to swim, you have to wear a swimsuit."

I frowned.

"You can use a towel to cover your body," he said.

I sighed. "Okay." I held up the floral one-piece. "This one."

He smiled. "Good choice. We're almost done. Follow me." He led me to a shelf lined with various, multicolored bottles. He pulled a small blue bottle with yellow lettering from a high shelf and handed it to me.

"It's sunscreen lotion to prevent sunburn. Anytime you go outside for a long period of time, you put it on to protect your skin."

I examined the bottle with interest. No wonder Americans had beautiful complexions. I had no idea sunburn could be prevented.

Peter paid for the lotion and swimwear, then drove us to Erb Park. I stared in awe at the pool, tennis court, playground, and pavilion. Several large trees were scattered around the grounds, which made the air much cooler than inside our house. We went to the playground first, and Peter and I pushed Nhia on the swing. He squealed and laughed, and I found myself wishing for a car yet again. Erb Park was too far from home to walk to.

Mother watched us with a broad smile. Then she bent forward and used her fingers to blow her nose onto the grass. She wiped her fingers on her pants.

Peter stared. "In America, we blow our nose into a tissue or handkerchief. If she needs to blow her nose again, I'll get her some toilet tissue from the bathroom."

Embarrassment flooded me. "Sorry. We do that in Thailand. No paper."

"I understand," he said, but I wasn't sure he did.

We had so much to learn. We had to learn the proper way to act in public, so that Nhia and Mother didn't embarrass Peter.

"There are only a few people in the pool now. It's a good time to swim. Can your mom push Nhia?" Peter asked.

"Mother, we're going swimming. Can you push Nhia and watch him?" I asked.

"Yes," she replied. "Don't go in the deep part until you can swim. Be careful."

"I know. Once I can swim, I'll teach Nhia and take him with me."

Peter slung his backpack over his shoulder, and we walked to the bath house which had been built underground with small hills on the left and right sides. Inside, two vending machines stood against the left wall, one with snacks and one with drinks.

Peter pulled my towel and swimwear from his backpack and handed them to me, then pointed toward the women's changing room on the right. "You can change in there. Put your clothes in a locker. Rub the sunscreen lotion on your body and meet me by the pool."

In the changing room, cream lockers lined one wall and cubicles and showers lined the wall on the opposite side with wooden benches in between. The room smelled of sweat and damp air. Two girls wearing two-piece suits talked while shoving their clothes inside the lockers. How could Americans go naked in public and not be ashamed? Would I be like them if I lived in America long enough?

I went into a cubicle and quickly changed, then wrapped the towel around me from my armpits to my thighs.

I emerged from the ladies' room to find Peter waiting outside the door. His towel covered him from the waist down, but at sight of his naked chest, I averted my eyes. I tried to concentrate on the two women and their children playing with plastic tubes and balls in the small pool, but from the corner of my eye, I saw him remove his towel.

"We'll go in the big pool," said Peter.

I yanked my eyes onto him, shocked at the bulge in his swim trunks. I spun and covered my mouth to stifle a scream. Peter grasped my hand. His touch sent a shock through my body.

"It's okay," he said.

Slowly, I faced him. My heart melted. His slender body and long legs and arms were so handsome. His skin was as white as his towel, a skin color my people considered beautiful.

"I'm sorry." Peter's mouth quirked upward, and he wrapped the towel back around his waist, but I recognized the satisfaction in his eyes.

"Sorry," I said. "I never see a man in underwear."

"I could tell," he said with a hint of laughter in his voice. "But remember, this isn't underwear. Wearing swimsuits are normal for Americans." Peter pointed at the two chairs next to the water. "Put your towel on the seat and try the water. I won't look." He faced the pool.

Slowly, I took off the towel. Suddenly, he turned, and I stepped back in alarm.

His eyes widened. "Sorry, I thought you were ready. You have a beautiful body." His expression softened.

"Mommy!" a girl shouted from the children's pool.

I blinked, and said, "Swim."

Peter laughed. "Yeah."

We got into the pool. The cool water soothed me, allowing me to relax and tuck in my thoughts and emotions. We stayed in the shallow part of the pool.

"Today I'll teach you the basic swimming skills," Peter said. "First step, learn to control your breathing and blow bubbles under the water. Look down at your feet while blowing bubbles and count to five. Watch me."

Peter took a big breath and plunged his face into the water. He blew out air and bubbles surfaced, creating the sound of a boiling pot. After a few seconds he lifted his face from the water.

Peter wiped the dripping water from his face then smiled. "You ready to try?"

It seemed easy enough. "Yes."

I inhaled, plunged my face into the water as he had, and began blowing bubbles. Water filled my mouth, and the salty taste and smell of chemicals nauseated me. I yanked my head from the water and coughed. I didn't know if I should spit out the water, so swallowed it. Feeling gross, I stuck out my tongue in an effort to clear the nasty taste.

Peter laughed. "Are you okay?"

My embarrassment deepened, but I knew he didn't mean to make fun of me. I supposed swallowing the water and sticking out my tongue must have looked funny. I didn't want to hurt his feelings, so I laughed, too, and flicked water at him. He scooped water and tossed it at me. We doused water at each other until we were both laughing hard.

When my laughter subsided, I said, "I drink dirty water. I don't want to get sick. My mother worry."

He shook his head. "A little bit of the water won't make you sick. Swimmers get water in their mouths all the time and don't get sick."

"All right. Teach me good this time."

"Sorry. I didn't do a good job the first time." He enunciated every word. "Blow bubbles through your mouth and nose but do not let water get in your mouth and nose."

Peter demonstrated. I tried again and got it this time.

He grinned. "You're doing great. Now practice a few times."

As I practiced controlling my breath and blowing bubbles, it got easier.

In between playing in the water, Peter showed me how to move my arms sideways and up-and-down. Then he showed me how to float face-up. I loved every minute in the pool and with him.

"Peter," a woman called.

He turned toward the speaker. I stood up and eased slightly to his side. Kate stood above us on the concrete in a navy, two-piece suit that accentuated her large breasts and round hips. Her red, curly hair fell across her shoulders.

"Hey," Peter said.

She stared at us. "Can I swim with you two?"

Peter looked over at me. "Um, we're about done."

We hadn't been in the water long, so I wondered if he didn't want her to swim with us. Kate shot me a glare. I dropped my gaze and studied my feet beneath the water.

"Can I talk to you, Peter?" she asked.

Peter got out of the pool. "I'll be back," he said, and followed Kate.

"Auntie Nou!"

I twisted around to see Nhia and Mother standing on top of the hill surrounding the pool. He waved at me.

"We'll meet you in a little bit," I called.

I waited until they had turned, then jumped out of the pool. Surrounded by so many other swimmers dressed as I was eased my discomfort. Still, I wrapped the towel around me. Maybe I wouldn't need the towel next time.

Peter and Kate stood near the men's changing room entrance. I strained to hear their conversation as I passed on my way to the ladies' locker room and heard Peter say, "I can't."

I slowed near the entrance as Kate said, "Only once a week," in a voice laced with frustration.

"I'm sorry. My schedule is full," Peter replied.

Two girls emerged from the women's entrance, and I hurried inside, afraid Peter or Kate might have seen me eavesdropping.

I showered, my thoughts absorbed with Peter and Kate. Kate seemed upset. I wouldn't interfere with Peter's relationship with Kate, but I had to know if there was something between them. I dressed and dried my hair, then found Peter waiting for me in the lobby with a pinched expression.

"You okay?" I asked.

He nodded. I handed him my swimwear and he put it in his backpack.

We took six steps, and I halted in front of Peter. "Kate look not happy. She angry at me?"

He leaned close. "No."

"Be honest. Kate your girlfriend?"

"Just a friend from high school."

I studied him and read only honesty in his expression. "What you talk about?"

Peter shrugged. "She wanted me to teach her advanced swimming lessons. I told her I don't have time. She wasn't happy."

My shoulders relaxed. "Thank you for take me here and teach me swimming."

He smiled softly. "You take learning seriously and always try your best. I admire you very much."

"Thank you."

He threaded his fingers through mine. My pulse fluttered.

"Auntie Nou!" Nhia called. He ran toward us with Mother walking slowly behind.

I yanked my hand from Peter's. He looked at me, his brow furrowed in a frown, but said nothing.

When Nhia reached me, I took his hand. "Did you have a good time?"

"Yes. Can we come back tomorrow?" he asked.

I shook my head. "I don't know. When we have a car, we can come here every day."

Mother arrived and we headed toward Peter's car. I couldn't stop thinking about Kate. I was certain she didn't like me. I hoped Peter was telling the truth about her not being his girlfriend. I didn't want to be Kate's enemy. My family and I were orphans without a clan or relatives to support and protect us. We couldn't afford any trouble.

15

July arrived and we finally received our AFDC money. After paying rent, two-hundred dollars remained. As we would no longer receive food vouchers from Peter's church, we had to save every penny for food. Xa and Auntie gave us food from their garden, which helped greatly.

On Tuesday, Nhia wanted to play in the library, and I needed new books. I pulled the stroller that Mary got us from the Goodwill store.

"Mother, Nhia and I are going to the library."

She shook her head. "Please don't go without Peter. I don't want those boys to hurt you."

My chest tightened. Was Mother right? Would the boys try to harm us? What would life be like if I always had to wait for Peter? Father used to say that fear wouldn't get us far in life if we wanted to pursue our dreams.

"Peter comes only three times a week," I said. "I want to go to the library every day." I squared my jaw in determination. "I won't let the boys stop us from learning. Peter said the library is a public place and we have a right to be there."

Mother pursed her lips in disapproval. "No. Stay home. I can't let anything happen to you two. I won't survive in this country without you."

I shook my head. "We can't let people bully us. Don't worry. We'll be okay."

Once outside, I pushed Nhia in the stroller, the American way. We reached Franklin Street, and I saw the redhaired boy and his friends up ahead. They each carried a plastic bag. My heart began to beat faster. We were only halfway to the library. I looked at the window where the woman had been the last time, but she wasn't there. The street was empty. If the boys caused trouble, we would have no help.

Should we turn back? Surely, there had to be someone in one of the buildings? Something hit my head with a splat. I cried out in pain. Thick yellow and white slimy stuff that looked like snot slid from my hair, down my cheek and onto my shoulder.

Egg.

Another egg hit my forehead as I yanked my gaze onto our attackers. I quickly wiped the sticky substance from my eyes and face.

"Stop!" I screamed.

Another egg hit my shoulder. Nhia shrieked as an egg hit his stroller. My chest burned with hot rage. The boys laughed scornfully.

"Why you do this?" I demanded.

"You don't belong here! Go back to your country!" yelled the redhead.

Their ignorance made me angrier. If I had a country, I wouldn't be here. "America my home. I not go anywhere!"

The blond boy threw another egg, but I easily dodged it. We didn't deserve to be treated like animals.

"Help!" I screamed. "Help us!"

Nhia wailed.

A blue car turned the corner onto the street, and the middle-aged driver rolled down his window and shouted, "Hey, boys! Knock it off!" as he slowed.

The boys raced away. The man pulled the car to the curb near us and got out.

He looked at me and Nhia in the egg-covered stroller and his face twisted in guilt. "I'm so sorry that those boys did this to you."

"Thank you for help," I said in a hoarse voice.

"Let me take you home. Where do you live?"

I didn't want to burden the kind man. "Not far. We go ourselves. Thank you."

He hesitated, then nodded. "All right but be careful."

The man left and I turned the stroller toward home with Nhia still crying. The redhead's words echoed in my head, and I stifled a sob. My people had no country to call home. We had always been a minority in someone else's land. Everywhere we went, we faced rejection, discrimination, and humiliation. I thought America was better than other countries, but I was wrong. Even here, people like the three boys hated us for no reason.

I sucked in several deep breaths. Eventually, I grew calmer, and reminded myself that a peach tree always has a few bad peaches. I couldn't allow bad people to make me fearful or degrade me.

By the time we arrived home, Nhia had stopped crying. He ran to Mother in the living room. She met him halfway, squatted, and hugged him.

One look at me and her face crumpled. "Those boys?"

I nodded.

"How dare they hurt my daughter?" she howled in fury. She released Nhia, came to me and stroked my egg-covered hair. "I'm sorry for being a mother who can't protect her daughter."

Nhia hugged my leg as I smoothed Mother's hair to comfort her. "It's not that you can't protect me," I told her. "We can't control other people. When we have a car, our lives will be better."

"That will be a huge relief." She wiped away her tears with the back of her hand.

I hugged her because I learned that it was the American way of offering comforting. Now that I was taller than her, she cried on my shoulder.

At last, my mother calmed down and took Nhia to the living room. I showered and allowed the cool water to soothe me. After I dressed in clean clothes, I joined my family in the living room on the sofa to watch TV.

As I tried to relax, I became aware of a throbbing ache on the spot on my forehead where one of the eggs had hit me. The pain reminded me of our struggles in America and made me appreciate the books we borrowed from the library even more. I would take nothing for granted.

But my determination didn't halt the memory of the eggs hitting my head or Nhia's cries of terror. I hurried to the bathroom, locked the door, and sat on the toilet with clenched fists. Why were the boys so cruel? A wave of humiliation burned clear to my soul. I clapped a hand over my mouth to muffle my sobs. I wouldn't let Mother and Nhia know of my weakness. They would lose hope if they knew. I took several slow deep breaths. No matter how many times I told myself to be strong, I failed. Could I remain calm if the boys caused more problems? If I defended my family, would we be deported to Laos?

16

The calendar hanging on the wall in the living room reminded me which day Peter would come. Today was Sunday, which meant he would come after church around noon. Excitement tingled in my stomach as I hurried to finish my chores. It had been only two days since I'd last seen him, but it seemed like forever.

I began cutting Nhia's hair in the kitchen. The phone rang.

"Xa, again?" I muttered. He called every day and showed up at my house whenever he wanted.

Mother picked up the phone, then said, "Peter."

I quickened my pace, scissors still in hand, and took the phone. "Hi, Peter," I said.

"Hey," he said. "I'm not going to church today. If it's ok, I'll come early to take you to the laundromat."

"Okay," I said.

"I'll be there soon."

I was still cutting Nhia's hair when Peter arrived with a fan. We greeted one another with broad smiles. Peter set the fan on the kitchen table.

"Thank you for the fan," I said.

"You're welcome. It's used but works."

He examined Nhia's hair. "I'm impressed. You're an exceptional barber."

I couldn't help but smile. "Thank you."

"Hi, Peter," Nhia said.

Peter and I looked at each other in surprise. This was the first time Nhia had spoken to anyone outside the family.

Peter squatted eye-level with Nhia and smiled. "Hi. I'm so happy you spoke to me."

Nhia pressed his lips into a line.

"Can you give me a high five?" Peter raised his hand with an opened palm. "All you have to do is slap my hand. Easy peasy."

Nhia shook his head.

Peter winked. "When you're ready, we can high five and play together."

Nhia giggled.

"Peter, you wait in the living room," I said, and began trimming Nhia's hair.

I bathed Nhia and cleaned the kitchen floor, then Peter and I left for the laundromat.

Once we got the laundry into the washing machines, Peter and I studied English grammar.

Two couples with young children arrived. A girl of about five with blonde hair watched us for a while as she sat with her parents two tables away.

"Mom, the girl over looks different," the little girl said in a loud voice. "I like her black hair."

"She has beautiful hair, but your hair is beautiful too," said her mother.

The girl touched her shoulder length blonde hair and smiled. She joined her little brother by the window, and they watched the passing cars on the street. Her parents glanced our way, then murmured something I couldn't hear.

"Peter," I whispered, "look like many family never see people like me."

Peter looked over his shoulder to the couple. "You're right."

"How you feel when people look at you and me together?"

"You would say, 'how do you feel?'" he corrected.

"How do you feel?" I repeated slowly.

He shrugged. "I don't care what they think. God wants us to love all people and help them. I'm living my life the way God wants me to, not based on somebody else's opinion."

What a brave soul! I looked at the couple again. They were pulling clothes from a washer. They didn't seem unfriendly. Not like the redhaired boy and his friends.

"Do you think most America think like you?" I asked.

"You would say, 'Americans' for the people who live in America," he said, then added, "I think most Americans would agree with me."

Our dryer stopped. I quickly loaded the clothes into a cart, then pushed the cart back at our table. Peter stood and took a shirt from the cart.

I waved him off as he began to fold the shirt. "A woman job. I can do it."

He folded the shirt neatly, then pulled another from the cart. "Remember, men and women are equal in America. We share duties."

Oh yes! He had told me this, but I forgot because in my culture, duties were gendered. Mai's husband Phia was one of the few Hmong men I had seen helping his wife with chores. My father and brother never did dishes, washed clothes, or helped with household chores. If Toua came to America, would he change like Phia?

"I wish for a husband that help and respect me," I said.

Peter paused in folding a towel. "You're an amazing girl. Your wish might come true." He paused. "I think it's time I tell you something."

I placed a folded shirt to the side. "What?"

"I love you."

I yanked my gaze onto his face. Peter loved me? How was that possible? I wasn't like him. I was uneducated.

"I love you too." My voice squeaked.

He grasped my hands and gently squeezed. We intertwined our fingers and couldn't stop smiling. I wanted to pull him close, but a good girl wouldn't initiate such intimate contact.

"Your mother and father okay you like me?" I asked.

"Yes. My mom likes you a lot."

Was a future with Peter, the handsomest, most caring, and thoughtful man I'd ever known possible? I'd love Mary to be my mother-in-law. My limbs felt light as a feather and a squeal escaped my lips. The couple near us glanced our way, and I remembered that we were in public. I pulled free of Peter's grasp.

"In America, it's okay to hold hands in public and even kiss," Peter said.

"Oh. But I'm shy."

We went back to folding clothes. My happiness faded as I recalled Mother. She liked Peter, but would she allow us to date? I prayed she would.

On the ride home, we held hands. I caressed his soft hand, then froze. My rough, dry hands must feel like sharp pebbles against his smooth skin.

I lowered my eyes to my lap. "Sorry, my hands not soft like your."

He rubbed my palm. "I don't mind."

"I wash dishes every day and my hands dry."

"I'll get you some lotion. After you wash dishes, you put lotion on to keep your hands soft.

I loved the lotion idea and loved learning new things. There were so many things I didn't know.

"If you're free, I would like to spend the rest of the day with you," Peter said.

I squeezed his hand. "I always free. I like you with me every day."

"If I didn't work and have other commitments, I would come every day."

If I could have him every day speaking English to me, I would learn English in no time.

We turned the corner onto our street and my breath caught. Xa's white, two-door car sat parked outside our house.

Peter parked behind him.

"Peter, that is Xa car," I said.

Peter turned off the ignition. "Who's Xa?"

"Auntie's son. He not my boyfriend, but he think he is."

He glanced at the car then looked back at me. "Hmm. I have a competitor." He gave me a slight smile. "As long as he's not your boyfriend, I'm good."

"I don't like him. I don't want him rude to you."

"Don't worry about me."

We got out of the car, took the baskets from the trunk, and carried them into the house. We opened the door to find Xa sitting at the kitchen table eating an apple. His eyes narrowed on Peter.

"Hi, Xa." I set my basket on the kitchen floor. "This is Peter. Our sponsor son," I said in English so Peter could understand.

Peter placed his basket next to mine and held out his hand, "Hi."

Xa hesitated, then stood and clasped Peter's hand. "Hi."

After the handshake, Peter and I brought the baskets to the bedroom. Auntie and Mother were talking in the living room. We returned to the kitchen.

Xa stood tall. "Peter, I'll take care Nou family from now on," he said in English.

"I like to help," Peter said.

Xa puffed out his chest. "Nou mother wants me to help the family. I know what they need. They trust me."

Peter looked at me. The air in the room felt thick. Had Mother told Xa that she wanted him to help us?

"I want Peter help," I said in English.

"Are you crazy!" Xa blurted in Hmong. "Do you think this white man cares about you and your family?"

"He has taken great care of us," I replied in Hmong.

Mother and Auntie came into the kitchen.

"Hi, Auntie." I gestured to Peter, and said in English, "This is Peter. He our sponsor son."

"Hi," Peter said.

"Hi." Her gaze shifted to me. "Nou, your mother wants to see my garden. She's excited. We've been waiting for you and need to go now."

"My mother can go with you. I have to go to the library," I said.

"I want a garden," Mother said. "I need you to check it out and see if we can grow our own."

She wanted me to go with them? I had promised to spend the day with Peter. My heart fell. I didn't want to disappoint him, but I had no choice.

I held back tears and looked at Peter. "My mother say I have to go to the garden. Sorry."

"It's all right. You go to the garden. Have fun."

He didn't seem angry, and I breathed easier. "Thank you."

Xa gave Peter a smug smile.

Peter left and I excused myself to the bathroom and applied sunscreen to my face, neck, and arms. I brought the sunscreen to the kitchen where everyone had gathered. Nhia clung to Mother's leg. I applied sunscreen to his arms and face. Then did the same for Mother.

"Auntie, do you want sunscreen to protect you from the sun?" I asked.

Surprise flashed across her face. "I didn't know there is such a thing. I've been using my bandana and hat to shield myself from the sun. I'd love to try it."

I applied sunscreen to Auntie's arms and neck but didn't ask Xa.

When we reached Xa's car, Auntie got into the back seat with Mother and Nhia.

"You sit with Xa in the front," she said. "You watch him drive and learn from him."

The back seat was crowded, and she had a good point. I did need to learn to drive. I sat with Xa in the front.

The long drive took us into a rural area with green fields that stretched far into the distance. Mother and Auntie chatted, which gave me excuse to remain silent. I didn't want to talk to Xa.

Auntie told Mother that her garden was on a farm that belonged to Uncle Shoua Nu's friend from work. They rented the small plot for ten dollars a summer and had grown a garden there for two summers.

We merged onto a dirt road where an old tractor, a truck, and a small car sat parked on the gravel driveway of a two-story, white house. Green corn plants covered the flat land for miles. Auntie's plot was near an old, red wooden barn. Her waist-high corn plants were in neat rows, and they danced and swayed in a warm breeze. Her cucumber and squash plants sprawled across the ground in beautiful vines. The cilantro and mustard greens were about a foot tall and ready to pick. Weeds had sprouted in much of the garden. Her garden reminded me of our fields in Laos on the hillside by our village.

"Your vegetables are growing well," Mother cried. "I feel like I'm back in Laos. I want a garden too."

Auntie beamed as she looked over her colorful garden. "It's late to start a garden, but next year we'll rent you a plot next to mine."

"I can't wait," Mother said. "I can help you weed. I have nothing to do and would love to keep busy."

"I'd love your help." Auntie crouched to check on her mustard greens.

Mother looked at her missing arm, then whispered to me, "I'll practice with one hand."

"I'll help," I said. "You can use a small hoe."

"Nou," Auntie said, "pick some vegetables for your family."

The blazing midafternoon sun beat down on us and I was glad for the sunscreen.

I hoisted Nhia onto Mother's back. "Mother, you should wait for us inside the barn."

"I want to check everything out first," she said.

She and Nhia went to the corn plants while I turned my attention to the cilantro patch. Xa joined me, but instead of helping, he watched as I worked.

"Good job picking," he said. "You're ready to be a wife."

I bristled. "No. I'm not ready."

Xa crossed his arms over his chest. "Your friend Peter might be handsome, but he's American. He helps you and tries to be nice just to make you fall in love. Once he has your body, he'll leave you."

Anger bubbled inside me. Out of respect for Auntie, I couldn't tell Xa how much I hated him. I sucked in a deep breath.

"You don't know Peter," I said through gritted teeth.

"He's too good for you. There's no way he'll marry you."

Could that be true? If Peter didn't think I was good, he wouldn't say he loved me, would he?

"Peter loves me," I snapped.

Xa scoffed. "He lied to you. You're new and know nothing about America. American divorce rate is high. Most Americans I work with are divorced. You know, decent Hmong men won't take a used woman or a woman who courts a white man. Stay away from Peter. He's spoiling you and ruining your life."

I stood and glared at him. "Enough of your talk. Leave me alone!"

He shrugged and returned to the car without another word. Mother might believe Xa was a decent man, but I knew better. Peter would be the ideal husband. Our cultural differences would be a challenge, but I believed that fate had brought our families together. Fate would guide me to the right man.

On our way home, we passed a field where several people crouched as they picked through dense green foliage.

"Auntie, what are the people doing in the field?" I asked.

"They're picking strawberries," Xa said. "I know the Hmong family working that field."

"Cher Thai Vang's family," Auntie said. "They live in Menasha, our city."

I was excited to hear they were from our Vang clan. "How many Hmong families live in Menasha?"

"Three. Us, the Vangs, and my father's family," Xa said. "If you want to earn money, you can pick strawberries with them. I heard the pay is $1.50 per hour."

In Laos, I hated weeding and farm work. If I had a choice, I'd never do it again. I did need to earn money, though.

"I want to work, but I don't have a car," I said.

"I'll give you a ride," Xa said.

I didn't want to ride with him. Plus, I needed to focus on my studies. "Very nice of you, but I'm not interested."

Mother and Auntie's lively conversations in the back seat resounded in the car.

Xa glanced at me. "If you don't like working, then get married. You can be a stay-at-home mom."

I was done talking with him. I couldn't wait to get home.

17

There weren't many people in the library at midday the following day. I sat on the carpet with Nhia on my lap as I read *Curious George* to him. A boy and his father read at the table nearby.

"Excuse me," a woman said.

I looked up to see Susan. Her long, brown hair cascaded down her shoulders.

"Hi," I said.

"Sorry to interrupt," she said. "I just wanted to say hi and get to know you."

"It's okay," I said. "Nhia, go play with the stuffed animal."

He glanced at Susan and scampered off to the playhouse.

Susan sat on the carpet next to me. "How do you like America so far?"

I shrugged. "Good."

"I'm glad." Her blue eyes bored into me. "I met up with Peter last week. He told me he tutors you. How's that going?"

Peter and Susan were seeing each other? What did this mean? I clenched my jaw to hide my confusion.

"Good. He a good teacher."

Her eyes widened. "He is?"

I nodded. "Yes. He teach me to read, write, and speak."

"Very well. I'm glad. What do you think of him?"

I stared at the floor not quite sure about the question. "What you mean?"

"Is Peter a good man?"

"Yes. Very good man and nice."

She gave a thin smile. "I have to go." She stood. "It was great seeing you."

"Nice seeing you too."

I watched her until she disappeared around the nearest shelf. Susan seemed nice and hadn't given me any dirty looks, but she made me uncomfortable.

Nhia and I played with the stuffed animals for a while, then we checked out books and walked home. We hadn't seen the redhead and his friends on the way to the library today and that gave me hope.

We reached the house and stopped at our mailbox. Excitement swept over me when I found a letter from Pheng. It had been almost two months since I sent letters to Pheng and Toua. I bounded up the stairs with Nhia trailing behind.

Pushing the door open, I called, "Mother!"

She hurried to the kitchen. "What?"

I held up the envelope. "A letter from Pheng."

Her eyes sparkled. "Read it."

Mother, Nhia, and I sat on the sofa as I read Pheng's letter aloud.

June 26, 1978
Dear Nou,

I received your letter today. It elevated my empty life and happiness swelled in my heart knowing that you, your mother, and Nhia are doing great and enjoying America. I miss you and Nhia very much. Every day, every moment, I wish to be with you and my son. I stop by the UNHCR office every day to check on our interview date. No luck so far, but I'm optimistic that one day I will reunite with you all in America.

I know you love my son and will raise him well and protect him. Thank you for all you do. When you read or play with him, I hope you think of me.

I'll write to you when we are coming. Take good care of yourself, your mother, and Nhia. I will see you in a few months.

Good-bye,
Pheng Yang

Today was July 24th, which meant the letter had taken almost a month to reach America. If Toua sent a letter, it should be here soon. When I received his letter, I would reply with the request for him to perform the tso plig. We had to get it done to ensure Mother's wellbeing.

I wrote a letter to Pheng immediately and included a picture of us, along with our phone number. Nhia and I started toward the post office, following the route Peter had shown me two weeks ago.

White clouds blocked the sun, and a cool breeze ruffled our hair as we strolled hand-in-hand on the sidewalk. Nhia pulled free of my hand and ran ahead. I chased him, laughing all the way to the post office where we deposited the letter.

On our way back home, Nhia ran several yards ahead of me. Suddenly, a bulldog raced from the yard of a nearby house. Nhia halted, then began to run when the dog veered in his direction. He screamed in terror. Panic shot through me, and I broke into a run as he fell on the sidewalk. The dog reached him. My heart twisted in my chest.

"Help!" I screamed.

A car crossing the street farther ahead slowed, then stopped on the street. A woman in her forties jumped from her car and ran toward Nhia.

"Get away from him!" she shouted at the dog.

The dog turned toward the houses and I caught sight of the redheaded boy who had thrown the eggs at us. He stood in front of the house where the dog had run from.

I reached Nhia, dropped to my knees, and pulled him close. He sobbed and

trembled uncontrollably.

"Shh," I soothed. "You're all right. I'm sorry."

The woman reached us. "Is he okay?" She squatted beside us.

"I don't know." Tears streamed down my cheeks.

I stared at the redhead. His smirk angered me. I pointed at him. "His dog. He make trouble."

The woman stood and shouted, "Boy, come over with your dog!"

"No dog. Nhia scare," I blurted.

The woman strode to the boy. I couldn't hear their conversation, but she returned shortly.

"The boy said his dog loves children and was just playing with your brother. Most dogs don't bite, and that dog isn't the type that hurts people."

Of course, she didn't know that the boy had attacked us before.

"Let's look at the baby," she said.

Nhia gripped me tightly.

"It's all right," I soothed. "The dog is gone."

The woman and I checked Nhia's body but found no teeth marks or bruises.

"Most dogs are nice pets," she said.

"Nhia scare of dog."

Her brow furrowed in worry. "Do you need a ride home?"

"No. Thank you for help. We are close to home."

She stood and looked round, then said, "You're sure?"

I scooped up Nhia. "Yes, thank you."

She seemed uncertain, then said, "Ok. Take care going home."

I nodded, then hurried toward home. I began to cry again. Nhia hadn't been hurt, but I had failed to protect him. Why did the redheaded boy hate us?

When we arrived home, I had wiped my tears away, but my red eyes gave me away.

"What happened?" Mother demanded.

I told her, and she took Nhia from me. "Were you scared?" she asked as she cuddled him on the sofa.

"Very scared," he whimpered. He still trembled, and huge tears rolled down his chubby cheeks.

Mother looked up. "When a person is this frightened, that means his soul has left his body. We must call Nhia's soul back or he might become sick."

My shoulders drooped. Where would we get live chickens for a *hu plig*, a soul calling ritual?

"Nou, do you hear me?" Mother said.

I blinked. "Yes."

"We'll call Auntie Shoua Nu to do the hu plig and Xa to buy live chickens for us. I'm sure they know farmers who have live chickens."

I rubbed my forehead with a palm to ease the tension. If I asked Xa for help, he would take that as a sign that he was our man.

I sat next to Mother on the sofa and took her hands in mine. "Mother, I think Nhia will be okay. We live in America now. It's a new country with new rules and new way of life. I don't think we can bring live chickens to the house. The landlord will kick us out if the people downstairs call the police on us again."

Mother narrowed her eyes. "Again?"

Oops. I silently kicked myself for my mistake.

"During the shamanic ritual, the woman downstairs called the police when Auntie stomped on the floor. I apologized to our neighbors but, of course, they don't understand our ways. Before coming here, we took the oath to be good citizens. If the police arrest us, they might send us back to Laos." I paused as memories of the canoeists we asked to help us cross the Mekong River from Laos to Thailand surfaced. My chest tightened. "Do you remember the canoeists telling us to return to Laos?"

Mother nodded. "Yes. We begged them, but they didn't care if we lived or died. I was so afraid."

"Me too."

"All right." She hung her head. "I hope Nhia will be okay." She stroked his head as he continued to sob.

Nhia wouldn't eat anything that night. The next day, he had a fever. I gave him Tylenol and his fever went down, but it rose again later.

"He's not getting better," said Mother. "We have to do hu plig."

It was my duty to make him better, so I agreed.

That evening, Mother called Auntie. After they spoke, Xa wanted to talk to me. Reluctantly, I took the phone from Mother.

"Nou, I'll help you take care of your family," he said. "After work tomorrow, I'll get two chickens from a farm and bring them over. We'll do the hu plig in the evening. How's that sound?"

"Very good." I was thrilled at the swift action. "Thank you."

"One more thing," he said. "You must respect me. Don't give me that evil, *I-hate-you,* look ever again." Without another word, he hung up.

I sank down on the sofa, put my elbows on my knees, and cradled my head in my hands. My inability to take care of my family tore at my dignity. I couldn't stand the thought of meeting Xa's demands and being extra nice to him.

The next evening, Auntie and Xa arrived with two live chickens in a brown box, mustard greens, and herbs. She also had a *kuam*, a divination tool made of a bull horn, and her metal hoop rattle.

My heart overflowed with gratitude. "Thank you, Auntie and Xa, for helping us." I did my best to smile.

"You're welcome," said Auntie. "I usually kill and pluck my chickens in our garage, but since you don't have one, you'll have to do it in the kitchen."

I scowled, not liking the idea of plucking chickens on the nice vinyl floor. "All right. I'll mop the floor after."

Auntie went to the living room where Mother tended to Nhia.

"How are you?" Xa asked.

"I'm fine."

He grabbed my hand. "I'm more than happy to help your family. If you need anything else, you let me know."

His touch left me cold. My instinct was to shove his hand away, but I had to give him more respect.

"Very kind of you." I managed a smile and gently pulled my hand free.

I had to get busy, so he wouldn't touch me again. I closed the windows so the noise wouldn't bother our neighbors, then filled a bowl with rice and stuck an egg and a stick of incense in the rice. Auntie and Mother entered the kitchen as I placed the bowl on a chair by the open door and set the box with the two live chickens next to it. I lit the incense, and its woody fragrance and smoke spiraled upward. I laid out a black garbage bag on the floor, then put a small plastic bowl on top of the bag.

"We must tiptoe," I said in a quiet voice, and pointed to the floor. "So we don't disturb our neighbors." To my relief, everyone nodded.

Auntie stood by the door with her metal hooped rattle, which contained multiple metal washers that clanged as she shook them. She uttered comforting words, asking Nhia's frightened, lost soul to return home. At last, she tossed the kuam on the floor. It landed with a thud with the pair of cut-split horns facing down. Despite my fear our downstairs neighbors might not like the noise, I wanted to cry with relief. This meant Nhia's soul had come home. The first round of the hu plig was done.

I removed a chicken from the box and pressed its beak tight to quiet its clucking. Mother held the chicken's feet and wings while I slit the neck with a knife. Blood splattered on the black trash bag. Mother let the chicken's blood drip in the small plastic bowl on the garbage bag. She then put the chicken in the basin, and we repeated the process with the other chicken. I wondered what Peter would think if he saw us. Would he still like me? Would he be interested in learning about my culture?

I dipped the chickens in hot, boiling water and held my breath as the stench of chicken dung filled the room. In Laos, our thatch huts allowed air to flow freely, but this American house trapped all smells inside. The smell became so overwhelming that Xa crinkled his nose and reopened the kitchen windows.

He leaned a hip against the sink counter and watched as I plucked the chicken. "You have skills," he said.

"Why don't you show me *your* skills?" I asked.

He laughed. "To be honest, I've never plucked a chicken."

Of course not. "Then you're not ready to be a husband."

Xa scoffed. "Killing chickens is woman's duty. A man proposes to a woman once he decides she's worthy to be his wife. That means he gets to observe her skills, not the other way around."

He went to the living room before I had a chance to respond. I could have used his help, but I remembered that he was the youngest child in his family. Auntie probably overindulged him, leaving him with few skills.

I cleaned the chickens, then boiled them, along with the egg. When the chickens were cooked enough to finish the ritual, I put them, the egg, lighted incense, and cooked rice together in the white plastic, oval platter and placed it on the chair by the door.

Auntie performed the second-time soul calling. Afterward, she put the platter on the table and examined the chickens' feet, eyes, and tongues.

"Everything looks good," she said. "Nhia's soul came home. He'll be well again."

Mother smiled. "Thank you so much for your help. We're lucky to have you."

"You're welcome."

Auntie took the egg, and Mother and I followed her to the living room. She extended the egg toward Nhia, but he didn't take it. Nhia was less afraid of women, but he didn't know Auntie well enough to take something from her. Mother took the egg and put it in his hand.

"It's the egg from the hu plig," she said. "You must eat it. Do you want to eat it now or later?"

"Later," Nhia whispered.

"You hold on to it," said Mother. "Your soul came home. You'll feel better soon."

I prayed she was right.

18

Nhia and I sat on the stairs for fresh air. After a week, Nhia was himself again and the knot in my chest had unfurled and the fog in my brain cleared.

The scorching sun baked us, and I started to sweat.

"Let's go under the stairs," I said.

Nhia nodded. We stood and went down beneath the stairs and sat on the ground. A food delivery truck with a picture of baked goods painted on the side passed by on the street. Although we just had lunch, my mouth watered at the beautiful pastries. August had arrived and it had been over two months since we came to America. I really wanted to learn how to cook American food for Peter in payment for helping me and my family. Guilt gnawed each time he came, and I had no good food to offer him. I was ashamed to offer him plain Hmong food, the only food I knew how to cook. I had been thinking about asking my downstairs neighbor to teach me how to cook American food but hadn't had the courage to ask.

"I'm taking fresh air out in the porch," Linda called from her porch.

"Okay," her husband replied.

Anticipation and fear swirled in my stomach. This was the perfect opportunity for me to talk to Linda about teaching me to cook American food.

"Nhia, do you want to meet our neighbors?" I asked.

He shook his head. "No."

"Stay here. I'll be back." I stood and walked to the side of the house opposite the driveway.

Linda sat on a brown wooden chair rocking herself.

I approached her. "Hi, Linda."

She smiled. "Hi, you remember my name, but I don't remember yours."

I smiled. "I am Nou."

She leaned forward on her chair. "Hi, Nou. How are you?"

"Good. How are you?"

She expelled a breath. "Okay, I suppose."

"I want to cook American food." I tried my best English. "Would you teach me?"

She frowned. "I'm sorry. I have pain and can't cook much anymore. My husband cooks sometimes and we eat frozen food and eat out."

My heart fell, but I still gave her a grateful smile. "It's okay. Sorry you have pain."

She leaned back on the chair and rocked herself. "Being old is no fun."

Mother called, "Nou, you have a phone call."

"Coming." I waved to Linda. "Very nice talk to you."

I ran upstairs with Nhia close behind. The phone lay on the kitchen table with its cord stretching long.

I picked it up. "Hello."

"Hi, Nou," Peter said. "If you're free, I'd like to take you on a date tonight."

"What is 'date'?"

"Go out to have fun together. You and me on a Friday night."

I gasped. I'd go anywhere with Peter—anytime. "Where?"

"To a theatre. A big place where a movie is shown on a big screen."

I squealed. "I want to go. I have to talk to my mother."

"Ok, ask her. I'd like to make the four-thirty show."

I turned to Mother, who sat at the table. "Mother, Peter wants to take me to watch a movie. This is another way for me to learn. Can I go?"

She hesitated. "A good, decent girl doesn't go out with a man alone."

"Please Mother. You know me. I won't do anything to shame you. I just want to learn. I'll be fine."

Her lips pressed together in thought. Finally, she said, "All right."

I replaced the phone to my ear, and said, "Peter, I can go."

"Perfect. I'll be there at four o'clock."

We said goodbye and I looked at the clock. Two p.m. I had two hours. I made dinner for Nhia and Mother, so I didn't have to cook later. At three-thirty p.m., I went to the bedroom and changed into a long, dark red dress with small white polka dots, a V-neck, and short puffy sleeves. In the bathroom, I applied foundation, eye shadow, and lipstick. I untied my long hair and let it fall to my shoulders. I hoped I proved worthy to go out in public with Peter.

As always, Peter arrived right on time. His tight, short sleeved shirt was tucked into the waist of his light brown khakis. He had trimmed his ear-length hair and parted it to one side. His broad smile and confidence made him so attractive.

My heart somersaulted.

Peter's eyebrows shot up. "Wow! You're beautiful."

I smiled shyly. "Thank you. You are handsome."

He grinned and handed me a small, plastic bottle. "It's lotion for your hands."

"Thank you."

"Should we go?"

"We talk to my mother," I said.

How I wished Peter could ask Mother for permission. That was our cultural norm, but the language barrier prevented them from communicating.

We went to the living room, where I set the lotion on top of the TV.

Mother said, "Hi."

"Hi, Choua," Peter replied.

She opened her mouth as if to say something, then looked at me. "He's our sponsor, and a good man. I trust him and you. Be home by eight o'clock."

"Thank you." I turned to Peter, and said, "We must be home by eight."

Peter smiled. "Thank you, Choua."

Mother nodded. "Nou, be a good girl."

"I will."

We went out to Peter's car.

He opened the passenger door for me with a flourish. "Your ride, m'lady." He made a low bow.

My stomach fluttered. "Thank you. All American men open door for women?" I asked as I slid into the seat.

He smiled. "When they remember."

He closed my door, walked around to the other side, and got into the driver's seat. He backed up into the street and drove. We held hands.

"Why you open the door for me every time?" I asked.

"Why do you?" he corrected.

"Why do you open the door for me?" I repeated.

He shrugged. "It's what a gentleman does. And I love you."

My stomach made another turn. I felt like I was flying. So, this was how a good man expressed love to a woman. This was how it felt to be loved. I wished the drive would never end but five minutes later, we arrived at the Viking Theater in downtown Appleton.

Peter parked the car on College Avenue, and we walked behind other couples holding hands and who were headed for the two-story concrete building. Inside the theatre lobby, the cool air welcomed us. Film posters hung on the walls, and a line of people formed at the concession stand. Although I felt eyes on us, having Peter with me gave me courage to hold my head high. Being different, I stood out, but I wasn't as nervous as I had been at Peter's graduation.

I gave Peter money to pay for my ticket, but he insisted on paying. He also bought us popcorn and two small drinks. We entered a huge, dark room with dim accent lighting on the aisles. Rows of seats on a sloped floor faced a giant screen on the opposite wall. We managed to find two seats in the middle section of the crowded theatre. We settled in the comfortable seats and Peter put his drink in the cup holder to his left and I did the same. Excitement washed over me.

"What do you think?" Peter asked.

"Very cool. Why no lights?"

"Are you afraid?" He held the popcorn bag closer to me.

I scooped up a handful of popcorn. "No."

"It's better to watch movies in the dark."

"Oh. Interesting." I popped popcorn in my mouth and chewed.

Previews filled the screen. The giant screen gave me the impression I sat only inches from the actors. The intense sound and color added to the excitement. What a difference between our small TV and this giant screen. A couple in front of us kissed. I wanted to cover my eyes, but reminded myself that displays of affection was normal for Americans. I looked around. The darkness made it difficult to see far, but a couple in our row four seats away kissed too.

Soon, the previews ended, and *Star Wars* began. Everything was good until the spaceships started zooming across the screen and fighting. Each scene made my stomach swirl and my head ache. I closed my eyes and pressed against the seat to lessen the hollow sensation in my belly.

Peter slid an arm around my shoulder and pulled me close. "Are you okay?" he whispered.

I opened my eyes and whispered, "Yes. Spaceship fly make me dizzy."

"I think it's because this is your first time seeing a big screen. Once you get used to it, you won't get dizzy anymore."

I hoped he was right.

His arm tightened around my shoulders. His sweet, fruity scent and warmth comforted me. I tried watching the movie and averted my eyes during the more violent scenes of spaceships fighting in space.

When the movie ended, we followed a stream of people, some holding hands, into a hallway and outside. As I squinted against the sunlight, feeling dizzy, Peter grasped my hand. I held tight. Seeing people holding hands in public, I felt less ashamed. I was still Mother's good girl because hand holding was a norm in America.

The sidewalk was packed with people from the theater and shops. We picked our way toward his car parked near a streetlight. Lines of cars stopped at the red light.

We reached the car, and I was sorry when he released my hand and opened the car door.

As Peter drove, I said, "Thank you for the movie. It is a good experience."

"What did you think of *Star Wars*?"

"I like it. Do you like it?"

"Oh. Yes. It's one of the best movies."

He turned into another street.

"How many movie you watch in theater?" I asked.

"Oh, too many to count. I like movies. You know, the sound and big screen."

Did he watch the movies with Susan or his male friends? I wanted to ask but didn't want to know the answer.

We arrived at a restaurant called Mary's Restaurant. He opened the restaurant door and held it for me. Inside looked similar to McDonald's, the only restaurant I had eaten in, except it was bigger and had beautiful wide, glass pendant lighting. The restaurant was half full of diners. A young, beautiful waitress with brown hair led us to a booth and gave us each a menu. Peter told her we'd take water for our drinks.

The menu overwhelmed me. There were many choices, and I didn't know enough English to know what to order.

"Peter, I order what you order." I set the menu on the table.

"I'll help you find something you like," he said.

"I eat any food."

Memories of our trek through the jungle unexpectedly surfaced. We had eaten what scarce food we could forage in the jungle. Mother, Nhia, and I had survived, but my father, sister, and so many others hadn't. I swallowed against the lump in my throat.

Peter's brow furrowed. "You okay?"

I released a long breath. "The journey to America. We eat leaves and bugs. We almost starve."

The waitress set our drinks on the table and Peter ordered tender chicken, baked beans, French fries, and rolls.

When she left, Peter covered my hand with his. As always, my skin tingled at his touch, and the warm spark rushed through my veins.

"I'm sorry for what you went through," he said.

"It's okay now. You make life good for me. I'm so happy with you."

I loved everything about him. His handsome face and his kind, caring heart. Xa didn't think I was good enough for Peter. Was I? Peter loved me, so I must be good enough for him. Xa said Peter would ruin my life. How could that be when Peter made me happy?

Thankfully, there were no Hmong around. If anyone saw me in public and alone with a white man, rumors would spread, and my reputation would be ruined. If Xa knew I was out with Peter alone, he'd be furious. But I didn't care.

Xa and his mother were like family. How I wished Xa would consider me a sister. I had lost my siblings and I missed them terribly.

Peter laced his fingers with mine. "I love you, Nou."

"I love you a lot," I replied.

The waitress interrupted us with our food. I surveyed the banquet. My stomach growled. I copied Peter's use of utensils and listened as he explained what a napkin is for and how to hold a knife. I cut my chicken and took a bite. It was crispy and delicious. Then I ate a spoonful of baked beans and loved the sweetness.

"Nou, I'm so proud of you for your hard work learning English and taking care of your family. You never complain. You're a caring, kind, hardworking, ambitious, and smart girl. We're here on a date, but I think we should celebrate your hard work."

Celebrate! I felt like I was floating in a cloud. I swallowed my food.

"Thank you."

A tear escaped my eye. I dabbed at my eyes with a napkin.

Peter grasped my hand and gently squeezed.

"You very kind," I said. "You understand my problems. You make me happy. You make me love life. I am lucky to meet you."

"I'm the lucky one," he said, and ate a fry.

He was so handsome with his straight nose and light brown hair. Why did American women divorce their husbands? American husbands and wives shared chores and had equal rights. If I could have Peter for my husband, I would never divorce him. I'd love, cherish, and support him and be patient and helpful. Heaven, if Peter could communicate with Mother and embrace our rituals, he'd be the perfect man.

I chewed the dinner roll. "Peter, thank you for the movie and food. I love everything. I love going out on date. I love to be with you. I learn so much. You the best teacher."

"Thanks. This is what people do, go out with the person you love and just have fun."

I grinned. "I love American culture."

Peter grinned back. "Good. Enjoy it."

We took our time eating, and I saved a few of my fries for Nhia because he loved them. The waitress brought the bill, and I asked for a to-go box. Peter checked his watch, and it was seven-thirty. We had to get home before eight o'clock.

On our way home, Peter told me that, besides swimming, he played tennis, volleyball, and cross country. I didn't know these sports, but I loved that he was telling me about his life.

When we pulled into the driveway, Peter parked the car and faced me. "Thank you for going out with me."

"Thank you for the fun night. I love it."

He smiled. "I'll see you Sunday."

Peter hugged me, then kissed me on the cheek. A powerful sensation coursed through me, giving me the courage to kiss his cheek.

"Good night," I said, and pulled away.

"Have a good night."

I got out and watched until his car disappeared around the corner. I sighed, already anticipating our next date. I couldn't wait to explore more things with Peter. He was the man who could fulfill my curiosity. My heart belonged to him.

19

Toua's letter arrived two weeks later. He wrote that his family was doing fine, and he was happy we were doing well. Receiving his letter assured me he had received my letter, which meant, I could send money for the soul releasing ritual.

"Mother, how much money should we send to Toua?" I asked.

She thought for several seconds. "After paying the bills and buying food, we have a hundred and fifty dollars left, but we need it for food for the rest of the month. Maybe send fifty dollars?"

"Hmm, will fifty dollars be enough?"

"I don't know," she replied.

"It's for both Der and Father. If we don't send enough, Toua won't be able to do it and we'll have to send again, which will take another month." I paused. "I suggest we send him one hundred dollars. I'll pick strawberries to make some extra money."

Mother's eyes widened in shock. "Pick strawberries? You hated weeding in Laos. Picking strawberries seems harder than weeding."

What choice did I have? Who would hire me for an office job when I couldn't read, write, or speak English fluently? I had no skills other than field work. No matter how much I hated working in the fields, I had to do something. My name meant *the sun*, the source of energy that was bright, hot, and powerful. I had to live up to my name.

"If Cher Thai's family can pick strawberries, I can too."

Tears sprang to Mother's eyes. "I'm so sorry. I should be the one working, not you. I have failed in my duty as a mother."

I embraced her and stroked her hair. "Remember, I'm your son. It's my duty to take care of you. Your duty as my mother is to be healthy and happy."

"I'm blessed you are mine," she sobbed. "Thank our ancestors and Heaven for giving you to me."

"I'm lucky to be your child. I am disappointed that I am not a son."

Mother wiped her tears with the back of her hands. "But you are a son to me."

Knowing that I was a son to her meant everything.

I composed a letter to Toua and enclosed a check of $100. Then went to the living room where Nhia watched TV. "Nhia, do you want to go to the post office with me?"

"No."

Since the dog incident, Nhia was frightened to leave the house. I walked to the post office alone and looked out for dogs and the redhaired boy.

That evening, I called Xa. He thanked me for calling. When I told him I had called to ask for Cher Thai's phone number, his voice lost its excitement. He didn't want to hang up after he gave me the phone number, but I explained I had to call Auntie Cher to ask for work, and he said goodbye.

I dialed the new number, and a woman answered.

"Are you Auntie Cher Thai?" I asked.

"Yes," she replied in a soft voice.

"I'm Nou Vang. I'm looking for work. I saw your family picking strawberries, and I'm wondering if I can join your family."

"How old are you?"

"Seventeen."

There was a pause. "Okay. Mr. Richard still needs workers."

I hesitated, then said, "I can't drive. Can you pick me up? I'll help pay for gas."

Another pause, and I feared I had asked too much. "Okay," she finally said. "When do you want to start?"

"As soon as possible."

"We'll pick you up tomorrow at seven a.m. Pack a lunch. Also, bring a hat and wear long sleeves."

"Thank you." I hated working in the fields, but it was a great relief to make the much-needed extra money.

"You talk to my son and give him your address," she said. "I can't write."

I gave her son our address, then thanked him and hung up.

I prepared tomorrow's food, so I could cook quickly in the morning, and Mother and Nhia would be able to eat. Next, I gave Nhia a bath. Then I dialed the Johnson's phone number.

"Hello," Peter answered.

"Hi, Peter, it's Nou."

"Nou." The tenderness in his voice seemed to caress me.

"I have job to pick strawberries tomorrow," I said. "I don't know when I get home. I'll call you to tutor me if I get home early."

"Are you sure you want to pick strawberries? That's hard work."

I kept quiet about my aversion to the job. I had to work. We needed more money. Plus, I didn't want him to continue buying me things.

"I want to try," I said.

"Okay. Be sure to use the sunscreen I gave you," he said.

"I will. I have to go sleep. Good night."

"Good night."

I lay in bed thinking about my new job. I wasn't excited about the physical labor, but I was looking forward to earning money. I hoped my mother would be proud of me and that Peter would know I didn't love him for his money.

20

The alarm shrieked at six o'clock the next morning. I dressed quickly, washed my face, and applied sunscreen. I went to the kitchen, cooked rice and boiled the chicken pieces from yesterday with herbs from Auntie's garden. I didn't want to wake Mother up just to fix her hair, so she'd have to wait until I returned. When the food was ready, I ate quickly and packed my lunch. There was enough food to last Mother and Nhia until I returned.

Auntie Cher Thai arrived at seven o'clock, as promised. I squeezed into the back of her small gray car with her boys, fourteen-year-old Leng and thirteen-year-old Keng. Her sixteen-year-old son, Fong, sat in the front seat with her. On the way to the farm, she told me she had two younger children at home with her mother-in-law. Her husband worked full-time, but the language barrier made it difficult for her to get a job. With young children to care for, fieldwork in the summer was her best option. She made her teenagers pick strawberries, tomatoes, and corn with her to keep them busy.

Keng's head rested on the seat, his eyes half closed.

"You look tired, Keng," I said.

He opened his eyes. "I haven't had enough sleep. Picking strawberries is hard work. When I'm seventeen like you, I hope I can get a job where I don't have to sit on the dirt and bend my back."

"Where can I get a job?" I asked.

"If you can't read and communicate well, you can work as a janitor in a company or a store," Fong said.

"Given a choice, I wouldn't do that either," I said. "For the time being, field work sounds better than being a janitor."

"If you all want good paying jobs, you must study hard," Auntie said. "Picking strawberries and tomatoes should teach you the importance of an education."

She was right. I loved school because I wanted to be a doctor and writer. This job was my next step in achieving those dreams.

When we arrived at the farm, Mr. Richard, a tall man with pleasant eyes and wrinkles creasing his forehead, greeted us warmly. He drove a truck filled with boxes and plastic buckets and we followed him to a nearby field. Auntie confirmed that he was kind and sometimes sent fruit and vegetables home with them.

Like Auntie, I put on my floppy hat even though I had on lots of sunscreen. Too much protection from the sun was better than not enough.

Auntie assigned us each a row of strawberries. I watched Auntie strip the fruit from the vines and copied her. At first, I crouched, but my back quickly began to ache. Then I knelt in the dirt and got the knees of my blue jeans dirty. My fingers were quick in stripping the strawberries and putting them in the Styrofoam pint boxes, but I couldn't keep up with Auntie's family.

In Laos, I thought weeding was backbreaking work. Today, I learned that picking strawberries was far worse. I hadn't done field work since we escaped last December, nine months ago, and my body was as stiff as the utility pole on the road near our house.

Occasionally, Fong picked up our full boxes and put them in

the truck for Mr. Richard to deliver to local stores. Sometimes, Leng helped Fong.

By lunchtime, the sun beat down on us. I used my collar to wipe the stinging sweat from my eyes. Every muscle in my body hurt and, as the afternoon wore on, I fell farther behind. Just as I was about to give up, Auntie came to help me.

Memories rose of Mother and Father working side by side next to my sister Der and me in our rice field in Laos. They took turns telling stories to pass the time. My chest tightened. Grieving for Father and Der would slow me even more, and I couldn't afford to get fired. Working hard would honor them, so I tried to move faster.

We finished at three o'clock. For six and a half hours, I earned $9.75 in cash and Mr. Richard tipped me an additional $0.25. The tip made me want to work harder next time. I appreciated that Mr. Richard paid us right away. The hard-earned money gave me pride and taught me to appreciate every penny earned. I also had a better understanding of how much time and money had gone into the things that people had provided for my family.

I could barely walk when we finally piled into Auntie's car, and I sank into the backseat with a long sigh. We were so tired that nobody spoke on the drive home.

We reached home at four o'clock, and I handed Auntie one dollar for gas.

She refused. "You can give me three dollars weekly. You won't make money if you give me a dollar a day."

"Thank you, Auntie." I got out of the car.

She drove away. Nhia and Mother were waiting for me at the top of the stairs.

Nhia hugged me when I reached them. "I missed you," he said. "Read to me."

"Later. Auntie is dirty and smelly."

We went inside and I called Peter and asked if he still wanted to tutor me. He said he'd be right over.

I just stepped from the shower when I heard tapping at the door. Quickly, I pulled on my clothes and ran to the door.

"Hi, Peter," I said.

His smile alleviated my body aches. Mother was in the living room where she couldn't see us, so we quickly hugged. I never hugged Peter or held hands with him in front of my mother. Such forms of public displays were a disgrace in our culture.

"How was your day?" Peter asked.

"Tired," I replied.

I half waddled to the table, my back and legs protesting all the way.

"You must be in a lot of pain."

I nodded as I eased myself into a chair next to the chair he chose. My damp hair wet my white V-neck shirt.

Peter handed me a book. "I bought you this dictionary to help you understand big words."

I turned the pages. The words were in alphabetical order with definitions.

"Thank you." I hugged him, then remembered Mother and pulled back. I glanced through the kitchen opening, but Mother wasn't peeking. I relaxed.

"You know what I need," I said. "How much?"

"Not much."

"Tell me."

His mouth tightened, then he said, "Two dollars and fifty cents."

I gasped. "A lot money. Two hours my hard work." I met his gaze. "Thank you so much. It mean a lot."

"I want to help improve your speech. Try not to leave out words when you talk."

"Okay. How I say the words is bad?"

"Your accent is okay. You're doing well with basic words."

In my notebook, he wrote *A lot of money. Two hours of my hard work*. He underlined the word *of*.

"When you speak, you tend to drop this word." Peter pointed to the underlined word. "I want you to say it slowly. The more you practice, the more you'll remember."

"Thank you for correct me," I said.

He wrote *Thank you for correcting me.*

I repeated the phrase a few times. English was so difficult. I was still confused with the past, present, and future tense. Peter said I would learn from reading. I had read many books from the library and was getting better, but I wasn't where I wanted to be. Now that I was working, I would have less time to read. What if I couldn't learn quickly enough to fulfill my dreams?

I shifted on the chair and grimaced when my legs protested in pain.

"I'm sorry you're in so much pain," Peter said. "If picking strawberries causes you pain, you shouldn't do it."

I couldn't tell him we were broke and had no money for food. I didn't want him to pity me.

"I want to buy a car." I spoke slowly in an effort to not leave out words. "When I can drive, I'll need money."

He nodded slowly. "That's a good goal. You're seventeen. You can take the driver's education class in high school and get your license. School starts in about two weeks."

I could learn to drive. "I cannot wait! How is it work?"

"Well, in tenth grade, you can take the class and learn to drive."

I frowned. "I will be in ten grade when school start?"

"Yes."

That meant I had only three years before heading off to college. If I didn't do well and earn good grades in high school, I wouldn't have a chance to get into college.

"Are you ok?" Peter asked.

I shook my head. "No. I scare to go to high school. I want to go to low grade."

Peter cocked his head. "You mean you want to go to junior high, right?"

"Yes."

"I think you're a little too old for junior high."

I held up one finger. "One year in junior high to get ready."

He thought for a moment. "I'll call the district and ask them if they'll allow you to start in ninth grade."

"Please, tell them I have to."

"Ok." He paused. "But if you're in junior high, you won't be able to take driver's ed until the following year when you're in high school."

I scowled. "I must learn to drive. My family need me to drive."

Peter studied me. "I'll ask if you can walk to West High School to take the driver's education class. I'll explain your situation to the superintendent."

I beamed. "Yes. Please. You are smart."

Peter laughed. "I'll let you know what I find out."

"Thank you."

I pulled the library books from the backpack, and we began reading. An hour later, we worked on division problems. Peter remained patient and taught me different ways to solve math problems. He truly wanted me to learn and succeed. I saw no indication of him being the kind of man Xa said he was. His dedication to my education was heartfelt.

After Peter left, I prepared food for tomorrow. Thankfully, Mother gave Nhia a bath. I was so lucky to have a mother who supported me. I read two books to Nhia, then went to bed at eight o'clock. I was almost asleep when Mother came to my room.

"Xa wants to talk to you on the phone."

I groaned. "I'm tired. Tell him I'm asleep."

Mother left the room as I snuggled beneath the blanket. A few minutes later, she returned and sat on the bed. She stroked my arm softly.

"Xa is handsome and seems like a decent man. You've been making excuses not to talk to him. Why don't you like him?"

I rolled over to face her. "He's too traditional. I want a man who supports me and treats me with respect. Someone who understands me and can cheer me up when I'm down. Someone I have feelings for."

Mother smoothed the hair from my forehead. "When it comes to love, Hmong men are introverts. Your father loved me, but he wouldn't tell or show me. We didn't hold hands and kiss like the people on TV. Completing our duties, making sure we had food on the table, and being faithful to each other were how we loved one another."

"We're in America now. The old way is boring," I replied.

Mother gave me a disapproving look. "I have a feeling you like Peter. Am I right?"

"Yes."

"Peter is handsome and a decent man, but he's American and we're Hmong. We're low-class. Even if he likes you, his parents won't approve. Xa told me that the Americans don't commit to marriage, so they divorce."

Why would Xa tell her that?

"That is one bad thing about the American culture," I agreed.

"Nou, I want you to marry a Hmong man, so when I die, he can help you provide me a good funeral. You know how important a funeral is to us. The ritual brings closure to a person's life and sends the soul to the ancestor's world. It's good that Xa is traditional because he will be willing to perform our rituals."

She was right, but how could I live with someone so different from me? I had promised Mother to do what a son would do, so it would be my responsibility to provide for her wishes. Mother trusted me and usually didn't question my decisions. For her to say these things, she must be concerned about Peter and me. I hated that my culture dictated my choice for a husband. My head pounded thinking about it.

"Mother, I have a bad headache. Can we talk later?"

She pulled the blanket up to my neck. "All right."

She left and I rolled onto my side. I loved my mother, my

culture, and who I was, but I also loved Peter and the American culture. Was there a way to balance the two worlds?

My heart felt heavy.

Der and Father, why did you leave me to suffer?

God and my ancestors, you expect too much from a teenager.

If Der and Father were present, I wouldn't be responsible for Mother and Nhia, and wouldn't have to worry about tradition and rituals. I would be able to date whoever I wanted and enjoy my new life. But they weren't here and, in the short time we'd been in America, the two worlds were already pulling me in two directions. I was totally stuck. But I knew one thing for sure.

If I had to marry a Hmong man, it wouldn't be Xa.

21

Sitting on the carpet in the bedroom, I recounted the money from working on the farm. After paying six dollars for gas, I had ninety-four dollars for the ten days I worked. This was the first money I had ever earned. I put the cash in a white envelope and tucked it under the mattress. Pain rippled across my back bending down. I breathed in relief for taking the day off from work to register for school. Registration started today, Monday.

Peter would be coming to take me to school soon, so I put on blue and brown plaid bell bottom pants and a white collared shirt. I wanted to look nice when going to places with Peter, and I wanted the school to know that I was a good, decent person. I gath-ered the AFDC stub, rent bill, and other bills and went to the living room. Mother and Nhia were watching TV.

"Mother, I'll be going with Peter to school to register me. He said there will be many people, so I can't take you and Nhia with me. Nhia will be afraid."

"I'd like to get out of the house, but it's okay. I'll talk to Auntie."

Her connection with Auntie had eased Mother's loneliness, but it pained me that I couldn't take her around.

I sat with her on the sofa. "Hopefully, we'd get a car by next year. I'd drive you to places."

Mother smiled.

I couldn't wait to take the driver's education class at West High School. Peter spoke with the school district, and they agreed to allow me to start in ninth grade and walk the four-minute walk to West High School for the class. He explained that they had no test to determine what grade I should be in, so they determined grade by a student's age. Everything was working out as planned, and I believed my ancestors and God had guided my life to ensure my success.

Peter arrived at ten a.m., and I hurried outside as he got out of the car. He opened the passenger door, and I slid inside. A few minutes later, we arrived at Wilson Junior High School, a huge, old brick building. The thought of finding my way in what I knew had to be a maze of hallways filled with students made me feel a little wobbly.

"This is your school," Peter said. "It's close enough to your house that the school bus won't pick you up, but it's too far to walk. You'll have to take the city bus. Students ride for free."

I had never taken the bus, and suddenly wondered if I was strong enough to accomplish my goal. *Heroes don't let fear stop them,* I reminded myself, and said in my bravest voice, "Okay."

We parked on the street and entered the lobby where two hallways intersected. The office was on our left. We turned right and entered the gym. Several dozen people milled around ten tables scattered across the gym floor. Peter led me to a table where another family sat, and he filled out several forms. A few people stared at me, but I had Peter, so wasn't too nervous. After he completed the last form, he handed me two forms for my mother to sign and dropped the rest at a table with a staff member.

He showed me the classrooms on the first floor, and we walked up the stairs to the second floor. This floor had one hallway with one girl's bathroom.

"I was a student here three years ago," Peter explained. "I know where everything is."

"Nice." I matched my steps with his.

A girl and her parents stepped on the second floor as we started down the stairs to the first floor.

"So, what do you think of the school?" Peter asked.

"A big school."

"Do you have any questions?"

I had about a million questions, but said, "Not right now."

"All right."

We reached the first floor and stepped past people who were coming in. Then Peter placed a hand on the small of my back and guided me around a large group of people in the hallway.

"Peter, I want to learn to cook American food," I said. "You know how to cook?"

He shrugged. "I know a little. I help my parents sometimes."

"Can you teach me?" I asked.

"Sure."

We reached the front door and exited the building.

"Can we cook today?" I asked.

Peter grasped my hand and interlocked his fingers with mine. "I'm free. I'll do anything for you."

"Thank you. Take me to the store, please."

At Piggy Wiggly, I pushed the cart while Peter gathered ingredients. He suggested we start with two of his favorite foods, pasta Alfredo and chocolate chip cookies. By the time we reached the register, we had many items in the cart. The food cost eight dollars. That money would normally feed my family for three days. American food consisted of too many expensive ingredients.

We arrived home at a quarter to twelve, just in time to make lunch. In the kitchen, we each tied on an apron. Peter gave me instructions, and I followed them. I gave him one large and one medium bowl. He measured flour, baking soda, salt, and baking powder in the large bowl. I mixed them while he creamed together the butter and sugar. Then he added eggs and vanilla and beat them until fluffy. When he poured them into the large bowl, Mother and Nhia came to the kitchen and watched.

Peter stopped mixing and asked, "Nhia, do you like cookies?"

Nhia's eyes sparkled. "Yes. When will they be ready?"

"About thirty minutes." Peter poured half of the chocolate chips into the mixture and put a handful of chocolate chips in Nhia's hand. "Eat them. They're really good."

Nhia put one in his mouth, chewed, and smiled. "I'm going to play outside. Will the cookies be ready when I come back?"

Peter's mouth fell open in surprise. "Your English is perfect!"

Nhia grinned.

Peter grinned back. "Go play. We'll call you when the cookies are ready."

Happiness swelled within me. In the past, Nhia had greeted Peter, but today he actually had a short conversation with Peter.

Nhia ate more chips as he and Mother went outside. When they closed the door behind them, Peter and I stared at each other in wide-eyed surprise.

"You reading to him, and the TV are teaching him well." Peter stirred the dough a little more. "Now we shape the dough into balls and place them on the cookie sheet."

I watched him and copied him. My cookies were small compared to his.

"Peter, why do you make big cookies?"

He smiled. "Why do you think?"

"Because you're big."

"Why are yours small?"

I laughed. "Because I'm short."

I froze when he tucked a strand of hair that had fallen into my eyes back behind my ear.

"Sorry. I got dough on your cheek." His eyes sparkled.

My heart danced against my chest.

"I love raw cookie dough," Peter said. "Can I use my mouth to get the dough off your cheek?"

I laughed and rubbed dough on his cheek. "I like raw cookie too. You go first."

He pressed his warm mouth against my cheek. I closed my eyes, and he kissed the other cheek. I opened my eyes, then I kissed his cheek where I'd smeared the dough.

"Mmm." I licked my lips. "You and the dough taste so good. I like eating raw cookie dough."

With a finger beneath my chin, Peter tilted my face upward. "Can I kiss your lips?"

My stomach fluttered, and all thoughts of Mother's desire for a Hmong son-in-law fled. "Yes. But I never kiss before. I don't know how."

His eyebrows shot up. "Are you serious?"

"Yes. My nephew the only person I kiss, and only on the cheek and forehead."

"Wow! We just touch our lips together, like kissing on the cheek."

"Okay."

Peter leaned in and gently pressed his lips to mine. He grasped my waist. I closed my eyes and melted against him. A jolt shot through me. After a few seconds, we broke the embrace. I wanted more, but my mother and Nhia could return any moment. Shame washed over me. I had disgraced Mother. I took a step back.

Peter's brow furrowed in concern. "Are you ok?"

I shook my head. "No. I shame my mother."

"By kissing me?"

"Yes."

Peter grasped my hands. "No. You didn't shame her. This is being in love. In America, we kiss, hug, and hold hands in front of our parents, and we don't shame them." He squeezed my hands and smiled.

"You are so good," I whispered.

"You are too."

"When are you go to school?"

"In September. But UW Oshkosh is only about thirty minutes away."

"Would you come back?"

Peter pulled me tight against his chest. "I'll visit you every weekend and maybe weekdays when I don't have class."

"I am happy you go to college to learn more. But I'll miss you."

"I'm going to miss you more." He kissed me on the forehead.

I took a deep breath, willing my heart to slow. "We go back to work."

I couldn't shake the butterflies in my stomach, so I filled two cups with water and gave one to Peter. After I emptied my cup, I felt calmer. His kiss was unbelievably good. Was I lucky to have kissed a white man? Was he fortunate to be the first man to kiss me?

While the cookies baked, I boiled the pasta while Peter cut the chicken breasts into thick strips, then cooked it in a large skillet.

The aroma of freshly baked chocolate chip cookies filled the kitchen. Peter pulled the baking pan from the oven, then put another in. My mouth watered at sight of the golden-brown cookies.

When the chicken strips were done, Peter transferred them to a bowl and started the sauce. He measured butter into the skillet. When it melted, he added cream cheese, then milk and Parmesan cheese. Removing the skillet from heat, he added the chicken. I drained the pasta and set it on the counter.

I stepped out onto the landing. Mother and Nhia were in the backyard with Nhia picking weed flowers.

"Cookies are ready," I called, and went back inside.

A moment later, the door swung open, and Nhia hurried to the table. He grabbed a cookie and stuffed it into his mouth. "Mmm!"

"Do you like it?" Peter asked.

"Yes. How many can I have?"

Peter looked at me.

"Two now and more later," I said.

Nhia grabbed another cookie.

"You like my cookies, so give me a high five." Peter raised his hand and Nhia slapped his palm. "Yay!"

Finally, Nhia was interacting with Peter. Mother smiled, and I gave her a cookie. She bit into it with a skeptical look.

"Very soft and good," she said after a few seconds. "Peter's a good cook."

"Yes, and we had fun cooking. I want a husband who will help me cook."

Mother cast a sideways glance at Peter. "We all want help, but don't set your expectations too high."

What was wrong with high expectations? I sighed. I hoped Mother would share my view soon and let go of her desire for a Hmong son-in-law. Peter was a good cook and a fun man.

As Mother and Nhia sat at the table, I grabbed a cookie and took a bite. I enjoyed the soft, chewy texture and delightful sweetness of the dough.

"Peter, your cookies are delicious. My mother loves them."

He smiled broadly. "Good."

Peter removed the last baking pan from the oven, turned off the heat, and joined us at the table. Nhia and I loved the pasta's rich buttery taste and asked for more. Mother ate a small plate and said it was okay.

Traditionally, cooking was a woman's duty in our culture, but today I learned that cooking together could bring a couple closer. My dream husband would be one who understood the importance of shared duties.

22

I pulled out the white envelope of money from under the mattress and added more money to it. I had made another fifty dollars toward a car payment from work. Yesterday was my last day of work, and I wouldn't miss the backbreaking labor as I was restless to start school tomorrow, Thursday, August 31. I put the envelope back and went to the living room to wait for Xa to take us shopping for school supplies. He had taken the day off from work today to help us because Peter was out of town for a vacation.

At ten o'clock, Auntie's robust voice echoed loudly in the kitchen as Mother greeted her. Mother's voice perked up as they spoke. Mother and I were best friends, but she needed someone like Auntie for a friend. Ever since she met Auntie, she had grown more and more happy.

I left Nhia on the sofa and went to the kitchen. I greeted Auntie and hugged her because I knew she liked to hug.

She grasped my hands and smiled. "You're a very kind girl."

"Thank you." I faced Xa. "Hi."

He smiled. "I'm looking forward to spending time with your family today."

I gave him a cool smile. I appreciated everything he'd done for us, but I wasn't so thrilled.

"We're going to my garden to pick vegetables first before going shopping," Auntie said. "Is everyone ready?"

"We're ready," Mother said in a light voice.

I couldn't go to the garden. It was not on my list of things to do. "Auntie, my mother will go with you," I said. "I have school tomorrow, so I need to take Nhia to the library. Also, I need rest."

Xa frowned. "You can go to the library after. You have the whole day."

"We have a lot to do today." I looked Auntie in the eye because I was good at making eye contact now. "I'm sorry. I promise to go with you the next time."

She nodded. "All right."

Auntie and Mother followed Xa outside.

After they left, I put Nhia in the stroller, and we went to the library. In the children's section, we played with the stuffed animals. My brown bear chased Nhia's monkey. Five minutes later, a slim boy about Nhia's age and man drew near us. While the man looked for books, the boy watched us.

"Do you want to play?" Nhia asked.

Pride filled me. Nhia was finally initiating contact with new people. The boy hurried to us and sat down with Nhia. I handed him the brown bear.

"What's your name?" I asked.

"Jack," he said softly.

Nhia said to Jack, "Your bear chases my monkey, okay?"

While they played, I picked out several books, then returned to the table where the young man sat and watched the boys play.

I sat across from him. "Hi. I am Nou."

He smiled. "I'm Henry. Nice to meet you. The boys are having a good time. Is he your son?"

"My nephew. Is the boy your son?"

The man nodded as the boys squealed in delight. "Yes."

"Thank you for let him play with Nhia," I said.

"Jack needs a friend. I would love for them to play together often."

"Yes," I agreed.

"Can I get your telephone number?" Henry asked.

I pulled my notebook from my backpack, wrote down our number, then tore the paper free and gave it to Henry.

He folded the paper, then put it in his pant pocket and stood. "I'll call and we'll arrange to meet at the library again." I nodded, then he faced the boys. "Hey bud, it's time to go. We'll come back and you can play with your new friend again."

Jack stood. "Bye."

"Bye." Nhia waved.

Nhia and I read and played for two hours. Then, we checked out new books and walked home.

We came home to a kitchen full of vegetables, a big bag of corn, several small bags of mustard greens, cilantro, green onions, hot peppers, tomatoes, and about thirty big cucumbers and squash. I couldn't believe all the food she'd gotten.

"These vegetables will last us several days and save us money!" Mother cried.

I hugged her. "When I can drive, I'll find you a place for a garden."

She smoothed my hair.

Xa returned after dropping his mother off at home. He drove us to the laundromat and helped me carry a basket of dirty clothes inside.

"I need to get something for my father," Xa said. "I'll be back to pick you all up."

I nodded and he left.

When we finished our laundry, we waited for him. To fill time, Nhia and I read. A ten-minute wait turned into twenty. I missed Peter and his promptness.

"What is taking Xa so long?" Mother asked, her expression tight.

"I don't know. Peter would never be late."

Disappointment flashed across Mother's face as she turned to the window.

Finally, Xa arrived thirty minutes late. I was angry at him for keeping us waiting but couldn't complain.

"Have you been waiting?" Xa asked.

I glared.

"I'm sorry. There was a traffic jam."

I forced a smile. "It's all right."

He leaned close and whispered in my ear, "You have patience. This is one reason you stole my heart."

I lifted a laundry basket, and he grabbed the other as we headed to his car with Nhia and Mother following behind.

Had he kept us waiting to test my patience? If so, he could test me all he wanted. The more he tested, the more he'd push me away. I wouldn't be disrespectful because I had to bring honor to my family and respect was a value of mine. But that didn't mean I had to love him.

After we dropped our clothes off at home, Xa drove us to Shopko. I picked out my school supplies while Mother and Nhia looked at toys. Once Xa helped me find everything on my list, he led me to a glass case full of watches.

"Which one do you like?"

I stared at the sparkling watches beneath the glass. I wanted one, but I knew what Xa was up to. In Laos, if a girl accepted a valuable gift from a man, it signified that she loved him and was willing to marry him.

"I don't like any of them," I lied.

Xa frowned, then waved over the saleswoman behind the counter.

"Show us that silver watch," he said in English.

"Of course." She pulled the watch from behind the glass and handed it to Xa.

"Let's try it on you and see how it looks," he said to me.

I raised my hand, and he fastened the shiny Seiko watch with its stainless-steel bezel and strap around my wrist. I couldn't take my eyes off it.

"It's beautiful on you." Xa turned to the saleswoman. "How much?"

"It's the last one," she said. "So, it's on sale for fifty dollars."

I quickly took off the watch and handed it to her. "Too much money."

Xa took it from her. "I'll pay for it."

"If you are going to buy it for me, please don't," I said flatly. "I don't need one."

I walked away to pay for my school supplies. When I glanced back, Xa was paying for the watch. I couldn't believe he would buy such an expensive watch.

When we arrived home, Xa helped carry everything inside. I busied myself with organizing my school supplies, aware that he was waiting for me so he could give me the watch. At last, he grabbed my arm and tried to put the watch around my wrist. I pulled away.

"We should talk outside." I opened the door, walked out onto the landing.

He followed and I waited for him to close the door behind him.

"Xa, it's nice of you to buy me the watch, but I don't need it," I said. "Sorry, I can't take it."

"Why is it so hard for you to take a small gift from me?" he demanded.

"If it's meant as a promised gift, I can't take it."

His eyes met mine. "I swear it's not a promised gift."

I looked down.

"Believe me. I won't lie to you. Can I put it on you, please?"

No matter how much I wanted the watch, I couldn't accept it. I didn't trust him. "No."

His face reddened. "My watch and I are worthless to you. I'll throw it away." He raised the hand gripping the watch and I realized he intended to throw it into our neighbor's side of the yard.

I grabbed his hand. "Don't throw it. We can't search for it in their yard."

"Will you accept it?"

What could I do? We were no longer in Laos. In America, he couldn't force me to marry him. I had to trust that the watch wasn't a promised gift.

"All right," I said.

Smiling, he put the Seiko watch on my wrist.

"Thank you."

"Thank you for accepting the watch. It's a small gift to help you start the school year." He glanced at his car. "I know you're busy, so I'll go home."

I tried to hide my relief. "All right. Bye."

"Good luck at school tomorrow."

I thanked him again, and he left. I should be grateful for the watch, but I wasn't because I didn't love him. What would Peter think if he knew I took a gift from another man? I hated to be unfaithful. I felt like an awful person.

That evening, I prepared food I could cook quickly tomorrow morning for Nhia and Mother before school. Mother assured me she could cook, but I knew she struggled with just one arm.

As I crawled into bed that night, I thought about tomorrow. My ability to read and speak simple sentences in English gave me confidence, but I couldn't help but wonder how the students would react to having an Asian girl in their school. At last, excitement and anxiety gave way to exhaustion, and I fell asleep.

23

The next morning, I fixed Mother's hair, then had a quick breakfast. I packed a sandwich for lunch and walked to the downtown bus station on College Avenue.

Peter told me to take Bus 4 route. All the city buses sat parked on the street. I found my bus and the driver punched my pass with a hole puncher. Two men sat in the middle section. I sat at the front. Four students, three boys and a girl, boarded and stared at me as they continued to the back.

At Wilson, the other students and I got off the bus. The breeze cooled my face as I waited outside near them. More students arrived, and some shouted in delight at seeing their friends and some hugged each other. Voices echoed all around the school. I felt many eyes on me and longed for my own friends.

When the bell rang, I followed everyone filed inside. An announcement on the intercom told us to report to homeroom. Peter had told me to get a schedule in the office. By the time I reached the office, the hallway was empty.

A middle-aged woman with brown, shoulder length hair sitting at the front desk asked, "Can I help you?"

"I need a schedule," I said.

"What's your name?"

"Nou Vang."

She disappeared into a small room then emerged with a paper and gave it to me. "You go straight to Room 130." She pointed to the hallway on my right. "Go all the way to the end."

"Thank you."

Anxiety swept over me as the bell rang again. I hurried to find Room 130. I was two steps inside when the teacher, a wrinkled man said, "Put your backpack in your locker."

I glanced behind me through the door at the rows of lockers that lined the wall. Which one was mine?

"What number?" I asked.

A brown-haired girl sitting near the door said, "I'll help her." She stood and walked to me. She looked at my schedule and pointed to a number on the top, then led me to the lockers in the hall.

"What's your name?" she asked.

"Nou. What's your name?"

"I'm Laura."

We scanned the numbers until we found mine. She showed me how to turn the lock using the combination on my schedule. What a friendly girl. I wished she would be my friend.

"Thank you for help me," I said.

"You're welcome. It's nice to meet you." She smiled.

"Same."

I put my school supplies and backpack in the locker, and we returned to the classroom. Three minutes later, the bell rang again, and everyone got up to leave. I didn't know where to go. Laura headed down the hall, chatting with some friends. I followed them into another classroom.

We sat, and the tall, dark-brown haired, male teacher looked at me and studied the paper he had on his hand. Then he walked over to me.

"Miss, what's your name?" he asked.

I told him my name.

"You're not on my list. Are you sure you're in the correct class?"

Everyone's eyes turned on me. My face grew hot in embarrassment. I stood to leave but didn't know where to go. My palms started to sweat. I remembered my schedule and pulled it from my pocket. Laura came over and looked at the paper.

"You need to go to Room 147." She pointed to the first column on the schedule. "This shows the period." She pointed at the next column. "This shows your classes. This one lists the teacher's name and room number."

I smiled thanks.

"I'll show you where Room 147 is." She glanced at the teacher, who nodded agreement.

"Thank you," I said in relief.

"Did you come to America recently?" she asked as we walked down the hallway.

Between my accent and my unfamiliarity with the schedule, the answer must have been obvious.

"Yes. In the summer."

"Your English is pretty good," she said.

"Thank you."

We turned a bend and stopped at Room 147.

"That's the room. Have a good day." Laura turned and hurried away before I could thank her.

I entered the class, and everyone's eyes shifted to me.

"You must be Nou Vang." This teacher smiled. Her cinnamon hair color matched well with her smooth, ashen skin.

I nodded.

She pointed to a seat in the front row, and I sat down.

"Welcome to math. I'm Mrs. Mattioli. I'm glad to have you in my class."

The tension in my shoulders eased a little. For the first time, I felt a sense of belonging as Mrs. Mattioli talked about class expectations, rules, grades, and the topics that would be covered in class. I loved math and excitement rippled through my stomach.

I had English and science next. My English teacher was a woman, and my science teacher a man. The thick textbooks they gave me sent a wave of panic through me. I tried reading a paragraph in my English textbook but understood only a few words. Should I have started in elementary school?

During lunch, everyone headed to the gym, which doubled as a cafeteria. I followed the other students, who chatted and laughed. Students filled the bleachers, where they ate their lunches.

I looked for Laura and spotted her among a cluster of girls. They huddled close, which left no room for me. I stood against the wall, hoping someone would wave at me and invite me to sit with her but no one looked in my direction.

I found three chairs between the sets of bleachers and sat on one. A plump woman supervisor walked by and smiled at me. More students arrived, and I looked for any Asian students. I spotted the redhaired boy with his friends. I turned away quickly, my pulse speeding. Oh God, it was a bad decision to attend this school. I could smell trouble. He hadn't seen me yet. I pulled the hood of my plaid flannel shirt over my head, then grabbed my lunch bag and scurried under the bleachers. The deafening drone of voices bore down on me. I had lost my appetite but forced myself to finish my food.

Hood over my head, I emerged from beneath the bleacher and approached the supervisor. I asked her to use the bathroom, then hurried from the gym when she gave permission. In the restroom, I felt safer, but I hated that I had to hide. How was I going to learn if I had to worry about my safety every day?

A few girls came to use the bathroom and talked about going outside to recess. Although I had my hood, I wouldn't risk going outside. I stayed in a stall until lunch was over.

I had history after lunch, and the textbook was as thick as the English and science textbooks. Could I keep up when I had so much to learn? How would I go to college if I struggled to read junior high textbooks?

When the last bell of the day rang, I picked my way through the sea of students toward my locker to get my backpack. The crowded hallways made my heart pound. What would I do if I missed my bus? Near my locker, I stopped in surprise at seeing Peter waiting for me. My heart burst with happiness. If I was an American girl, I would have thrown myself into his arms. His broad smile completely healed my frayed nerves. I weaved through the crowd and stopped when we were six inches apart.

"How was your first day?" he asked.

The students near my locker turned to stare at us.

"You surprise me," I blurted.

"I can tell."

"I thought you on vacation." I smiled.

The locker next to mine slammed shut and the boy left.

"I got home an hour ago," Peter said.

"Peter?" a girl called.

We turned to face the speaker. Two girls approached us.

"Hi, Liz and Ava," Peter said.

"Hi," the girls said in unison.

The tall, long brown-haired girl said, "What are you doing here?"

Peter glanced at me and back to the girls. "This is Nou Vang. My family sponsored her family from a Thai refugee camp and I'm picking her up."

"Cool." She smiled at me.

She seemed nice, and I returned the smile.

"Nou, this is Liz Anderson, Susan's little cousin," Peter said. "And this is Ava Morgan, Liz's friend."

"Nice meeting you," Liz said.

"Nice meeting you too," I said.

Lockers being slammed shut and farewells surrounded us and in the halls.

"Gotta go," Liz said. "Mom's waiting."

"Take it easy," Peter said.

"Thanks."

The girls waved, then hurried to their lockers on the opposite wall.

I stepped closer to my locker and opened it. Quickly, I took my backpack and stuffed my books inside, and we started down the hallway.

We reached Peter's car, and he opened the door for me. I got inside, then tossed my backpack in the backseat as he slid into the driver's seat. Peter grasped my hand and our eyes locked.

"I missed you." I couldn't mask my cracking voice.

"I missed you too."

He kissed me. A tear slid down my cheek.

Peter gently wiped the tear away with a thumb. "Are you ok?"

I nodded against the lump in my throat. "My first day not very good."

His brow furrowed. "I'm so sorry."

"Seeing you, I am so happy. You the only friend I have. You cheer me up. You talk to me and my sadness go away."

Peter pulled me close. "Am I that important to you?"

"Yes. You very important to me."

He kissed my head. "Thank you for telling me."

I pulled free, and he started the car. We held hands as he drove.

"Why you come to school?" I asked.

"I wanted to check on you and pick you up."

I squeezed his hand. "Very nice of you. Thank you."

Peter turned down an unfamiliar street.

"Where we going?" I asked.

"You had a rough day. You don't need the stress of cooking dinner, so I'm buying dinner." He grinned. "McDonalds."

How thoughtful. But I didn't want him to spend money on us. He had done so much already.

"I can cook. Just go home."

Despite my protests, he went to McDonalds and bought food.

When we arrived home, Mother and Nhia waved from the living room window. I held up the McDonalds bag and Nhia's eyes widened. He loved chicken nuggets and French fries.

Nhia met us at the door and Peter handed him his food.

Nhia hugged him. "Thank you."

Tears pressed against the backs of my eyes. Finally, Nhia trusted Peter and was using good manners.

I hugged Nhia. "Good boy. I'm pleased that you thanked Peter. You're doing a good job."

Nhia and Mother went to the living room with their food while Peter and I ate at the table. After eating, we looked at my textbooks.

"They are so hard," I murmured.

"Don't worry. With your determination, you'll be reading them in no time." He winked.

"Thank you. You make me believe myself."

A knock sounded at the door. My pulse jumped. It had to be Xa. Who else would visit without calling?

I opened the door and Xa smiled and held up two plastic bags of vegetables. Despite my anger, I had to be respectful. After all, he was bringing us food.

"Hi," I said in a polite voice. "I asked you to call before coming."

He shrugged. "Sorry. I wanted to check on how your first day of school went." Xa entered, then stopped short, his eyes on Peter.

"Good evening," Peter said in a tense voice.

Xa set the bags on the floor. "What are you doing here? I told you I take care of Nou and her family. They don't need your help anymore."

"Nou needs my help," Peter said. He pointed to the textbooks on the table. "We're in the middle of a reading lesson—which you interrupted."

Xa's face reddened.

I stepped between them, facing Peter, and begged with my eyes for him to leave. "You tutor me another time. Okay?"

Peter hesitated, then stood.

"You leave Nou alone today on," Xa said in a grating voice.

"You're the one to leave Nou alone before I call the police," Peter snapped, then left.

I spun to face Xa. "Peter is my tutor and I need his help. You have no right to tell him anything. You were rude!"

"I'm sorry, Nou. When I see him with you, my anger gets the better of me."

Mother entered the kitchen. She greeted Xa, then said to me, "What's going on?"

Xa glanced from me to Mother. "Auntie, Peter is teaching Nou bad things. Like to hate her culture, disrespect parents, and do whatever she wants." Xa eyed me. "You see, she doesn't respect Hmong men anymore."

Fury shot through me. "Liar!"

Mother stared at me in disappointment. "You've been rude to Xa, and I've noticed that you don't embrace our traditions much anymore."

She began to cry and Xa stroked her hair to comfort her. My mother's tears pained me—as Xa knew they would. I wouldn't further disappoint her by arguing with him now, but I would deal with him later.

"Xa, please leave," I said. "I need to study."

He hesitated. "I can't help you with reading, but I would do anything for you. You don't need to read to be successful in America."

Clearly, he didn't support my dreams.

Anger bubbled in me. "Go!"

He left and Mother motioned for me to sit at the table. We both sat, and she met my gaze. "Nou, I'm sorry if I'm not a good mother. I don't know what I did in my past life or this life to deserve this unimageable suffering." Tears streamed down her cheeks.

I stroked her hair.

"You are my only remaining child, and all the pressure is on you because you are my only hope. You bring me happiness and you always work hard. I am so proud of you." She wiped her eyes with the back of her hand. "I want to remind you that you have freedom in this country, but you should never forget your culture, traditions, and values."

I wrapped my arms around her. "I know."

"We have no family here and we can't be rude to anyone, including Xa. We need his family's help," she said. "I know you won't shame me."

"I won't," I said softly. "We took the oath to be good citizens. We don't want to be sent back."

A thudding ache pulsed in my head, and I could no longer listen to her. I didn't even want to read. "I need a nap," I said, and went to bed.

As I lay in bed, my heart cried out for a girlfriend to talk to. I wanted to vent so badly that my chest hurt. Did other teenagers have problems like mine?

24

My science, English, and history classes grew more difficult over the next two weeks. In addition, I feared for my safety, so I ate under the bleachers and hid in the bathroom during recess. I loved school and tried my best, but those three classes overwhelmed me so much that I often ended up in tears. So far, no one seemed to notice when I lowered my head and wiped my eyes.

The only class I enjoyed was math. Every day, Mrs. Mattioli had the math *Problem of the Day,* which encouraged me to go to class early, so I had enough time to work on the problem.

Today's Problem of the Day was 20N-2=58, which was easy because I had studied Algebra over the weekend. I worked on the problem while other students chatted with their friends before the bell rang. The girl in the row on my right remained quiet. She didn't seem to have friends in the class. Last week on Friday she said hi to me, but she didn't seem to notice me now. My first week in school, people had stared at me. Now they acted like I was invisible.

When the bell rang, everyone began to work on the problem.

Mrs. Mattioli walked around the room. She stopped at my desk and checked my answer.

"Good job," she said softly. "Can you do the problem on the board for us today?"

My stomach swirled in nervousness, but I got the correct answer so at least I wouldn't embarrass myself.

"Sure," I said.

Mrs. Mattioli went to the front of the room. "All right class, I'd like Nou to solve this problem for us today."

I must show the class I could do math even though I struggled in other subjects. I went to the chalkboard and solved the problem step by step.

"3 is the correct answer," Mrs. Mattioli said. "Check your answer. If you don't have that number, turn to a neighbor and see if she/he can help. If not, I'll help."

I returned to my seat and the girl on my right turned to me. "Hi," she said. "I'm Emily."

I smiled. "Hi."

Emily's long auburn hair cascaded down around her shoulders and thick bangs hung across her forehead like a paintbrush. Like me, she didn't wear makeup, but she was beautiful with a soft, pale complexion.

"Now that I see the steps on the board, I know how you got 3 for the answer, but how do you know to add or subtract?" she asked.

"When is subtraction, you add the number." It was hard to explain with my limited English, so I demonstrated in my notebook.

She beamed. "Oh. I get it. Thanks."

For the first time since school started, my spirit brightened. "You are welcome."

She closed her notebook. "Are you new to America?"

I nodded. "Three months in America."

"How do you like it?"

"It's good."

Mrs. Mattioli began her lesson. Emily gave me a final smile, then turned her attention to the chalkboard.

My heart soared. I had helped Emily by solving the *Problem of the Day*.

The bell rang for second period, science class. I dragged my feet to the class. Last week, we had our first lab. I couldn't find a partner, so I had to write the report alone. I got an F. I was so embarrassed and discouraged.

I barely got to my desk when the second bell chimed. A few students hurried in as Mr. Miller took attendance. Mr. Miller began his lecture on the earth's structures. Even with the diagrams he showed us, nothing made sense to me. Mr. Miller talked too fast, and I didn't know the terminology. Tears threatened and I drew in a deep breath. I had to talk to Mr. Miller. I couldn't fail this class.

During independent reading and work time, I raised my hand. Mr. Miller came to my desk.

"Mr. Miller. Reading is hard for me. I don't understand science." I worked to keep my voice light.

"How long have you been in America?" he asked.

"Three months. I have no education in my country."

His eyes widened in shock. "Thanks for letting me know. I'll talk to the principal Mr. Sherman and see what we can do for you."

"I want to learn science," I said.

He smiled gently. "Got it. I'm proud of you for advocating for yourself."

I didn't know the new word, but it must be a good one. "Mr. Miller, you say the word adv.... I cannot say it. Write for me."

In my notebook, he wrote *advocate*. "It means to speak out to get help. You know you're having trouble learning science and you asked for help." He paused. "We'll figure out a plan to help you."

"My mother cannot help me," I blurted. "I have to ask for help."

"You're doing an amazing job advocating for yourself."

The knot in my chest unfurled.

During lunch, as I was on my way to the gym, Emily found me. Standing side-by-side, I saw that Emily and I were the same height.

"Can I join you?" she asked.

"Yes!" I cried. "I would love to eat with you."

We walked to the area between the two sets of bleachers where the three chairs still sat. With Emily, I felt safer in the lunchroom. If someone bullied me, she might back me up. Today, I didn't need to hide under the bleachers or hide in the bathroom. But I did pull my hood over my head.

"We can eat here." I nodded toward the chairs.

Emily looked around. "Do you always eat here?"

"Yes." I pointed to a spot under the bleachers. "There."

She frowned. "Why under there?"

"I feel safe there."

We sat on the wood chairs. She tucked her hair behind her ears and pulled a sandwich from her lunch bag. Her eyes flicked to my hood, but she said nothing. I was glad because I didn't want to explain the redhaired boy to her.

"Thanks for your help in math today. You're pretty good at math." She took a bite of her sandwich.

"A little. I like math."

She scrunched her nose. "I hate math. I wanted to talk to you but wasn't sure how. I guess talking in math class broke the ice."

I swallowed my food. "I'm the same. I worry people don't like me."

"I like you. If you want, we can eat together every day." She returned her attention to her sandwich. "I'd love to have a friend."

I gasped in joy. "I like to be your friend. I don't have one."

Emily looked up. "Me either. Let's be friends." She raised her hand for a high five, and I slapped her palm. "I used to have friends, but they've been mean to me. I'm staying away from them," she said.

I smiled. "Okay. You are my friend now."

She stuffed the remainder of her sandwich in her lunch bag. "Let's go out for recess."

I hesitated, then nodded. I was tired of hiding.

We went to the track field behind the school. Some kids walked on the track, some played balls on the field while others hung around with friends by the shed near the track. Emily and I walked. A gust of warm wind jerked my hood off one side of my face, and I quickly pulled it back into place.

"Do you have brother and sister?" I asked.

"I have an older sister in high school and a younger half-sister in sixth grade."

The runners shot past us, and we stopped to watch them.

"Your parents are divorced?" I immediately regretted the question.

"Yep. My mother has custody of my sister and me. We visit our father on weekends."

We began walking again.

"Your parents are okay they don't have boys?" I asked.

She shrugged. "They wanted a son, but they don't care that they don't have one."

I studied her. "American parents love boy and girl the same?"

"Yeah. They're treated the same if that's what you're asking," Emily said. "Daughters have the same opportunity as sons."

"That's nice. I like that. I wish my culture is like that."

Emily frowned. "Your culture doesn't value girls? That's insane."

"Because we girls cannot do...um culture ritual."

She shook her head in disbelief.

A group of boys strolled near us.

"She's hot—for a Chinese," one said.

The others laughed.

I opened my mouth to say I wasn't Chinese when Emily shouted, "Get lost, losers!"

The cheeks of the boy who'd spoken reddened, and he said, "Looks who's talking; the *loser* who's friends with the Chinese girl."

I frowned. "I'm not Chinese."

The boys burst out laughing.

"Shut your mouth, Mark Langstrom, or I'll kick your butt!" Emily shouted.

She grabbed my hand and pulled me across the field, away from the boys.

"Why they laughing?" I asked.

"Because they're jerks," she said in a fierce voice.

Then I understood. "They make fun of me."

Emily looked at me, then slung an arm around my shoulder and continued walking. "They're jerks to everyone. Mark is on the football team, and he thinks that makes him special."

I looked over my shoulder at the boys, who were now walking as if nothing had happened.

"Forget them," Emily said. "They're not worth the trouble."

I looked at Emily and my heart swelled. I had made a very good friend today.

When I arrived home that afternoon after school, Nhia ran to hug me. I carried him to the living room, where we played clapping games on the carpet.

Mother came from the bathroom and sat on the sofa. "You seem happy today. Is school better?"

I grinned. "No. But I made a friend." I didn't tell her what the boys had said. I didn't care. I had a new friend, and she was looking out for me.

Mother's face brightened. "A new friend? That's wonderful! I did my best to cook dinner."

"I can do it. It's my duty."

"You've been doing everything, which only makes me more disabled. I need to learn to do things so I can help you achieve your dreams."

"I appreciate it."

I ate quickly and began my homework. I opened my history textbook and noticed the empty chair that Peter usually sat when tutoring me. My heart ached. Since Peter started school, he visited on weekends and called only twice a week because long-distance phone calls were expensive. His parents helped pay for his apartment rental, which left little money for our calls. Was he having as difficult a time adjusting to the new routine as me?

25

Two days later in math class, an announcement came over the intercom, "Nou Vang, please report to the office."

All eyes shifted to me. Anxiety washed over me. Why was I being called to the office? Was I being taken out of school? I had stayed clear of the redheaded boy. Had he said something about me?

As I stood to leave, Emily whispered, "Hope everything is okay."

I gave her a tight smile.

I forced each foot in front of the other and reached the office to find the principal waiting for me.

"Hello," Mr. Sherman said. The skin around his eyes crinkled as he smiled. He seemed friendly, but people in authority could make trouble for me.

"Hi."

He gestured for me to follow him. We walked to a room filled with awards in frames on the wall and a huge desk with a comfortable leather chair.

"Have a sit." Mr. Sherman pointed to the three chairs in front of his desk and sat behind the desk.

I sat in the middle chair.

"How are you today?" he asked.

I twisted my hands in my lap. "Okay."

"How do you pronounce your name?"

I said my name.

"Nou, you did the right thing by sharing your struggle to read with Mr. Miller. He and I discussed your situation. He said you study hard, but the language barrier makes it difficult for you to grasp the concepts."

I nodded. "Yes. The textbooks are hard. I read picture books and understand them. I learn from my tutor. I don't learn in class."

Mr. Sherman leaned forward. "You have a tutor? That's excellent."

I shook my head. "Not anymore. He went to college."

"I see." Mr. Sherman sat back. "To be honest, we aren't prepared for your situation. You are our first foreign student from the refugee camp. I spoke with your English and history teachers. We all agree it's best to place you in seventh-grade science and English classes. The pace is slower, and the reading is easier. What do you think?"

The tension in my stomach eased. They were moving me down two grade levels. "Okay."

"Good. You're doing well enough in history to keep you in that class. I have your new schedule. You'll start tomorrow." He picked up a sheet of paper from his desk and handed it to me."

"Thank you for helping me."

Mr. Sherman smiled. "You're welcome. You'll have Mrs. Bell for English and Mr. Jacobson for science."

I couldn't believe my good fortune. "Okay."

I now had English and history in the morning and math and science in the afternoon. I no longer had math with Emily. I was disappointed, but she and I could still have lunch together.

The next day, I went to Mrs. Bell's class and found the

redhaired boy staring at me from his seat in the middle row. My heart sped up. Freckles painted his nose and the area under his eyes. Still, his frown made his face seem even more unkind up close.

Mrs. Bell was a young, beautiful woman with hair the color of golden apples. She directed me to an empty seat in the back row. The redhead's eyes followed me, and a sly smile touched his mouth as I sat down.

Oh Heaven, this class would be a nightmare. The schedule change was a big mistake. He was younger than I, but America was his country. He had family and friends. If he caused trouble and blamed me, who would believe me? I was a refugee, a girl with only a mother and a young nephew for support.

I considered telling Mrs. Bell that I wanted to go back to my old English class. But I needed this class, and running away wouldn't solve anything. Maybe the redhead would leave me alone if I ignored him.

Mrs. Bell handed me a sheet of paper titled, "Demonstration Speech." She asked everyone to get out their papers, then she reviewed the requirements. A small table at the front of the class was covered with baking ingredients, a bag of flour, a carton of eggs, a bottle of oil, sugar, a whisk, a bowl, and measuring cups. Mrs. Bell modeled a demonstration speech using the items on the table. She talked about making eye contact with the audience and speaking clearly and loudly. Her cheerful voice and enthusiasm made everything interesting. Our homework was to create our own speech about a subject that interested us.

The redhead shot me another sly smile. I tensed with memory of the eggs he had thrown at me and Nhia and his shouts for me to go back to my country. Why did he hate me?

When the bell chimed at the end of class, he left. I waited a few seconds, then picked up my books and headed for the door. I stepped into the hallway to find him standing outside the door.

My breath caught. I started walking toward history class. He kept pace beside me.

"Nou, what are you doing for your speech?" His mouth twisted into a mean smile.

How did he know my name? Mrs. Bell hadn't introduced me to the class. I wanted to tell him to leave me alone, but being rude would get me in trouble.

"You speak English funny. You can't give a speech," he sneered. "You'll fail, bitch!"

Anger shot through me. I sidestepped a group of students. He stopped walking beside me and I quickened my pace. I took several deep breaths. I knew what to do. I would prove to him I was smart, despite the language barrier that made me appear unintelligent.

During lunch, Emily asked about my new English class. Although she had backed me up when Mark Langstrom made fun of me, I didn't know her well enough tell her about the redhead. Instead, I opened my notebook to the page where I had written *demonstration* and showed it to her.

"Tell me to say this."

"Oh. Demonstration."

"Dimontration."

She laughed softly. "Your accent is funny. Say dem-on-stray-shun."

I bit into my peanut butter sandwich as I looked down into my lap.

"Geez, Nou, I didn't mean to be rude. Sorry."

I chewed and swallowed. "I'm not mad. I'm hungry."

Emily touched my shoulder. "Repeat after me. Dem-on-stray-shun."

I repeated the word until I got the pronunciation correct.

"I'm doing a demonstration," I said the word slowly. "I have a speech for English. I don't know what to do."

Emily drank from her water bottle. "Hmm. In seventh grade, I did mine on how to take care of my dog. I brought a stuffed animal for the demonstration."

"In Laos, I have a dog. The enemy kill him." My chest constricted at the memory.

"Oh. Sorry." Emily touched my hair. "You have beautiful hair. How about hair care?"

I nodded slowly. "Good idea. Thank you."

I had to find more ideas. Maybe something I was good at, like embroidery. I'd make a list when I got home.

As usual, when I got home from school, if Mother hadn't cooked, I cooked. Today, I cooked and by the time I finished washing dishes and ready for homework, it was seven o'clock. I had just finished math homework when a knock came at the door. Would it be Xa or Peter? I opened the door. Xa stood with bags of squash and cucumbers in hand.

"Help me bring them inside," he said. "There are more in the car."

Mother came into the kitchen and helped us bring in the food.

"Thank you for feeding us, Xa" Mother said.

"You're welcome, Auntie. My mother and I just came from the garden. I dropped her off and came here." Xa looked at me. "Sorry, I didn't have time to call ahead."

At least he acknowledged that he should have called.

"It's all right," I said.

I gave him a cup of water, and he sat at the table. I began cleaning the vegetables.

Mother stood on the opposite side of the table from Xa. "Xa, you must be tired from work and taking your mother to her garden."

"Very tired but as her only child now, I must do my duty."

"You're a good son."

Xa finished his water. "Thank you, Auntie."

"Refill Xa's cup," Mother said.

Didn't she see I was busy? I wanted to refuse, but Xa had said that I disrespected Hmong man, and I couldn't prove him right. I refilled his cup. Mother helped put the clean vegetables in the refrigerator, then she went to the living room. I wished Xa would leave, so I could finish my homework. He smiled as I sat at the table and started to do my science worksheet.

"You don't need to study so hard," he said. "Take time to enjoy life."

"I want to go to college."

He snorted. "You think you can go to college?"

"Yes," I replied.

He tapped the table with his fingers. "A diploma will get you a good job. But you must be a good wife and mother."

I looked at him. "I have dreams."

He plucked an orange from the fruit basket on the table. "Can you peel it for me?"

I bit back a scold. A dutiful daughter cooked for a guest and since I hadn't cooked for Xa, I had to give in to this small request. I peeled the orange. I hoped my future husband wouldn't demand that I do every little thing for him.

He watched me with sparkling eyes. "I want you to tear off each segment and put them in a bowl for me." He was testing my patience, like most Hmong men would before they decided to marry. Although I wouldn't marry him, I couldn't disappoint my mother. I put the orange segments in a bowl, then returned to my homework as he ate.

"Thanks for peeling the orange for me." He popped the last piece of orange into his mouth. "I'm exhausted, so I'll head home."

I hid my relief as best I could. "Thank you for the vegetables. It's very kind of you and Auntie."

"I'll bring more next week." Xa went to the living room where Mother sat on the couch while Nhia watched TV. "Auntie, is Peter still coming to tutor Nou?"

"He went to school and stopped tutoring her," she replied.

"Good. He better leave Nou alone. He's spoiled her enough."

Anger boiled up in me and I wanted to shout that Xa had no say in my life. But I knew Xa would only use that as an excuse to prove to Mother that Peter was spoiling me. What would Xa do when he learned that Peter was still visiting me?

26

In English class the next day as Mrs. Bell began the lesson, the redhead entered the classroom and walked straight to his desk without giving her his late pass.

"Jacob Shine, do you have a late pass?" she asked.

"No." He set his books on his desk and flopped down into his seat.

"Go back to the office and get one," she said.

"Ok," he replied. "First, I need to sharpen my pencil."

Mrs. Bell frowned but nodded.

Jacob walked past my desk to the pencil sharpener on the counter at the back of the room. Behind me, the turn of the pencil sharpener ground his pencil to a point, then stopped. I tensed. On his way back to his seat, I started when he dropped a note on my desk. I cast a quick glance around. No one seemed to notice, so I quickly slipped the note inside my notebook.

Jacob left his pencil on his desk, then left. When he returned with his late pass, he gave Mrs. Bell the pass, then sat down. When she wasn't looking, he would glance back at me. I knew he wanted to see my reaction to the note, but I wouldn't give him the satisfaction. I planned to read it during my next class.

When I took my seat in history class an hour later, I unfolded the paper.

Nou, the sponger,

You dirty Oriental. Why did you come to my country? Go back to your country, sponger! Don't come to my school. You don't need an education. No one will hire you. The government brought you here for prostitution. Haha.... Prostitution suits you. My dad will pay you to sleep with my older brother. When is a good date? Must let me know soon.

Sincerely,
    The American Protector

I pulled out my dictionary and looked up *sponger* but couldn't find the word. Then I looked up the word *prostitute* and my stomach turned. I had to know the meaning of *sponger*. Class hadn't started and Mr. Jones stood at the podium waiting as students entered. I wrote the word in my notebook, then went to Mr. Jones.

"Hi, Mr. Jones," I said.

"Hi, what can I do for you?"

I showed him the word. "Can you tell me the meaning?"

He looked at the word for a few seconds. "The informal meaning would be people who get money or food from others in order to live. The other meaning is someone that sponges."

"Thank you," I said.

I walked back to my seat lightheaded. How did Jacob know we received money from the AFDC program? We qualified for the aid. We didn't beg his family for money. Peter's family and his church supported us financially, but they did so willingly. What right did Jacob have to call me a sponger?

I reread the letter. *Sponger* and *prostitute* were the worst labels in my society. I thought of Mark Langstrom and his friends, and how they had made fun of me. Were all American men like this? My head throbbed. I forced back tears and jumped when the bell rang to signal the start of class. Had I been brought to America to be a prostitute? Was Peter one of the men I would serve? A wave of nausea rolled over me and I thought I might vomit. I stood and hurried to where Mr. Jones stood at the blackboard.

"You look sick," he said. "Go to the bathroom or the office."

"Bathroom," I managed.

I ran down the hall. Thankfully, no one was in the bathroom. I crammed myself in the stall and dropped onto the toilet lid in time to let my tears fall. Ten minutes later, I felt better, but I couldn't return to class with red eyes. I left the stall and splashed water on my eyes at the sink, but the redness made plain the fact I'd been crying. I would have to wait until my eyes were clear. I returned to the stall and sat on the toilet.

Five minutes later, the bathroom door swung open.

"Nou," a girl I didn't know said. "Are you in here?"

My heart began to pound. "Yes," I replied in a small voice.

"Are you okay?"

I swallowed and hoped my voice didn't crack. "A little."

"Mr. Jones said if you are sick, you need to go to the office and lie down there or go home."

"Okay. Thank you."

The door swung shut and her footsteps trailed off. My mind whirled. I wanted to stay in school, but I knew I couldn't face anyone after that note.

I returned to Mr. Jones' classroom, gathered my belongings, and went to the office. I told the secretary I was sick. They said I could go home. I didn't know what time the city bus would come, and I didn't want to wait. Our house was a mile away, but I hoped the walk would cool me off, and set off at a slow walk.

My mind whirled as I searched for a solution to end the redhead's bullying. Swearing, fighting, tattling, or cursing would escalate the problem, and I worried the government would send us back to Laos if I caused trouble. We took the oath to be good citizens, so I had to avoid trouble at all costs. I wasn't a coward. After Father was killed by the Communists soldiers who chased us through the jungles of Laos, I led my family to safety in Thailand.

If Father was here, what advice would he give? He always told us that communication was the key to understanding each other. But I didn't want to talk to Jacob, much less understand him. What should I do?

As the cool air kissed my face, I thought of the demonstration speech I had to do in English class. Emily was kind to suggest haircare, but haircare wasn't important. I wanted something interesting and meaningful. Then I knew what I should talk about. Instead of a demonstration speech, I could give a speech about why my family came to America and the tragedy of our trek.

If Jacob and the rest of the class knew about us, maybe they would accept us and respect me. On Monday, I would convince Mrs. Bell to allow me to tell my story.

My heart felt lighter.

Mother stood at the window as I neared the driveway. I waved at her. Surprise crossed her face, and she met me at the door.

"Why are you home early? Are you all right?"

"I was sick earlier but now I feel better after walking home."

She felt my forehead. "You don't have a fever."

"I was sick emotionally."

She smoothed my hair. "How can I help?"

"Be my mother and stay healthy. If you and Nhia are healthy, I can deal with the problems at school. Don't worry about me. I think I have a solution."

We entered the living room. Nhia ran to me and clung to my

leg as he babbled about a Disney show he was watching. Having a family waiting at home for me warmed my heart and gave me purpose.

I spent the afternoon reflecting on my reaction to the redhead's letter. My anger and hurt had cost me half a day of education. I would never again miss school over another person's words.

In English class on Monday, I approached Mrs. Bell during work time. "Mrs. Bell," I whispered. "I want to tell you something."

Her blue eyes met mine. "Of course. What is it?"

"My family is new here. The students don't understand us. I want to tell the class my story to replace the demonstration speech. I think it helps students understand me."

She beamed. "What a wonderful idea."

What a nice teacher. I put my hands together in front of me. "Thank you."

"I'm looking forward to getting to know you better," she said.

"Can I go first on Monday next week?" I asked.

Her brows rose. "So, you want to go first on the first day of presentations?"

I nodded. "I don't speak good English. But I have to show the class that I am brave."

She gave me a broad smile. "I'm proud of you, Nou. Of course, you can present first. You speak English well. You have an accent, but it will get better."

"Thank you."

As I returned to my desk, Jacob dropped me another note on his way to the pencil sharpener. I opened it right away this time.

Sponger,

Have you decided on a date yet? My brother can't wait to meet you.

Sincerely,
The American Protector

I tore a sheet of paper from my notebook and wrote back.

Dear The American Protector,

I will let you know after the presentations. Thank you for your patience.

Sincerely,
The Dreamer

As soon as the bell rang, I caught up with Jacob in the hallway and handed him the note. He read it and laughed, but I didn't care. I wouldn't allow him to deter me from my goal of showing the class that my family and I were people just like them.

When I arrived home, Xa called and asked about school. I admitted that school was difficult but didn't mention Jacob. If Xa knew what he wrote to me, he would tell Mother even more negative things about Americans and maybe even the students at my school. There was no telling what kind of problems he might cause.

After I hung up, the phone rang again. I picked it up. "Hello."

"Hi, Nou," Peter said.

"Peter!" I cried. "I miss you."

"I miss you too. I'm coming home on Sunday morning to see you."

My heart soared. He'd attended a conference last weekend and hadn't come home. "Good. We have breakfast together."

"Perfect," he replied.

I wiped away a tear with my hand. "Can you help me with my speech?"

"Sure. What's the speech about?"

"About why my family came to America."

"Okay. We'll work on it. It'd be better if we could start on Saturday, but I can't miss marching band practice. The coach is very strict."

A strand of hair fell across my eye, and I tucked it behind my ear. "It's okay. I'm glad you're coming on Sunday."

"I wanted to see you. How's school?"

I sniffled. "Hard without you. I'll tell more when you come. I can't wait to see you."

"Me too. Talk to you later."

We said goodbye, and I placed the phone back on the cradle. Sunday would be two weeks since I'd last seen Peter and seemed like a lifetime away. I had to have my speech done before he arrived. Thought of the pile of homework and the added work of the speech overwhelmed me. No. I would not fear the hard work it would take to attain my dream.

27

Excitement kept me awake most of Saturday night and, at six o'clock Sunday morning, I got up, washed my face, and painted my face with makeup. I put sausage links in the oven, put rice in the rice cooker, and made scrambled eggs. Peter said he ate links, scrambled eggs, and pancakes for breakfast, but I didn't know how to cook pancakes, so he'd have to eat rice instead.

After I cooked, I stood at the living room window and watched for Peter. At nine o'clock, his blue car pulled up to the curb in front of our house. I raced down the stairs.

He met me at the bottom of the stairs. I glanced over my shoulder to see if Mother was looking out the window, and when I didn't see her, I hugged Peter. His deep blue eyes locked with mine and we kissed. I pulled away. I felt ashamed but how could I help myself? I was in love.

Peter warmed my heart and brightened my day. I wondered what it would be like to live with him. I imagined us having a great time reading, cooking, going out, and doing chores together. I imagined our tall children with dark brown hair, light colored skin, and long eyelashes. We would have a perfect life. Were such things possible?

We climbed the stairs and went inside.

Mother stood at the sink washing her hands. She glanced over her shoulder and said, "Hi, Peter."

"Hi, Choua," he replied. "How are you?"

Mother paused in washing her hands and looked at me in question. I translated for her.

"It's so hard to talk to him." She turned off the water. "Tell him I'm doing well."

I translated the part that she was doing well.

Peter nodded. "It's difficult to communicate with her. Have you tried teaching her English?"

"Yes. She wants to speak English, but it's so hard. She is old and can't learn."

"Wow! You said that in perfect English. Since you started school, your reading and speech skills have improved tremendously." His eyes sparkled. "I'm sure your mother will learn English from you as time passes."

I hoped he was right. Would he be interested in learning Hmong, so he could communicate with Mother?

She faced us and dried her hands on her pants.

Peter's gaze sharpened and he looked at me. "Don't you have towels or paper towels to dry your hands with?"

I frowned in confusion, then my cheeks warmed in embarrassment. "We don't have money for towels."

Mother glanced at me, and I realized she didn't understand us. I wasn't sure what to say. If I told her Peter was asking about towels, she would wonder the same thing I wondered, why would we buy towels—especially paper towels—when we needed to save money for a car?

She left the room and I pointed to the table, and said to Peter, "Sit. We'll eat breakfast."

Peter sat and I served him scrambled eggs, sausage links, rice, and a cup of orange juice. I served myself the same and sat beside him.

He smiled. "Thanks for cooking breakfast. Are your mother and Nhia eating?"

I gulped down my food. "They ate. Sorry, you eat rice, not pancakes."

He ate a spoonful of rice. "It's not bad."

I gave him an uncertain smile. We ate rice at every meal. Hopefully, he would learn to like rice as much as we did.

After we ate and I cleaned the table, we sat side by side and I gave Peter the speech written on the front and back of a single page. The speech had taken me five hours over five days to write in English.

He read the title out loud, "Why we came to America," then looked at me. "What made you choose this subject?"

I didn't want Peter to pity me or worry about me, so I had decided not to tell him about Jacob.

"Some kids at school are mean to me. I think if I tell them about my family they'll understand."

"I wouldn't have thought of that." He locked eyes with mine. "Kids at school are bullying you?"

I studied the paper he still held.

He placed a finger beneath my chin and tilted my face upward so that our eyes met.

"If they're bullying you, tell me," he said.

I had to tell him. I chose my words carefully and enunciated them well, "When I took Nhia to the library in June, three boys threw eggs at us and told us to go back to our country."

His mouth thinned. "Why didn't you tell me? I'm your sponsor. I'm supposed to protect you."

I averted my eyes in shame. "I didn't want you to worry. I wanted to go to the library when I want to. If you know the problem, you want to drive me, and I didn't want you to take me every time." I looked up at him. "The boy that threw egg at me is in my class. I think the speech might help him understand me. If it doesn't, I'll let you know."

He laid the paper on the table and grasped my hands. "From now on, you let me know when people bully you."

"I will. Work on my speech now. There are mistakes in the paper."

He gave me a gentle smile. "I'll correct them for you."

Peter read the speech in silence, his mouth pressed tightly together. At last, he looked up, and I was shocked at the tears in his eyes.

He laid the paper on the table and placed his hand over it reverently. "That is incredible. If you can make me cry, you'll make other kids cry too. If this speech doesn't touch the bully, then he's a complete fool."

I looked away, embarrassed. "I hope people care."

"People will care because it is good...and true."

I prayed he was right.

We examined every line together. I showed him where my limited English hadn't conveyed the feeling or message I wanted, and he helped me revise. We edited and rewrote the speech three more times until I was satisfied with a shorter, more precise piece.

I rose and stood at the opposite end of the table to practice. Peter set the time for three minutes, the required duration. I enunciated each word carefully while making eye contact as much as possible.

After the fifth reading, Peter clapped. "Excellent."

I burst into tears. Peter jumped to his feet, took two quick steps to me, and wiped away my tears with his thumbs. I glanced down the hallway, checking for Mother. She wasn't peeking at us.

"You are a determined girl." Peter whispered. "I wish I had your drive."

"I have no choice. Only hard work will get my family to pros-per-i-ty."

He laughed and gave me a high five. "Good job."

"Your dictionary helps me," I said.

"Keep up the good work. You're on your way to achieving your goals."

"Thank you so much for helping me. I believe God loves me and sent you to help me."

He chuckled and eased closer about to kiss my cheek when Nhia burst into the kitchen. Peter took quick a step back, mouth downturned in a frown.

"Auntie Nou," Nhia said.

"What?"

He hugged my leg. "Can we go outside to play ball?"

I stroked his hair. "Later. I'm working on my school project."

"Please," he begged.

I looked at Peter. He nodded.

"All right, Nhia," I said. "Only because you said 'please'. Go get your ball."

Nhia hurried to his room.

"When will Nhia's father come to America to raise his child?" Peter asked.

I started. "I-I don't know. Soon, I hope."

Peter nodded slowly. "It's got to be difficult for you and your mother to take care of him."

I opened my mouth to say that we loved Nhia and would take care of him as long as necessary, but Nhia came back with the ball I'd sewn out of an old black T-shirt.

"Mother," I called to the living room, "do you want to go outside with us?"

"Sure," she called back, and joined us in the kitchen.

Peter eyed the ball skeptically as we walked down the stairs. "You call that a ball?"

I nodded. "Yes. I made it to play a ball tossing game for the New Year celebration."

He smiled. Normally his beautiful smile would chase away any sadness in my heart, but I couldn't forget his question, *"When will Nhia's father come to America to raise his child?"*

"Let's give this ball a try," he said.

In the backyard, Peter and I tossed the ball a few times, then he said, "Now it's Nhia's turn."

Peter squatted eye-level with Nhia and tossed the ball to him. Nhia missed more often than he caught the ball and ended up chasing it.

"Nhia isn't afraid of Peter anymore," Mother said. "Peter's nice."

"Yes," I said. "Peter's a decent man."

Ten minutes later, Nhia plopped down on the grass.

Peter squatted down next to him. "Are you tired?"

"Yes," he replied.

Peter ruffled his hair, then stood, and faced us. "The ball is hard. I'll get him a Nerf ball to play with." He looked at his watch. "Shall we go to the laundromat?"

"Xa took us yesterday. I let him because you are busy." Although Mother didn't understand English, Nhia did, so I mouthed, "I love you only."

He smiled. "I understand. I'd better head home and check on my parents before driving back to school."

"Okay. Thank you for playing with Nhia and helping me with my speech."

"I'd love to play with him again sometime." Peter waved to Mother. "Bye, Choua."

"Bye," Mother said.

"Good luck on your speech," Peter said. "Let me know how it goes."

"Thank you. I'll let you know."

I loved having Peter here, but his visits were always bittersweet when he left. I couldn't wait for the day when he finished school and returned to Appleton for good.

From the moment I arrived at school the following morning, my mind was fixed on my speech. As the time drew near, my stomach knotted tighter and tighter. Although I felt warm, I shivered as I walked to English class. Not only was this my first speech, but a bully would be watching and listening to my every word. If I failed to educate him and get him to empathize, he might terrorize me even more.

Mrs. Bell reviewed the expectations for both the speaker and the audience. Then she explained to the class that instead of a demonstration speech, I would do a presentation about my family's journey to America. She called me to the front of the classroom.

I drew in a deep breath and took from my notebook the picture of my family that Mary had taken the day of Peter's graduation. My heart fluttered as I rose and walked to the blackboard where she stood.

"Mrs. Bell, can I show this picture?"

"Of course. We'll use the projector."

She pulled the overhead projector from the corner to where I stood, then plugged it in and placed the picture of me, mother, and Nhia in the middle on its smooth glass. She pulled the screen down over the blackboard then turned on the projector. The image filled the screen.

"My name is Nou Vang. I am a dreamer. I would like to tell you how and why my family came to America." I pointed to the picture. "My mother, my nephew, and I risked our lives to come here to be free. My mother was shot during our escape through the jungle, and she had to have her arm amputated. My sister, my nephew's mother, was also shot during our journey. As she lay dying, I promised her I would keep her son safe. I dreamed of coming to America, where I could raise him in peace and safety."

Jacob stared at me. I gathered my courage and locked eyes with him. "America didn't want communism to spread in Southeast Asia, so the government got involved in the Vietnam War. Another war known as the Secret War started in my country Laos. The American CIA recruited the Hmong, my people, to fight in the Secret War. My father fought as a CIA soldier and was shot on the leg."

I paused and took a deep breath to fight tears. "When the Americans withdrew from the war, the enemy took revenge and burned my village—and many other villages—and killed many people. My family fled from village to village in fear for our lives. In the end, we were forced to leave our country or be killed. During our hazardous trek through the jungle, the Communists looked for us and eventually killed my father and sister. We ate ferns, vines, insects and whatever we could find to stay alive. Some children died from starvation. My nephew almost died. He is traumatized and afraid of people."

My heart pounded. All eyes remained locked on me.

"I brought my mother and nephew to America for a better life. I take care of them. I love stories, and this passion keeps me motivated to learn. My family and my love of learning keeps me strong and gives me a purpose. I hope one day that I'll be able to read any book, write my stories to share with the world, and become a doctor. I believe education is the road to being self-sufficient. I want to be a good citizen and contribute to my community. I don't want any trouble, and hope that people won't cause me trouble. My family suffered much sorrow to come to America. America is my home now. We want peace. Thank you for listening to my story."

Everyone clapped, including Jacob, who stared at me in an odd way. A few students raised their hands for questions.

I looked at Mrs. Bell. "Mrs. Bell, should I answer questions?"

"Answer two questions."

I pointed at Billy, the curly brown-haired boy in the front row.

He asked, "How did you learn to speak and read English in just four months?"

"My sponsor's son tutored me twice a week at first, then three times a week. I go to the library almost every day, and I read every day."

"What do you like about America?" asked Jenny, who had an oval face with long blonde hair.

"Freedom, education, food, and equal rights for all."

The class clapped again. I returned to my seat, feeling breathless and light-headed.

After the last student gave their presentation, we had one minute before class dismissal and the students near me turned to me.

Jimmy, a cute boy with a long face, said, "You're amazing. I like that you shared your story."

"Yeah, your speech was great," said Sara. Her big glasses covered her green eyes. "I learned a lot about you today."

Amy, always dressed in matching clothes, chimed in, "I can't imagine what you went through."

I smiled. "Thank you for understanding me."

The bell rang. Everyone stood and headed for the door.

When I reached the front of the room, Mrs. Bell motioned me aside. The tenderness in her eyes tugged at my heart.

"Thank you for sharing your story," she said. "I'm so sorry for the tragedies your family went through. I didn't know you had to work so hard to learn English, or that you're the caretaker for your disabled mother and traumatized nephew. You're an incredible person. You must be traumatized too."

I nodded. "But I must be strong for my mother and nephew. They're the reason I work hard."

She smiled. "You're doing a wonderful job."

"Thank you."

She hugged me and her orange blossom scent filled my nose.

I walked to my next class feeling weightless. When the bell rang for lunch, I hurried to the gym to share my presentation news with Emily, only to find her absent. Though I missed her, I felt as though I walked on a cloud for the rest of the day.

As soon as I arrived home, Peter called. "How was your speech?" he asked.

"I did all right." My chest swelled with pride and excitement. "Some students talked to me today. They never talk to me before. I think they respect me more now."

"That is something to celebrate," Peter said. "I'm proud of you, Miss Nou."

I clasped my hand on my chest. "Thank you. I was able to do the presentation because you helped me. You are my success."

He laughed. "You give me too much credit. You did all the work. I'm glad things went well. I'll talk to you later. I love you."

"I love you too."

We said goodbye. I replaced the phone on the cradle and leaned against the wall.

I hoped Jacob would stop bullying me.

28

The next day, I reached English class to find Amy waiting outside the door.

"Hi." She smiled.

"Hi."

"I told my parents your story. You know what they said? They said you're marvelous and a devoted daughter."

"Thank you. Very kind of them."

I caught sight of Jacob in the hallway. He slowed and stared at us as he entered the classroom.

Lisa stopped beside us. "Your story made me cry. I don't know how you handled all that. If I were you, I would have been terrified."

"I appreciate you understanding me," I said.

Several students brushed past us into the classroom, and we hurried inside to our seats. The bell rang. Jacob got up, pencil in hand, and dropped another note on his way to the pencil sharpener. I unfolded the paper and read.

Dear the Dreamer,

I'm sorry. I have never been to other places and never understood people like you. I was worried you would steal my sister's future husband. I understand you now. Thanks for teaching us about your journey and your life.

I hope you accept my apology.

Jacob

I took a deep breath and sat straighter. My plan had worked. Pride flooded me. Mrs. Bell began class, but I reread the third sentence in Jacob's note.

I was worried you would steal my sister's future husband.

Who was his sister? Jacob's red hair and facial features reminded me of Kate. Could they be siblings? In between student speakers, I wrote a note to Jacob.

Dear Jacob,

I accept your apology. I hope you don't hurt anyone again.

PS Who is your sister?

Sincerely,
The Dreamer

When the bell rang, I hurried after Jacob and caught up with him in the hallway, then gave him the note.

He read it, then said, "You don't need to know her name," and hurried away.

At lunch, I waited for Emily at the gym entrance. She was

absent yesterday and I couldn't wait to talk to her. I hoped she was here today.

At last, I caught sight of her walking toward the gym.

I waved. "Hi."

"Hi." She stopped next to me. "Good job on your speech."

I raised my brows in surprise. "How do you know?"

Emily smiled. "I heard some students talking about it this morning. They said you're brave."

I laughed. "Wow! Nice."

We entered the gym and went to our chairs only to see them gone. We sat on the first row of bleachers and took out our sandwiches.

"Emily."

She looked at me. "What?"

"Can you help me?"

"Sure. What is it?" She took a bite of her peanut butter and jelly sandwich.

"Jacob Shine in my English class wrote bad stuff to me. He has a sister. I want to know her name. Can you find Jacob's sister's name for me?"

She swallowed her food. "How will knowing who his sister is help you?"

"I want to know, so I can avoid problems."

She took another bite of her sandwich. "What bad stuff did he write to you?"

"He wrote I am a sponger and prostitute."

Her eyes widened. "What a jerk! If he continues to call you names, I'll—oh, I'll do something."

"I don't want trouble for you," I said.

She chuckled. "I'm not afraid. I'll find out his sister's name for you."

I recalled how she had taken up for me against Mark Langstrom and his friends the first day I met her. I didn't think Emily was afraid of anything.

"Thank you so much," I said.

She pulled a cookie from her lunch bag. "Are you done with your math homework?"

"Yes. Do you have math homework?" I asked.

"I don't understand some of the problems."

I took a drink from my water bottle. "I can help you after school. If you like, I can tutor you after school every week."

Her mouth dropped open. "Geez, that's so nice of you. My mom will love that. I can do Monday and Wednesday after school."

"Good. You can ride the bus with me, or your mother can drive you to my house. Then we walk to the library."

"It's getting cold. We should have my mother drive us to the library."

I nodded. "I like it. Your mother can pick me up from my house."

"Deal." Her shoulders dropped. "Oops. I can't do it this week or next week. My mom is out of town. How about the first week in November?"

"I'm ready when you are ready."

"You're the best." She smiled broadly.

I smiled back. I couldn't believe I had knowledge my friend needed. I would help her as Peter had helped me.

29

November arrived. I opened the door to find the stairs covered with snow. I crouched and plunged my hand into a drift two inches high until my fingers tingled. I stood and gazed out on the beautiful, colorless world. Snow blanketed the street and sidewalk. Even the green bush near the stairs was covered in white. I would need a warmer jacket. No one had shoveled the sidewalk, so by the time I reached the bus station, my white sneakers were caked with snow. I shook them off before stepping on the bus.

At school, the sidewalks and front concrete steps were shoveled. A few students enjoyed a snowball fight.

In my third period history class, an announcement came over the intercom that I should come to the office.

When I arrived, Mrs. Young, the secretary, pointed me to the table where a telephone sat. "There's a phone call for you."

My hand shook as I picked up the receiver. "Hello."

"Nou, it's your mother," Mother said in a strangled voice. "Nhia and I went outside to play in the snow, and he fell. He has been crying for an hour and won't stop. He wants you. I don't know what to do anymore."

My heart began to hammer. "Is he hurt?"

"Yes."

Memory of my sister Der falling in the rice field when she'd been shot rushed to the surface and I began to shake. I blew out several deep breaths.

"Okay. I'm coming home," I managed, and hung up the phone. I turned to Mrs. Young. "My nephew fell and is hurt. I have to go home. I need a ride."

"Does he need to go to the hospital?" she asked.

My throat constricted. "I don't know. I have to check on him."

"I'll check with our counselor, Mrs. Henderson. She might be able to drive you home. Go get your things from class."

"Thank you."

I feared my legs would give way as I hurried down the hallway.

In the classroom, I went to Mr. Jones, where he sat at his desk. "I have to go home," I said hoarsely.

His brow furrowed in concern. "Is everything okay?"

I only shook my head, then got my books from my desk. I went to my locker, put my books in my backpack, then headed to the office. Mrs. Henderson and I arrived at the same time. We hurried to her dark red car, and she pulled out of the parking lot. My hands and legs shook.

Mrs. Henderson patted my shoulder. "Take deep breaths. Your mother is with your nephew. He'll be all right."

I twisted my hands to control my panic. "My mother doesn't speak English. She has only one arm. A traumatized woman. She is scared. I take care of them."

Mrs. Henderson gave my arm one more pat. "I'm sorry that everything is on your shoulders. Let me know if you need anything."

"I will. Thank you."

I directed her home. Five minutes later, she parked the car in front of our house.

"Should I come in to make sure he's okay?" Mrs. Henderson asked.

"Yes, please."

We hurried from the car, up the stairs, and into the house. I continued to the living room with Mrs. Henderson close behind. Mother sat beside Nhia, who lay on the sofa. Both had red eyes, and Nhia moaned softly.

"Hi," Mother said to Mrs. Henderson.

"Hi."

I sat on the sofa and pulled Nhia onto my lap. He wrapped his small arms around me, buried his face against me, and burst into tears.

"Shhhh. You'll be okay." I stroked his head.

Mother brought a chair from the kitchen for Mrs. Henderson, and she sat down.

"Sorry you had to come home," Mother said as she sat on the sofa. "I'm exhausted trying to quiet him."

I rocked Nhia, and he began to calm down. "Where did he fall?"

"We didn't know the snow was slippery. He went down the stairs too quickly, slipped, and fell about halfway down."

I should have told them to be careful. In truth, I should have taken the time to clear the snow off the stairs before leaving for school. I had so much to learn. I gently removed Nhia's t-shirt. His eyes landed on Mrs. Henderson, and he wailed in fright.

"It's okay," I told him. "She's my teacher. She's here to help."

Nhia clung to me.

"Mrs. Henderson, Nhia is afraid of you," I said. "I think he's okay. You can go."

She stood. "Okay. Call me if you need anything."

"Yes. Thank you."

Mrs. Henderson left, and Nhia's sobs subsided.

I removed his pants and examined his body. His back and buttocks were bruised and scratched.

"Does your head hurt?" I asked as I helped him get dressed.

He nodded. "Yes."

I remembered when Mother had felt sick a few months ago. "Mother, do we still have Tylenol?"

She shook her head. "We're out."

I should have asked Mrs. Henderson to buy us Tylenol before she left. I would call Peter after his last class. I hugged Nhia close and told him folktales until he fell asleep, then put him in bed.

At two o'clock, I called Peter.

After the third ring, he said, "Hello."

"Peter, I need your help," I said.

"Nou, what's wrong?"

Just hearing his voice soothed my anxiety. "Nhia fell on the stairs. He's hurt. We need medicine."

"Oh, poor kid. Children's Tylenol?" he asked.

I sniffled. "Apple sauce too."

"Okay. I'll be there soon."

"See you soon," I said, and placed the phone back on the cradle.

When Mother announced from the window that Peter had arrived forty-five minutes later, I hurried outside to wait for him at the top of the stairs. He carried a bouquet of multicolored daisies in one hand and a paper bag in the other. He smiled as he climbed the stairs, then stopped one step below me.

"For you, to cheer you up." He handed me the bouquet. "You must be stressed."

Tears filled my eyes, and he pulled me tight against him.

"I missed you," I said.

He pulled back. "I missed you too."

"Sorry you have to drive thirty minutes here," I said.

"I would drive thirty hours to see you. Shall we look in on the patient?"

Inside, I put the flowers on the table while he placed the shopping bag on the counter and removed the medicines, one bottle of children's liquid Tylenol and one bottle of adult Tylenol, and a jar of apple sauce. Together, we went into the living room. Mother greeted Peter.

"It's good to see you," he said.

I grabbed my purse, fished out a five-dollar bill, and handed it to Peter.

"They didn't cost that much," he said.

"Take it, please," I begged.

He glanced at Mother, then took the bill and stuffed it into his pants pocket.

Peter sat on the sofa with Nhia, who had woken up half an hour ago. "Nhia, where does it hurt?"

"My head and back," Nhia said softly.

"Can you tell me what happen?"

"I slid on the stairs and hurt myself." Nhia's eyes brimmed with tears.

I couldn't believe how good Nhia's English was. In a month, he'd be four. Soon, he could be Mother's translator.

I went to the kitchen, mixed a spoon of apple sauce with two drops of Children's Tylenol in a small bowl, and carried it to the living room.

"Here." I knelt in front of Nhia and held out a spoonful of applesauce.

Nhia narrowed his eyes, then he gave in and ate it. Then I read to him.

Mother called Auntie about Nhia's fall. For Mother, talking to Auntie, the shaman, was like consulting a doctor. This was her way of helping. I hated that talking to Auntie meant Xa had to be involved. Xa wasn't good for Peter and me. I considered telling Mother to end the call but, like always, I had to be a dutiful daughter and respect her. Which meant, I had to remain positive and hope for the best.

Mother finally ended the call. "Auntie told me that she knows *khawv koob* and can help. Khawv koob will heal the small cut on the back of Nhia's head faster. She and Xa are coming now."

Of course, I wanted to help Nhia get better, and the Khawv koob—an art of magical healing—was very powerful. But the more we asked Auntie for help, the more we owed her and her family, specifically, Xa. My heart raced. Would Xa confront Peter again?

"Peter, Xa and Auntie are coming to help Nhia." My voice shook slightly, despite my effort to sound calm. "You should go home now. I don't want Xa to be rude to you."

His expression remained impassive. "I'm not leaving. I'm not afraid of him."

"I don't want problem." I begged.

"I won't create a problem for you."

What did that even mean?

30

Fifteen minutes later, Auntie and Xa arrived. Mother remained in the living room with Nhia while Peter and I opened the door for them. If Xa wanted to create problems, I preferred he do so in the kitchen. At least, that way, I might have an easier time forcing him to leave, if necessary. Xa entered followed by Auntie.

His gaze locked onto Peter, and he halted. "I told you to leave Nou alone. I told you I will take care Nou family. Why you here?"

"Nhia got hurt," Peter replied in a calm voice. "I brought medicine for him."

Auntie looked from one to the other. She didn't speak English, but she couldn't miss the men's tense body language.

She turned to me, and said, "If your family needs anything, let Xa know. He's a helpful man."

I nodded but had no intention of calling Xa for help.

Everyone went to the living room. Auntie sat on the sofa with Mother and Nhia. I got a chair from the kitchen, put it by the wall adjacent to the sofa, and invited Xa to sit. Then I set a chair for myself next to Peter. He smiled. I smiled back. Xa cleared his throat and threw me a narrow-eyed look. Peter locked eyes with him. My dependency on these men had led to hard feelings. All because I was unable to take care of my family properly. All because I was just a daughter and not a son.

Auntie started the khawv koob, chanting softly in an unfamiliar language for about two minutes, then blew air on Nhia's wounds.

"Nhia's wounds would heal soon," she said confidently. "I'd need to repeat the khawv koob three times for best result."

"Thank you so much," said Mother.

"You're welcome. I'll come again tomorrow and one more time after that."

Peter and I looked at each other.

"What did she say?" he asked.

"I don't know the chanting. But she said Nhia would get better," I said.

Peter gave a tight-lipped smile. "It's interesting. Does it really work? I've never seen someone treated this way."

"You question my mother khawv koob?" Xa's voice rose. "Show respect for my culture."

Everyone turned to Xa and Peter.

Peter's expression darkened. "Sorry, I meant to ask how it works. I should get going." He stood and faced me. "Call me if you need anything."

"Okay. Thanks for coming."

I ignored Xa's stare and walked Peter to the door.

He pulled me close for a hug, then stepped back. "I'm sorry, Nou. I didn't mean to disrespect your mother's friend."

"I know."

After closing the door behind Peter, I turned to see Xa standing in the hallway with narrowed eyes. I lowered my gaze and started for the living room.

He grabbed my hand. "Tell Peter to keep his hands off you."

"I don't know why you're angry." I yanked free of his grasp. "You're not my boyfriend. I can date whoever I want."

"The next time he touches you, I'll punch him." He stepped closer.

I shoved him away. "Don't shame our people by hurting anyone. We're a minority. People will hate us."

"You're afraid because you're a woman. As a man, I won't let others crush us."

Blood pounded in my ears. "I know you had a bad experience in the war, but you have no right to touch me."

"Nou, I'm trying to protect you. Peter will only love you when you are beautiful. If you want your marriage to last, you have to marry me."

I stood as tall as I could and lifted my chin. "Peter loves me. If I marry him, he won't divorce me."

His face reddened and his gaze shifted past me. "Peter gave those flowers to you?"

I whirled to run to where the flowers sat on the table, but Xa pushed past me. He snatched them and crushed them between his hands. I swallowed a scream. I couldn't frighten Nhia or Mother, but I burned with hatred for Xa.

"You had no right," I said through clenched teeth.

Something in my voice must have surprised him. He looked down at the ruined flowers in his hands as if noticing them for the first time.

"I'm sorry," he said softly. "Nou, I wasn't thinking. I'm so sorry."

I turned on my heel, hurried down the hall to the bathroom, and locked myself inside. I lowered the toilet seat and sat, sucking in deep breaths. I never wanted to see him again. What could I do to stop relying on Xa and Auntie? I closed my eyes and tried to think of a solution.

About five minutes later, footsteps approached, then stopped at the door.

"Nou," Mother called. "Are you in the bathroom?"

"Yes. Do you need to use it?"

"No. Are you all right?"

I stood and opened the door.

"I heard you and Xa argue and saw the crushed flowers." Mother's voice sounded tight. "Did Xa ruin the flowers?"

I nodded. "Yes. He had no right to do that. The flowers cost Peter a lot of money."

Mother shook her head. "Xa is impulsive and has problems controlling his anger. He's not like Pheng."

"We don't need him to help us," I blurted.

Mother sighed. "We need Auntie."

Not if we could find another shaman.

We went to bed early that night. Nhia slept between Mother and me, snuggled against me as I cradled him and whispered soothing noises until he fell asleep.

In the middle of the night, he cried out in pain.

Mother switched on the light, and I felt Nhia's cheek and temple. "He has a fever." She scrambled out of bed. "I'll get the medicine."

Mother returned with apple sauce and Tylenol. I gave Nhia the medicine, but he kept crying.

I carried him to the living room and turned on the TV. Mother sat with us and, after a while, Nhia fell asleep. Still, he kept jerking awake and crying out in fear.

Mother's face clouded with worry. "We have to do hu plig."

I was exhausted. I didn't want to see Xa and ask him to get live chickens for us.

"Mother, we should go to church. That way, we won't need to rely on Auntie. We burden her too much."

Mother glared. "I told you that I don't want to convert. I have only a few years left to live. When I die, I want to be with your father, the ancestors, and my children. Our religion is a lot of work, but that is what we believe."

I crossed my arms over my chest. "Other Hmong like Mai's family converted to Christianity. We can too. We don't need to keep asking Xa and Auntie for help."

"Auntie likes helping us. If you don't like Xa, that's one thing but you shouldn't use that to force me to convert. I want you to be proud of our culture and religion."

"I am proud. But I've had enough of discrimination, getting bullied, depending on others, and being held hostage to rituals." I sighed. "Can we just not do the soul calling?"

"You don't want Nhia to get better? What's wrong with you?" Her voice rose. "You don't seem like my daughter anymore. Are you brainwashed?"

My temples throbbed and the volcano of emotion that had been boiling inside me erupted. "You don't understand what I'm going through! You don't know how much I sacrifice for you and Nhia!"

Mother jerked in shock, and Nhia startled awake. He began crying again. I pulled him onto my lap.

"I'm sorry," I whispered.

I didn't meet Mother's eyes as I rocked him back and forth, stroking his head. Shame flooded me. I had never raised my voice to my mother. I was a bad daughter. I wished Pheng was here to care for his son. When would he come to America?

Eventually, Nhia fell asleep again. I carried him to the bedroom and laid him on the bed. Then I returned to the living room. Mother sat in the dark as the television flashed light across her face.

I knelt before her. "Mother, I'm sorry. It's been a long day, and I'm tired."

She stroked my hair. "I know. I'm tired too. I'm sorry." Her voice cracked. "I know how hard it is for you to care for me and Nhia. I'm sorry I'm not helpful and we have to rely on others."

"It's not you. It's us having no family. If Father, Toua, and Der were here, we would be fine." At the thought of them, I burst into tears.

Mother and I cried together. She and I slept little that night.

The following morning, I wanted to go to school, but I had to stay home to care for my family and myself. I took a Tylenol capsule for my headache and called the school to report my absence. Mrs. Young knew my situation and accepted my call without talking to Mother.

Later that evening, Xa and Auntie came over to do khawv koob for Nhia again. Xa's eyes remained locked on me all evening, but I kept my distance.

After Auntie finished the khawv koob, Mother said to her, "I'm sorry to ask you again, but Nhia is sick, and we need you to do hu plig for him."

Auntie felt Nhia's head. "He has a fever. Tomorrow is Saturday. Xa doesn't have work and can get chickens. Let's do it tomorrow. I'll do the last khawv koob and hu plig after that."

Mother smiled. "You're very kind. Thank you for all you do for my family."

"I love your family," Auntie said. "I'm glad I can help."

After Xa and Auntie left, I reflected on our dependence on them. I had vowed to my sister that I would care for her son. I had vowed to Mother that I would be her son and take care of her. Auntie made Mother happy. There was simply no way I could avoid Xa.

Xa wanted to make me feel weak.

But I am not weak.

31

A hand shook me awake.

"Wake up," Mother said. "Xa and Auntie are here."

I sat up and realized I had dozed off with Nhia on the sofa. His fever had kept me awake all night. I looked at the clock. It was ten minutes before one.

Mother crossed to the window. "They're on their way up."

I stood and stretched. The nap had helped. I went to the door and waited.

When they reached the stop of the stairs, I opened the door. "Hi, Auntie."

She frowned. "You don't look well. Are you sick?"

"I'm okay. It's just lack of sleep."

Mother came to the kitchen and greeted Auntie, and they went to the living room.

Xa still stood outside.

"Are you coming in?" I asked.

"Nou, you're going with me to get chickens from the farm," Xa said. "Get your purse. I'll wait for you in the car."

I narrowed my eyes. "How far is it?"

"About an hour's drive."

I twisted my hands. The farm was so far away. I didn't feel safe going with him alone. "My mother wants to go too," I lied. "Please wait. Once Auntie is done, we'll all go."

Xa shook his head. "My mother wants to teach your mother khawv koob. They don't need to go. I won't bite."

I hesitated.

"Do you want to get chickens or not?" he demanded.

I huffed. "Fine."

I grabbed my purse from the bedroom and went outside. Xa sat in his car with the engine running. I opened the passenger's side of the two-door car and bent the front seat forward to go to the back seat.

"Sit in the front with me," Xa said,

I hesitated, then pushed the backrest back to its upright position and got into the front.

Xa glanced at me several times before saying, "Are you sick?"

"I'm just tired. Nhia kept me up all night."

"That's what happens when you have a child."

I yawned.

"You have acquired skills from caring for Nhia," he said. "You're ready to be a mother."

I leaned my head against the headrest. "No. It's too hard to be a mother." I needed to change the subject. "Why do we have to go so far to get live chickens? Aren't there farms nearby that raise chickens?"

"The nearby farms have only cows. The farm we're going to belongs to a coworker's relative who has chickens."

Snow blanketed the fields and the colorless world stretched out before me. I fought to keep my eyes open but finally gave in and let them close.

A thumping sound woke me. I bolted upright and looked around. Xa was pulling off onto a lightly plowed side road.

"Are we there?" I asked.

He put the car in park and left the engine running. "No. We're stopping for a short break."

"How long did I sleep?"

Xa twisted to face me. "Thirty minutes. Are you feeling better?"

I shrugged. "A little."

He took out a small white box from his coat pocket and opened it. A beautiful silver ring sparkled against the black velvet lining.

"Nou, in America, a man gives a woman a ring when they are getting married. I love you." His eyes glistened. "Would you please marry me?"

I stiffened but tried to keep my revulsion out of my voice. "That's very nice. But I'm not ready to get married."

Xa pulled the silver ring from the box and held it up. "I am ready. Give me your hand. I want to put this ring on your finger."

I balled my hands into fists in my lap. My heart thumped.

"Don't be afraid," he said.

I shifted so my back was braced against the door.

"Please marry me, Nou."

"I'm sorry. I can't." Guilt knotted my stomach.

His eyes narrowed.

"Look, I'm overwhelmed with everything. I'm just not ready," I said.

"When *will* you be ready?"

I shrugged. "Maybe a long time from now. Not until I have a good job."

"You must marry while you're still beautiful. When you're a spinster, men won't look at you."

Frustration welled up in me. He wasn't getting the hint that he wasn't the man for me. Maybe the war had damaged his brain. I'd had enough of his pressing me.

"I'm sorry, but you aren't the one, and I'm tired of your attention. Now can we just go get chickens?"

He leaned closer. "I may not be as handsome as Peter, but my father was a high-ranking officer in Laos, and I was a soldier. If we were there, girls would be chasing me and begging me to be their husband. You would have to fight hard for me."

I gave a hollow laugh. "But we aren't in Laos."

He snorted. "That's the only reason I have to work so hard for your love. No matter how much my mother and I help your family, you still don't appreciate me."

"I appreciate all the help you and Auntie have given us," I said with feeling. "If you want me to thank you every day, I will. But I can't be your girlfriend or marry you."

He lowered his head and closed his eyes. The car engine's steady hum reminded me that I was far from home. Despite the car's warmth, I shivered.

"Why don't you like me?" he whispered.

"You're handsome and a good man," I said. "But I have dreams. And you and I have different views about life."

He took a deep breath. "Nou, I don't have anyone to give the ring to if you won't marry me. Consider it a present. You don't have to marry me. It's not a promised gift." He held it up again and looked into my eyes.

I shook my head. "Keep it until you find the love of your life. She'll appreciate it."

"It's hard to find a wife when there are so few Hmong around. You are the only girl in the area."

"More people will come."

He shook the ring at me. "I bought the ring for you. I'm happy to give it to you even if you don't love me and don't want to marry me. Keep it as a memory of me. I might be ugly, but this ring isn't. Just remember that I love you."

I clasped my hands tightly together on my lap and shook my head.

"Fine." He placed the ring on my lap.

"I don't want your ring." I put it on his lap.

"I hate myself." His eyes glistened with tears. "If you don't take my ring, please come to my funeral."

I stared. Surely, he wouldn't harm himself?

He began to cry. "I'm worthless. I don't want to live."

My heartbeat accelerated. He was out of his head. I had no idea what he might do. If he harmed himself, who would care for Auntie?

"Please calm down," I said in panic.

"Don't bother trying to save me," he said between wracking sobs.

"Calm down. I'll take your ring."

Tears streamed down his cheeks. "Do you know how it feels to be rejected?"

"I do know." I picked up the ring.

He began to calm down. I finally exhaled.

"Will you wear the ring?" he asked.

"Maybe. Or I'll keep it safe."

"Thank you."

He wiped away his tears and I shifted back into my seat as he put the car in gear and pulled back onto the main road. My heartbeat gradually slowed. A while later, we arrived at the farm. He opened his door, and I opened mine to follow him.

"You stay in the car," he said. "I'll get the chickens."

"I'll help."

He spun and pointed at me. "Woman, stay in the car."

I pressed my lips together in frustration but closed the door. Through the window, I saw a man emerge from the house and lead Xa to a red barn. Ten minutes later, Xa returned with two chickens in a brown box. He put the box in the trunk, then got back behind the wheel. On the way home, I didn't want to talk to him, so I pretended to sleep.

Once we arrived home, Auntie began the soul calling. Mother sat at the kitchen table while I cleaned the rice cooker's pot. My hands shook with the memory of Xa's outburst, and the pot slipped from my hands. It hit the floor with a clang. Mother looked at me. I avoided her eyes and picked up the pot. I finished cleaning it, then got the rice cooking, and headed to the bathroom. Mother followed. I slowed and peeked into the living room, in hopes she would go sit on the sofa. Xa rested on the sofa and Nhia sat on the carpet in a corner reading. I continued toward the bathroom with Mother close behind.

In the hallway, she whispered, "You look upset. Did Xa anger you?"

"Yes. I hate him," I whispered. I didn't want Mother to worry, so didn't tell her about the ring or his outburst.

Mother frowned. "I'm sorry you have to put up with him. I wish there was another shaman in the area. Remember that we need Auntie's help, so please be polite."

I nodded. "I know."

Mother went back to the kitchen.

After the hu plig, I cooked the chicken quickly, and we ate dinner. In appreciation of Auntie's time, dedication, and her khawv koob, Mother gave her twenty dollars and thanked her. She accepted the money. I breathed a sigh of relief. Maybe by paying her, I would be less obligated to Xa.

As Xa and Auntie started to leave, he said, "Nou, would you turn on the outside lights for us?"

I stood and followed them to the door. I flipped the switch. Auntie walked out and started down the stairs.

"Bye, Auntie," I said.

She waved. "Bye."

Xa halted beside me and smiled. "Thank you for taking the ring. I'm going to take you out for dinner tomorrow. I'll come around four-thirty."

Why didn't he ask if I wanted to go instead of demanding? "Sorry, I can't go with you. I'm busy with homework."

His smile faded. "You can do homework after. You won't have

to cook for your mother and Nhia. I'll get them food when I send you home."

I looked down at the floor, but said in a firm voice, "I can't go."

"Okay. Um...my mother wants you to see our house. She has been asking. If you can't have dinner, a quick visit would make her happy."

I looked at him and frowned. If Auntie wanted me to see their house, she'd have asked me herself. "I don't have time to visit." I sounded rude and was glad Mother was in the living room.

Xa hesitated, then whispered, "The elders said that in love, the more you hate that person, the more likely you'll marry him. Hate me all you like."

He turned and stepped outside. I slammed the door shut.

I didn't believe such nonsense.

32

On Monday morning as I put my backpack in my locker, someone bumped into me on my shoulder. I looked behind me and a boy said, "Watch out gook!"

Gook? Did he mean, "Nou"? Did he mean, "watch out, Nou"? Why was I at fault when he bumped into me?

Liz and Ava broke into wild snickers at their lockers. I looked from where the boy had disappeared into the crowd back at them. Were Liz and Ava laughing at me? I sighed heavily. I knew some kids didn't like me. I pulled my books from my locker and headed to class.

When I arrived in English class, Mrs. Bell beckoned me to her desk. "A new Hmong family arrived last week, and we have a girl in seventh grade," she said. "Her name is Mee Thao. She doesn't speak English. We put her with you in this class and your science class. Do you think you can help her?"

Hope sprang to life inside me. The Hmong community would soon grow if more families kept coming. I wondered if either of Mee's parents were a shaman.

"Yes," I said. "I'll try my best."

Mrs. Bell smiled and patted my arm. "I knew you would. Thank you, Nou. She'll sit next to you. I'll move Sara to the empty seat by the corner."

I went to my seat. A few minutes later, a girl with an oval face and long black hair tied at the back of her head walked in.

I jumped to my feet and hurried to her. "Hi, Mee," I spoke Hmong cheerfully. "I'm Nou Vang."

"Nou, I'm lucky to be in this class with you." Tears shimmered in her eyes. "I was terrified the whole time in homeroom."

"I know what you mean."

I led her to our desks, and we sat.

"When did your family arrive in Appleton?" I whispered.

"Wednesday, before the snow. I registered on Friday, and today is my first day."

"You did well in finding this class on your first day. Do you understand your schedule?"

She pulled out a paper in a folder. "Our sponsor, a woman, showed me the classes on Friday, so I kind of know where to go."

I gave a single nod. "Good."

Mrs. Bell cleared her throat, and everyone quieted. I studied Mee's schedule. She had math next.

When Mrs. Bell explained the assignment, Mee looked at me with a blank expression. I understood her frustration. I took notes in English and Hmong so I could explain to Mee later.

During independent reading time, I whispered, "Mee, do you understand any words in the textbook?"

She shook her head.

"Don't worry. After I read, I'll explain everything. Do you have a phone number?"

Mee wrote her number on a sheet in her notebook, then tore it out and handed it to me. I got out my dictionary and translated unknown words. The translation slowed my reading, and I was still working when the other students finished.

Jacob glanced at Mee and me. I didn't care that he was done early. The reading was difficult. I was only halfway finished when the bell finally chimed.

"I'll finish the work at home and call you," I told Mee.

She nodded.

"Meet me by the office, and we'll go to lunch together," I said.

Her expression relaxed. "Thank you."

Although Mee knew where her math class was, I walked her there to ease her anxiety. Then I went to my class.

At lunchtime, Emily joined Mee and me by the office near the gym entrance.

"Emily, this is Mee Thao. She is a new student. She doesn't speak English."

"Welcome to Wilson." Emily smiled. Her bangs were getting longer; they almost reached her big blue eyes.

"Mee, this is Emily Hill," I said in Hmong. "She's my American friend."

Mee nodded. We went inside the gym and sat on the bleachers to eat our lunches. Emily had a sandwich, chips, and soda. Mee had rice and sausage. I had rice and chicken wings. Emily stared at our food for a few seconds, then shrugged and took a bite of her sandwich.

"Why didn't you come to school on Friday?" Emily asked after she swallowed.

"My nephew fell from the stairs and got hurt."

"Oh, I'm sorry." She shoved a chip in her mouth.

"He's better now," I said.

Mee's eyes flicked from Emily to me, her expression blank. She didn't ask what we were talking about, so I didn't translate.

During recess, we walked around the football field with other students. A few boys threw snowballs at each other, and the supervisor scolded them. A girl and boy held hands as they walked in front of us. I thought of Peter and how much I missed him. He had brought me a bouquet of red tulips on Sunday. I kissed the flowers before I left for school, imagining they were his lips.

"They're such a cute couple," Emily said in a dreamy voice. "It's cool they're the same height."

Their brown hair made them a perfect match too.

"They are cute," I said.

Would people say Peter and I were cute? I doubted it. Physically, Xa and I would make a cute couple. Images of Xa proposing and forcing me to take the ring flashed through my mind. I bit my bottom lip. He frightened me. My emotions rushed to the surface. I needed to share with Emily.

"Emily, I want to tell you something."

She looked at me. "What is it?"

"A Hmong guy likes me. He asked to marry me."

Emily's eyes widened. "Did you say yes?"

I shook my head. "I don't like him."

"Good. When did he ask you?"

"On Saturday. He scares me. He hates Peter, my sponsor's son."

Emily stopped walking. Mee and I halted.

"Why does he hate Peter?" Emily asked.

"Umm, Peter is my boyfriend."

Emily gaped. "You date your sponsor's son?"

"Well, we love each other."

Mee stared at us in confusion. "What are you two talking about?"

"I'll tell you later," I said in Hmong.

"Okay. I get it now," Emily interrupted. "You don't love the Hmong guy, but he loves you and asked to marry you."

I nodded. "I hate him, but he calls me almost every day."

"Tell him to stop calling you. If he continues to annoy you, that's called harassment. You can report it to the police."

"Oh." I wondered if I could do that. "My mother needs his mother's help. It's not easy in my culture to be rude."

Emily tossed her head. "I don't know about your culture, but in America, you have rights. No one can force you to do things that are bad and violate your rights."

If reporting Xa to the police was my right, maybe I could use that right if he tried to hurt me. The bell rang, signaling the end of recess.

As we headed inside, Mee grabbed my arm. "Nou, why do the Americans hiss like a snake when they talk?"

I laughed. "I asked the same question when I came to America, but as you learn the language, you don't hear the hissing much anymore. I think it has to do with the *s* sound. Many words have the *s* in it."

"Yes, I think you're right."

"Nou," Emily interrupted, "my mom is home and can pick you up at five to go to the library. I really need help with math. Do you think we can go today?"

"Today is okay. Bring your calculator."

Emily beamed. "Thank you. See you at five." She waved at Mee, then disappeared in the crowd.

Mee and I picked our way through the crowded hallway to her locker, then I told her I could call her after school and went to my locker.

When I arrived home after school, Mother and Nhia waved at me from the window as I approached the driveway. I waved back and hurried up the stairs. The smell of roasted pork and green onion crushed with hot pepper and cilantro filled the air.

"You cooked." I hugged her. "Smells delicious." I went into the living room where Nhia sat on the sofa, watching TV. "Hey kiddo. Are you still in pain?"

He whimpered as he shifted. "A little."

I kissed him on the forehead. "Soon, you'll be your old self."

In the kitchen, I put the food on the table, and we sat to eat. Nhia sat on the chair next to me with Mother on the opposite side.

"Mother, thank you for cooking dinner." I bit into the pork rib.

"I'm getting better at using one hand."

"Good. I'll continue to prepare food for you to cook." I drank water from my cup. "I'm going to the library to help my friend Emily with her math homework. Her mom will pick me up and drive us there."

Mother's expression brightened. "I'm proud of you. You're not only our backbone but are helpful to others, as well."

"Thank you."

I worked on history homework after I washed the dishes and cleaned the table. When Emily arrived, I put on Xa's watch because the library second floor's clock broke and hadn't been replaced. I hated to admit it, but the watch had come in handy the few times I needed it.

Her mother dropped us off at the library. We went to the youth area on the second floor and worked on Emily's math homework. Math came easily for me. Emily was easily distracted by people's movements and conversations, but I kept her on task.

As I coaxed her on how to find the area of a rectangle, heavy footsteps approached from behind. From the corner of my eye, I glimpsed a dark-haired young man. My heart raced. Xa? He hurried past me to the bookshelves to my left and I realized he wasn't Xa. How foolish of me to have thought he had followed me to the library. Oh no, were the panic attacks I had experienced in Laos returning?

"Are you ok?" Emily asked.

I released a breath and pointed to the man by the bookshelf. "I thought that man was Xa. You know, the Hmong guy I told you about."

Emily stared at me. "Geez, you're that afraid of him?"

"He's not nice. I dislike him."

"If he comes here, I'll kick his butt for you."

Could she really do that?

"Nou," a soft feminine voice said.

Emily and I both looked up. Susan waved at us from over the book on the bookshelf where she stood. I waved back. She emerged from the aisle and came to our table. She wore her brown hair up in a tight ponytail.

"Hi, Susan. You come home from the university?"

"Yes. I needed a book for a class." She showed us a thick book. "Are you two studying?"

"Yes," I said. "This is Emily."

"Hi, Emily. Nice meeting you."

"Nice meeting you too," Emily said.

Susan hugged her book to her chest. "I spoke to Peter on the phone the other day, Nou. He couldn't say enough good things about you."

My heart began to beat fast.

"He went on and on about how smart you are, and ambitious, and how you're learning English at an incredible rate. Keep up the good work."

Peter and Susan still talked to each other? Why hadn't Peter told me?

"Thank you," I murmured.

"You're welcome. Say, would you mind giving me your phone number? I'd like to know more about your traditions. Plus, maybe I can help you sometime."

I wondered what she was up to, but said, "Sure." I wrote my phone number on a page from my notebook and gave it to her.

"Thanks," she said. "Talk to you soon."

We said our goodbyes.

"Is Peter dating her too?" Emily asked after she left.

I stared at the table, hoping Peter wasn't dating both of us. "I don't know. She's his ex-girlfriend. She dumped him because he didn't go to college."

"Hmm."

I didn't want to know what that "hmm" meant. "No more talking. Back to work."

I tried to forget about Susan's visit, but I couldn't ignore the sick feeling in my gut.

33

As our group ate lunch the following Wednesday, I noticed that Mee didn't have a lunch bag. She opened her sketchbook to draw.

"Hey, Mee, did you forget to bring a lunch?"

She looked up at me. "I packed it. Just forgot to grab it."

Good thing I brought rice and roasted pork ribs in two Tupperware containers. I combined the food in two containers and gave Mee one. Emily brought a plastic fork and spoon for her spaghetti and shared her spoon.

"Would you like some spaghetti?" Emily asked her.

Mee looked at me in question. I translated. She nodded. Emily forked some noodles into Mee's container and a few into mine. I ate my noodles, savoring the sweet and sour tomato sauce taste.

"Emily, it's good," I said. "Thanks. Do you want to try rice?"

She forked some rice into her mouth and chewed slowly. "It tastes like nothing."

"Rice is plain. You have to eat with pork. Hmong food is plain."

Emily sipped her bottle of juice. "Do you eat rice a lot?"

"Rice is the main crop in Laos, so I grew up eating it every day." I spooned rice into my mouth and took a bite of the rib.

Due to the minus twenty-five degrees temperature, recess was inside today, so we took our time eating. The chattering voices echoed around the gym.

I turned to Mee. She had finished her food. "You can thank Emily for her food. I'll teach you. Do you know how to read Hmong?"

She shook her head. "No."

"It's okay. Can I use a page in your sketchbook?"

Mee opened the book to the last page and handed it to me. I took out the pen in my pants pocket and wrote *thank*. I pointed to the word and said, "The sound of this word is *teeb* in Hmong. You know the flashlight."

Her eyes glistened. "Oh. I understand."

I wrote *you* and said, "This word alone is you, but when it is added to the word *thank*, the sound is like the letter q in the alphabet."

"I know the letter q."

"Good. Now say thank you."

She took a breath and said, "Thank you."

I patted her on the shoulder like how others had done for me. "Good job."

Mee looked at Emily and said, "Thank you."

Emily smiled. "Good job, girl. You spoke English!"

Mee grinned.

I put my containers in my lunch bag and opened Mee's sketch book. She had drawn Hmong refugees fleeing the war and their lives in the camp.

"You can draw!" I cried.

Mee beamed. "In Thailand, my cousin taught me to draw. He drew many story cloths for friends. He made money drawing."

"Did you draw story cloths too?"

"Yes. I made money too."

I stared at her. "Can you draw me one?"

"Sure," Mee said.

Excitement rushed through me. "I want to make my sponsor's son Peter a story cloth. I'd like you to draw my story. I'll call you."

"How big do you want it to be?" she asked.

I eyed the banners hanging on the gym wall. "Hmm. Maybe that size?" I pointed to a banner."

"Okay. That's about thirty inches by forty inches."

"I'll get you cloth."

"No need. My mother brought a roll from Thailand. I'll use that."

I couldn't believe it. "I'll pay you."

"No. You've helped me a lot in class. Don't pay me."

"Well...." No matter what she said, I would pay her, but I said, "I appreciate that. Thank you."

Emily stared at us. I felt bad that I had to speak in Hmong. I was relieved that my two friends understood when I switched languages. One didn't question me when I talked to the other, which helped our friendship.

"Emily, did you find out anything about Jacob's sister?" I asked.

She shrugged. "Not yet. Sorry. I only know a few people. Finding out about his sister is harder than I thought. I talked to two seventh graders and haven't heard from them. I'll let you know as soon as I hear anything. If I can't find out through people I know, I'll talk to the bully myself."

"Thank you for helping. It's cold. Will your mother take us to the library tonight?"

"Yes."

I shifted my attention to Mee. "Mee, do you want to come to the library with us?"

Her expression dulled. "I'd love to, but my family doesn't have a car."

"When I can drive and have a car, we'll be able to study and do things together."

She nodded. "I can't wait."

I looked at both my friends. Not so long ago, I was a loner who ate under the bleachers and hid during recess. Now I had two friends, who supported me.

When the bell rang, Emily said, "See you at five tonight."

"Yeah," I said. "Bye." I waved and headed to my locker.

I caught sight of Mark Langstrom up ahead and lowered my gaze. He whispered something to the boy he was with as he passed me but said nothing to me.

I neared my locker and overheard someone say, "I can't believe she's dating Peter Johnson. Doesn't she see herself in the mirror."

I turned toward the speaker. Three girls I had seen with Liz Anderson stared at me. They quickly turned and disappeared into the crowd.

How did they know I was dating Peter? When Liz and Ava saw Peter picking me up from school, Peter told them he was my sponsor. Did he tell Liz I was his girlfriend? Peter and I were different, but we loved each other. What was wrong with that? Why were people so cruel?

School ended at three thirty-five p.m. The city bus didn't come for another ten minutes, so I took my time. The hallways were practically abandoned when I exited the building and stepped out into the frigid afternoon. As I neared the bus stop, a white car slowed, then stopped in front of me. The car looked familiar, then I realized it was Xa's car. Sure enough, I glimpsed him in the driver's seat in the instant before the driver's side door opened and he got out.

I frowned. "What are you doing here?"

"Picking you up." He smiled as his eyes landed on the watch on my wrist. "The watch looks nice on you. I'm glad you're wearing it."

"It's been useful."

He held out a hand to take my bookbag as he rounded the hood.

I held my bag tightly. "Why are you picking me up?"

"Your mother wanted me to take you to the store to buy juice for Nhia. He's been asking for juice all day and she doesn't want you taking the bus to the store in this cold weather. I told her I'd pick you up and go straight to the store."

He was right. We had run out of juice, but I didn't like Mother calling him. I hesitated.

Xa locked eyes with me. "Nou, I don't like Peter and hate it when he's with you, but you know I'd never hurt you. Come on. I'm getting cold. Let's go."

I didn't have much choice and climbed into the back seat. He gave a faint smile.

He pulled the car from the curb, and said, "I had a bad day at work today. Would you like to hear about it?"

"Sure."

"I work in assembly lines and one machine broke and the others didn't work properly, so the supervisors made us clean the building. My coworkers whined all day long, driving me crazy. Some people chose to go home without pay. I stayed because I need the money."

His job sounded stressful. Xa rambled on. He turned down an unfamiliar street.

"Why are we going this way?" I demanded.

"Another way to the store," he said in a smooth voice, but something felt wrong.

A block later, he parked behind a blue car. A young man got out of the car.

Hair rose on the back of my neck. "What are we doing here? Who is that guy?"

"He's my half-brother. He's going to the store with us."

Xa got out of the car and slipped into the backseat behind the driver's seat. His half-brother got in behind the wheel.

I pressed myself into the corner. "What's going on, Xa?"

He scooted closer. "My brother will drive us to the store."

"You're lying!" I lunged between the front seat and the door for the door handle, but Xa yanked me back onto the seat.

"Calm down," he ordered. "Please don't try to escape a running car. You'll get yourself killed."

I thrashed, but he dragged me against him and clamped my arms to my sides.

"I'm warning you," he growled. "I love you very much, and I'm taking you to be my wife."

"No!" I kicked his shin.

I broke free, but Xa pushed me down on the seat and flipped me face-down with my arms behind me.

"Stop! Don't do this!" I shouted.

I kicked the seat, but he sat on my legs as he bound my wrists with thin twine. Where had he gotten the rope? My heart thudded. The twine cut into my wrists. I bucked with all my strength, but he was too strong. With one knee on the floorboard, he held me down with the other knee while he bound my feet.

Tears coursed down my face. Once finished, Xa pulled me upright in the seat and hugged me close. Neither man responded to my screams or cries for help. I realized my only option was to talk my way out.

I took a deep breath. "Xa, please don't do this. Take me home, and we'll talk with my mother and your parents. Communication is the best way for a happy marriage."

He scoffed. "You rejected my proposal. There's no other way."

"This way only works in Laos. We're in America now. Forcing me to marry you won't work."

"You want to bet?"

"You'll go to jail for this! Do you understand?" I shouted.

"Not if the Hmong community sanctions the marriage."

Was he right? I was a girl and with no male family. Who would care about me? My stomach turned to jelly. If I lost my body to

Xa, I would be forced to be his wife. My dream to go to college and a life with Peter would be shattered. A knot squeezed my chest tight. I breathed deeply and closed my eyes.

I had to escape.

I went limp.

34

Xa's half-brother parked the car on the driveway of a small, corner white ranch house. Ranch houses lined the street with a few two-story houses. The half-brother opened the car door. Xa got out, then scooped me up into his arms and walked to the house. He stopped at the threshold. An older man inside the door murmured while he swung a chicken over our heads. With a start, I realized he was performing the *lwm qaib*, a ritual to ward off any evil spirits that might have traveled with the groom and bride on their way home.

"Uncle, I don't want to marry Xa!" I cried. "Please stop him."

The man didn't look my way. I thrashed, but Xa held me tight as the man completed the ritual. Then he carried me inside and into a bedroom at the back of the house. He laid me on a bed I realized must be his bed. I began to imagine what he planned to do and began to tremble.

"Can you untie me?" My voice choked with anguish. "My wrists and ankles hurt."

He gazed down at me. "Later, wife. Stay still in bed."

"Arrgh!" I snarled.

He left the room and closed the door. I rolled to the bed's edge and managed to pull myself upright. I stood and took several small jumps across the carpet to the door. I pressed my ear to the wood and strained to hear the conversation in the next room.

"The messengers left to notify her mother," Xa said. "They should be there already."

"Good," a man replied. "As part of the notification process, a gift of money must be given to Nou's mother. Did you give the messengers enough money?"

"I gave twenty dollars for the gift and one hundred dollars extra in case the messengers have to bribe her mother to accept the marriage and not call the police."

I gasped. Would Mother take their money? She better not. I took a deep breath to calm the rush of blood through my head. The clink of glasses and cutlery resounded in the kitchen.

"Mother, is the food ready?" Xa asked.

"Yes. Take some for her," Auntie said.

Auntie was in on my abduction? I couldn't believe it. I hopped back to the bed and flopped down on the mattress an instant before the door opened. Xa entered with a bowl of rice and a bowl of pork stir-fry. He set the food at the foot of the bed. He left, then returned with a plate, spoon, and chair.

He moved the food to the chair, then looked at me. "I know you're hungry."

"I'm not."

He waited a few seconds, then pulled me to a sitting position and slid me to the bed's edge so I faced the chair where the food waited. Then he sat beside me.

"I'll feed you. I'm sorry that I must marry you this way. This is the choice you gave me."

I gave him the evil stare. "My choice doesn't have anything to do with this. Kidnaping isn't a choice. We have nothing in common, and I don't love you. My values and respect for you prevented me from being rude. Now, I see I should have put you in your place from the beginning. I won't marry you! Let me go."

His expression turned cunning. "You are my wife now and will be my wife forever."

"I don't love you!" I spat.

His lips curled upward in a hideous grin. "After tonight, you'll love me."

A cold sickening feeling settled in the pit of my stomach.

"Once I have your body, a decent man won't want you," he said.

"I don't care. We're in America now. It's not like in the village where everyone will know and look down on me."

In truth, I cared. But I had to convince him somehow.

Xa sneered. "You may live in America, but you're Hmong. The Hmong community will tell everyone you're ruined."

I realized arguing was a waste of time. So far, my tactics of screaming, asking for help, and telling him I didn't love him weren't working. My only choice was to escape. Although my stomach didn't want food, I needed energy.

"I'm hungry. Untie me so I can eat."

"I'll feed you." Xa picked up the spoon and bowl of rice.

"I don't need you to feed me. I can do it myself."

Xa scooped up a spoonful of rice and held it up. "I'll untie you after I have made you my wife. Would you like to be my wife now, so I can untie you?"

I swallowed. "No. Feed me."

I ate the entire bowl of rice and all the pork. Then I laid down on the bed without a word.

"Get some rest." Xa picked up the chair and dishes and pulled the door shut when he left.

I waited a few minutes to make sure he wasn't coming back, then got to my feet. I glanced at the alarm clock on the side table. The digital face read 4:35 p.m. Only an hour had passed since Xa kidnapped me, yet it felt like hours. I hopped to the window, then nosed my way between the opening in the curtain and looked outside. The streetlights cast a glow across the empty, nearly dark street. The window was only about three feet above the ground. If I could free my hands and feet, I could escape through the window.

Men's muffled voices emanated from the living room. I hopped to the door and pressed by ear against the wood.

"Nou's mother called but your phone number was disconnected. She was furious and demanded that you call her."

"I'll call her tomorrow morning," Xa said. "Did she take the money?"

"No."

Of course not. I had never been so grateful for my mother.

"She wanted to speak with Nou and refused to talk to us," the man said. "After I explained to her that Nou likes you and accepted your gifts of a watch and a ring, she calmed down."

Anger flared. "Liar!" I cried. "He tricked me! You tricked me into taking the gifts!"

I banged my shoulder against the door. Quick footsteps approached and I hopped backward so quickly, I nearly fell over. The door burst open. Xa and Auntie stared at me.

"You lied to my mother," I spat.

Xa scooped me up and tossed me onto the bed.

"Liar! I've never liked you!" I screamed.

His eyes narrowed.

"I'll talk to her," Auntie said.

Xa walked out and slammed the door shut behind him.

I pushed myself to a sitting position and looked at Auntie. "Auntie, you must help me. I can't marry Xa. You must convince him to let me go home. Please."

She sat on the edge of the bed. "He loves you and will be a good husband."

"I don't love him!" I cried as much in frustration as fear.

Auntie smoothed my hair. "You'll learn to love him. He's a good man and will take good care of you. As women, we want husbands who will take care of us and love us. He's what you need."

"I can't marry him."

"I said the same thing when Xa's father kidnapped me for his wife. He wasn't attractive, but he was smart and ambitious. I fell in love after a month of living together."

Good for her. That wouldn't happen for Xa and me. I had dreams, and I wouldn't even try to live up to his old-fashioned expectations for a wife.

"Auntie, we don't live in the old country anymore. It is wrong to practice bride kidnapping. It worked for you and Uncle, but I can't accept it."

Auntie stroked my hair. "We live in the new world, but it's our tradition. We're Hmong. Please don't tell the authorities. The messengers told your mother not to call the police."

Mother wouldn't know how to call the police.

"I don't want to marry Xa," I said through clenched teeth. "How many times do I have to tell you?"

"Xa and I love you. I want you to be my daughter-in-law. Your mother and I get along very well. We will be a happy family with all of us living under one roof."

She wouldn't help me. I had to try to get her to untie me. I twisted my mouth downward to show I was in pain. "Auntie, my wrists and ankles hurt very bad. Can you untie me?"

She looked at my feet then my hands behind my back. Sorrow crossed her features. "I can't. Xa will kill me." Tears abruptly spilled from her eyes. "I rely on him for everything."

Sadly, I knew this part was true. Her husband was legally married to another woman, but in the eyes of the Hmong community, still married to her, as well. But because he was old, it was Xa's responsibility to care for his mother.

"I'm sorry, I can't stop him," Auntie murmured.

Fury shot through me. "He's your son. You *can* stop him and help me."

She shook her head. "In America, I'm a child. I can't do anything."

My heart fell. I took a deep breath. I had to try a different tactic.

"I need to call my mother. She'll be worried."

"She knows you're safe with us."

What a stubborn woman! Auntie might not be able to stop Xa, but she could at least untie me. I no longer liked or respected her.

"I'm tired and need sleep," I lied.

She rose and I scooted up on the bed, my back to her. I lay perfectly still until the door clicked shut.

35

I turned onto my back and studied the room. It was a plain room with a bed, a nightstand, and dresser. On top of the wooden dresser sat a frame with a black and white picture of Xa in his soldier uniform. He was about sixteen and handsome.

Xa had been right. If we had won the Secret War, he would be of high status and would have many girls to choose from in Laos. I wouldn't have had a chance to capture his attention. I should be grateful and accept this marriage. But I loved Peter. He was the man of my dreams. My chest tightened. Were my dreams gone?

No. Heroes didn't give up. No matter how difficult, the hero Nuj Nplhaib continued to chase and fight the tigers who took his beautiful girlfriend, Ntxawm. I must fight for my freedom and dreams. I could be like Superman and save myself. Why couldn't I fly like Superman? I wiggled my wrists in an attempt to loosen the rope, but the rough twine cut through my flesh. I bit back a cry of frustration. I couldn't save myself while bound.

"Peter, help me," I murmured. "You have to help me." I heaved a deep breath. "God, you brought Peter to my life to help me. Please bring me to him pure. Don't allow Xa to rob me of my pride, my youth, and my future. Please help me."

I couldn't hold back the tears, but I was determined that Xa wouldn't hear my sobs, so I turned my face into the quilt. My heartbeat pounded in my ears. Screeching tires outside brought my tears to a halt. I sat upright.

The clock read 5:25. Emily and her mom were supposed to pick me up at five. Maybe they were still at my home and trying to figure out what happened to me.

"Father, my ancestors, and God, please make Emily call the police," I prayed. "Urge Mother to have them call Peter. They must help me get out of here as soon as possible."

Thinking about Emily calling the police and Peter coming to help me, sent a renewed strength into my limbs—until I realized that, even if Emily asked, Mother couldn't tell her what happened to me.

My head felt heavy, and an ache pulsed through my body. Had coming to America without my brother been a mistake? I hadn't believed something like this could happen in America. How could I have been so naïve?

A red light flashed past the window. I scooted to the edge of the bed and hopped to the window. I poked my head through the opening in the curtain and spotted a police car at the end of the block. I opened my mouth to scream, then stopped. Even if I yelled for help, the police wouldn't hear me. The car turned the corner. Was the police car a coincidence, or had Emily or Peter called them?

Five minutes later, another police car drove past. Hope surged. I had to get out through the window. If they drove past again, they would help me. I turned and looked around the room for something sharp to cut my bonds with.

My heart jumped into my throat when the door opened. Xa stood in the doorway.

"Are you trying to escape?" He strode to me.

"No," I whispered. "I miss my family and was just looking out the window."

He narrowed his eyes. "Don't try to break the window. There's barbed wire outside. I don't want you to get hurt."

Barbed wire outside a home in Appleton? Was that possible?

Xa picked me up and carried me to the bed. I looked through the open door into the hallway. The house was quiet. Had the men left?

"After I shower, I'll be ready for bed," Xa said.

Fear coursed through me. I jammed my eyes shut. When I heard the door creak, I opened my eyes and released my pent-up breath. I had to do something. But what? I got up and hopped to the closed door, then tried to open it but found the door locked. I hopped to the window and, this time, pulled one side of the curtain to the side with my teeth. The dim light from the street didn't provide enough light for me to discern if there was any barbed wire below the window.

Another police car drove past. I had never seen a single police car on my street. Surely, the police were looking for me. I turned and hopped to the bed. I dropped to my knees and looked under the bed. More rope lay spread across the carpet. Was Xa going to tie me up in bed? The room began to spin around me. I had to escape.

The bathroom door creaked open. I rolled onto my back and sat upright against the side of the bed. The bedroom door opened, and Xa walked in with a white towel wrapped around his waist. He closed the door and removed the towel. I started to squeeze my eyes closed, but saw he wore pajamas. He sat cross-legged on the carpet beside me. I scooted away from him.

"You looked pale when I took off my towel." He grinned. "You thought I was naked. That proved you haven't seen a naked man. I love a pure girl. You're worth all the trouble you caused me." He reached up to tuck a loose strand of my hair behind my ear.

"Don't touch me!" I began hyperventilating and the room spun.

I listed to the right and Xa caught me.

"What happened?" he demanded.

I wheezed for air.

"Mother, come quick! Nou is fainting! Hurry!"

He lifted me onto the bed. Auntie hurried in.

Like my mother, she felt my forehead. "You're shaking. Take slow, deep breaths."

I breathed in slowly.

"Xa, untie her," Auntie ordered.

Xa untied my wrists and ankles, revealing red, painful welts. The watch band slipped onto the red welt. I unclasped the band and let the watch drop onto the bed.

"Keep your watch," I snapped.

"It's yours. I'll put it in a safe place until your wrists are healed," he said.

Auntie smoothed my hair. "I'm sorry things had to come to this. I'm sorry you got hurt." She instructed Xa to bring ointment from the bathroom. He hurried away and returned quickly with a small jar of ointment. Auntie sat on the edge of the bed and applied ointment to the wounds.

"Auntie, can you have Xa take me home? Please. I want to go home," I begged softly.

She looked at me. "You can't go home. We already did the lwm qaib. You're Xa's wife now."

My breath caught in my throat. Was it true that I couldn't go home? I didn't care. I had to go home. I didn't come to America to be forced into marriage.

"Auntie, I'm afraid of Xa. Can I at least sleep with you tonight?" My voice wobbled. "I promise just tonight until I feel better."

Auntie looked at Xa.

"No. Nou will sleep with me," Xa said, his voice firm.

I had to buy time and figure out a plan. "Auntie, stories calm me. Can you tell me about your young self and your life with Uncle?"

Xa left the room and Auntie began her story. She told me how she had been a beautiful girl my age when Uncle, a young soldier, kidnapped her. He loved her, and they were happy, until she aged, and Uncle married a second wife. They lived under one roof until the Communists invaded Laos. Because Uncle was a high-ranking officer, he and the family were air lifted to a refugee camp in Thailand.

In America, Uncle couldn't have two wives, so on paper, Auntie was a divorcee. She had eight children, three sons and five daughters. Two of her married daughters moved to California and the rest stayed in Thailand. Xa was the youngest and only son with her now.

I asked her to tell me more stories and she told the folk tales of *Nuj Nplhaib thiab Ntxawm* and *Niam Nkauj Suag Paj*. Xa returned to the room.

When Auntie finished the second story, Xa said, "No more stories."

Auntie smoothed my hair. "It's my bedtime."

She left and Xa locked the door.

The air around us grew thick. Xa stepped toward me with a smile. I felt like I was being buried alive. My brain shut down. I closed my eyes and tried to summon courage. The mattress dipped with his weight as he sat on the bed beside me. Not seeing him, my nerves calmed a little and the word *rights* flashed in my head. I had the *right* to choose my husband and future. I wouldn't let fear rule me. I would free myself.

I opened my eyes.

He smiled a satisfied smile that boiled my blood. "Would you like to change? I bought you pajamas."

"I have a stomachache. I have to use the bathroom." I masked my shaky voice as best as I could.

He opened the door. I hurried across the hall to the restroom. He followed me and prevented me from closing and locking the door.

"Seriously, I can't poop with you watching me," I said.

"Yes, you can, if you have to."

I crossed my arms over my chest and stared.

"Do you want to use the bathroom or not?" Xa asked impatiently.

"I can't do it with you watching."

Xa clicked his tongue. "Come out from there."

"Turn around, then."

Sighing, he faced the hall. Once I had finished, I stood and pulled up my jeans. As soon as I flushed the toilet, he turned around.

"Bedtime," he said.

He wouldn't let me out of his sight. I put the lid down and sat on the toilet.

Some elders say that sons typically follow in their fathers' footsteps. Xa did to me what his father had done to his mother. That meant when he tired of his first wife, he would marry a second wife.

That first wife wouldn't be me.

36

I needed to study the layout of the house. Maybe I could find a way to escape.

"Xa, can we watch TV?" I asked. "I have a stomachache and can't sleep."

He sighed in frustration. "It's passed my bedtime. I'm tired."

"Just a little, until my stomach feels better. If you love me, you'll listen to me."

He thought for a minute. "All right."

I fought to contain my relief. "Thank you."

We sat on the living room sofa and Xa turned on the TV. I allowed him to wrap one arm around my shoulders and hold my hand. His touch made my skin crawl, but I forced myself to lean against him.

As I pretended to watch TV, I rubbed my neck, so that I could turn my head to study the house. The front door was to the left of the sofa and the kitchen was located through a door to my right. The bathroom and two bedrooms were on the left side of the house down a narrow hallway. Shoes sat in a neat row on a mat near the door. I didn't see mine anywhere. Where had Xa hidden my shoes? A pair of slippers sat to the left of the couch near Xa. They must be Auntie's.

Xa kissed my hand. "Nou, I love you very much. You're everything I need in a wife. I have no words to describe you, but I'll try so that you can understand why I would die for you." He kissed my head.

I had heard a story of two lovers who committed suicide because their parents disapprove of their marriage. Would Xa really die for love? Guilt niggled at the possibility that I was being too harsh toward him. I pushed away the impulse. I loved Peter. He was my strength.

"Go on," I said.

"You're beautiful. You're kind when you aren't angry. You're smart, a hard worker, patient, and caring. I want to be the best husband I can be."

"Please be nice to me, then," I said.

He kissed my head again. His kissing felt like a thousand crabs crawling on me.

"I will," he said. "I didn't mean to hurt you. I want you so much, and you left me no choice but to force you to be my wife. I'm very sorry."

I pulled my hand away. "If you wait until I have a job, I might marry you without force."

"I thought about that, but I can't stand Peter touching you. He's around you too much, spoiling you and ruining your life."

Spoiling me? I suppose from Xa's perspective that was true. After all, he wanted a wife who waited on him and obeyed his every command, not a wife who demanded respect.

Still, I couldn't keep but ask, "How is Peter ruining my life?"

"Decent Hmong men only want subservient Hmong women. He's filling your head with all kinds of ideas that make you disrespect a good man like me."

I was right. His version of a wife was a servant.

"I'm not a subservient type of girl." I gave an airy laugh. "I'm serious. Can you please take me home?"

He grasped my hand again and squeezed it. "You're the girl I want. You're not too spoiled yet. You must understand that some Americans are nice, but some aren't." His expression darkened. "Some of my coworkers were mean to me and told me to go back to my country. I was bullied at school. Random people called me and told me to go back to my country. I learned to stay away from Americans, and I want you to do the same."

So, my family wasn't alone in facing discrimination. "I know some Americans hate us," I said. "But we shouldn't let the bad Americans teach us to hate and fear the good ones."

"Americans can't be trusted," he shot back. "Nou, I decided to marry you so I can protect you."

No doubt, he believed what he was saying. He warned me to stay away from Peter. When I disobeyed him, he told himself that marrying me was the only way to protect me. My brother would disapprove of my relationship with Peter, too—particularly if he experienced racial discrimination. But Xa's reasoning was a too-convenient reason to take what he wanted.

A wife and daughter-in-law had many responsibilities, and I already had enough with my own family. Plus, I didn't love Xa.

We sat in silence. I pretended to watch TV, while wracking my brain for a plan of escape. Xa remained glued to my side. With every passing minute, my hope of rescue faded. Emily hadn't called the police, after all. I'd been fooling myself.

"We've been watching TV for a long time now," Xa finally said. "It's time for bed. Please don't make me force you."

A fireball of anger and resentment burned in my chest.

"I'm not ready." My voice shook.

He grasped my chin and forced my face upward to meet his gaze. "I think you will never be ready."

"I'll go to bed if you promise not to touch me," I said.

"I can't do that."

He stood and reached for my arm. I knocked his hand away. Xa scooped me off the sofa and carried me down the hallway. I pummeled his chest with my fists and kicked, but he clamped his arms more tightly around me.

We reached his bedroom. Xa kicked the door shut and tossed me onto the mattress. I rolled across the mattress and jumped to my feet on the other side of the bed.

"Help! Auntie, please help me!" I screamed.

His mother didn't come to help me.

Xa vaulted over the bed and grabbed me. This was my last chance for escape. I could do this. I had led my family through the jungle to safety. I could save myself. I shoved him with all my might. He stumbled backward and crashed into the wall, then crumpled to the carpet.

I stared in horror at his motionless body. Oh God, had I killed him?

Run! a voice in my head shouted.

Eyes locked on Xa, I skirted the foot of the bed, then lunged for the door. I threw the door open and raced down the hallway to the living room. I scooped up the slippers near the sofa and burst through the door and out into the frigid air. I skidded to a stop at the curb, breathing heavily.

The streetlights cast soft light across the snow-covered ground. I shivered at the eerie silence. The world seemed deserted. Xa's house sat on the corner. Memory of him lying on the carpet flashed in my mind's eye. I began to shake. What if I killed him? Would anyone believe that he had kidnapped me? Auntie would tell the police that I, his wife, had killed him.

But I wasn't his wife.

I glanced back at his house, then ran across the street. A large tree sat close to the nearest house. Lots of boot prints filled the snow-covered yard. Children must live in the house. I hurried across the yard to the tree and collapsed behind it, my back against the trunk. Cold shot through my bare feet like tiny tendrils, and I realized I was barefoot. I still gripped the slippers and quickly put them on. They would be of little help, but at least my feet weren't in direct contact with the snow.

No one stirred in the house in front of me. Might the people help me if I pounded on their door? Would the ruckus wake Auntie and would she notify Xa? I turned and peeked around the tree just as Xa stumbled out of the house wrapped in a thick winter coat. My heart leapt into my throat. He stopped at the street, looked left, then right. I huddled close to the tree, my teeth chattering so loud, I feared he would hear me.

He hurried to the left toward the intersection, then stopped and scanned the street in all directions. He started at a run and disappeared around the corner. I glanced over my shoulder at the house that belonged to the yard where I was hiding. Was this my chance to see if the people there would help me? What if Xa returned before someone answered the door? Or worse, what if the people in the house turned me away? I nearly cried when Xa returned seconds later. I crouched low behind the house as he hurried up the walkway to his house, then disappeared inside. If he decided to search for me in his car, he'd catch me in no time.

I had to move. *Now.*

I hunched low, ran across the yard to the next house, and plastered myself against the side of the garage. A light suddenly shone in Xa's living room. He'd woken Auntie. I raced around the garage and house and didn't look back until I had turned the corner. I gasped for air and the freezing wind ripped through my thin shirt.

I stumbled, caught myself, and ran down the sidewalk as fast as I could. How much longer before I lost feeling in my feet? Already, I wasn't sure if I could feel my pinkie toes.

"Please, Father," I rasped, "don't let Xa drive down this street."

I thought I heard the hum of a car engine and the world spun around me. No, I couldn't faint. Xa would surely find me. I turned another corner and gasped at sight of soft light emanating from a house up ahead.

I pumped my freezing legs faster and swung my arms in an effort to bring feeling back into my hands. If I died, who would care for Mother and Nhia?

"Father, help me," I whispered. "Mother and Nhia need me. Save me." My mouth felt numb. "God, help me. Give me wings to the house with the lights on."

Finally, I stumbled up the porch steps as the world spun. I pounded on the door.

Then everything went black.

37

I blinked my eyes open to a grass roof above me. The murmur of voices wafted toward me. I sat up. Where had a thatch hut come from? I looked down and realized I was sitting on my old bamboo cot in Laos. I shifted and caught sight of two people sitting around the fire pit, their backs to me. I couldn't believe my eyes.

I jumped out of bed. "Father! Der!"

They turned to face me. Father looked so thin that his bones were visible beneath his skin, and I barely recognized him. Der, however, looked exactly as I remember, beautiful with long hair and light-colored skin.

"You're up," Father said.

"Hello, Nou," Der said.

"I can't believe we're together again. I missed you both so much." I stretched out my arms to hug Der, but she held up her hand.

"Don't touch us."

I let my arms fall back to my sides and sank onto a short stool next to her. "Why can't I touch you? I want to feel your warmth and hold your hands."

Der's eyes shimmered with tears. "I'm sorry, you just can't."

Father's features twisted with grief. "We're just visiting."

"I don't understand." I looked around the hut. Everything looked the same as it had before we fled the Communists, the mud stove, fire pit, dining area and four bamboo cots.

"You live with your family," Der said. "Mother and Nhia."

I glanced around the hut again. "Where are they?"

"You'll see them soon," Father said.

Confusion rattled my brain, but I didn't care. Der and Father were here. My heart somersaulted in joy.

"How are you doing?" I asked.

Father smiled. "Fine. Finally, we can move on to the next chapter of our lives. Thank you for releasing our souls. We'll be on our way."

"Thank you for taking care of my son," Der said.

I stared in confusion. "Your son?"

"I left him in your care. Remember Nhia?"

"No." I shook my head. "Der, I miss you so much. I want to be your sister forever. I want to go with you and Father."

"You can't," Der said. "Mother and Nhia need you."

I stamped my foot on the floor. "Father, I need you and Der. Please take me with you."

Father shook his head. "You can't go with us. You have duties to finish."

They stood and walked toward the door.

My heart ripped in half. "Don't leave me! Please don't leave me!"

I jumped to my feet and took a step toward them. They turned to face me.

"You can't go with us," Father said in an authoritative voice. "Take care of your mother and Nhia. You are your mother's only hope. Don't disappoint her."

I stood rooted to the spot as they opened the door. The hollowness in my stomach gnawed like a monster.

Then I remembered what I had to say before it was too late. "Father, Der, I love you!"

They looked over their shoulders and said in unison, "We love you too. Goodbye."

"Goodbye," I whispered.

They exited and closed the door behind them. I couldn't believe they left me with an impossible task. The room spun and I collapsed onto the dirt floor. A sob wracked me.

"Father, you're not being fair. Why do you give me a difficult job? I can't do it alone. I hate my life."

From afar, a child called in a faint voice, "Auntie Nou. Auntie Nou." The voice came closer. "Auntie Nou!"

The shout broke the spell, and I snapped my eyes open. A child's face hovered an inch above mine, eyes as big as an owl's.

"Auntie Nou. She's awake!"

I blinked. Nhia sat on the bed beside me. He kissed my cheek.

A woman smoothed my hair. "My daughter, you are awake."

I squinted. "Mother?"

Tears rimmed her eyes.

I lay in a hospital bed. How had I gotten here? I closed my eyes. However I'd gotten here, my prayers had been heard. I had escaped Xa.

I started to speak, then felt something down my throat. I looked down at the tube taped to my mouth. I tried to swallow, but the tube gagged me. What had happened? Nhia grasped my hand, and I gently squeezed his chubby fingers.

A nurse in a white uniform entered the room. She smiled at me. "You're awake. The doctor said you'd wake up, and here you are. My name is Amanda. I'm going to remove the tube from your throat. Ok?"

I nodded. She gently peeled back the tape that held the tube in place, then eased the tube free of my throat. I took a slow breath. My throat felt dry as sandpaper, but the pain had subsided. The nurse put the items on a nearby cart, then grasped my free wrist to check my pulse. I looked into Mother's bloodshot eyes. She touched my forehead with a warm hand.

"Mother, you've been crying?" My groggy voice didn't sound like me.

"Yes. I thought I would lose you."

I smiled as best I could. "We're a family again."

The nurse laid my hand on the bed, then wrote on a paper clipped to a clipboard. "Do you need anything?" she asked.

I didn't exactly know what I needed. I was glad to be safe. "No."

"All right. If you need anything, just press the button on the railing." She pointed to the railing to my right, then left the room.

Movement in the corner of my eye caught my attention and I started upon realizing a man and woman sat in chairs in the corner to my far right. The woman was Auntie. I would have shouted for her to leave, but the man stood and took two steps to my bed. Could it be?

"Peter?" I whispered.

"Thank God, you're awake." His eyes looked dull and tired.

Joy burst inside me. "Peter."

He took my hand in his. I tried to sit up.

"Wait." Peter pressed a button on the bed and the bed lifted so that I was in a more upright position.

Then he hugged me. My heart nearly burst. Finally, I was with the man of my dreams. Tears burned my eyes. Mother cleared her throat and Peter pulled away. I had hugged my boyfriend in front of my mother and should have felt terrible, but I didn't care anymore. I needed his hug for courage and strength.

"I was so worried. I prayed for your recovery," Peter said.

"Thank you," I replied, a little breathless.

Peter went to his chair and returned with half a dozen red roses wrapped in beautiful paper. "They're for you, sweetheart."

My heart melted. I took the roses. "Thank you."

"I'm so sorry I wasn't there to help you when Xa kidnapped you," he said.

"It's okay. I thought about you and Emily calling the police to help me."

"Emily did call the police. Then she called me. When Emily got to your house, your mother couldn't tell her what happened, but your nephew translated for her. When I arrived, I talked to Nhia, and he told me what your mother had told him."

My chest burst with pride. I squeezed Nhia's hand. "Nhia, your English saved me."

"I love you, Auntie Nou," he said.

"I love you too."

I looked at Peter. "What did Nhia tell you?"

"That Xa took you to be his wife. Your mother hadn't spoken to you, so she wasn't sure whether or not Xa had forced you."

I nodded, unable to speak.

"Give me the flowers," Mother said. "You should rest."

I gave her the roses. She set them on the cart, then gave me a cup of warm water. Auntie stood and came to stand next to Mother.

My breathing accelerated. "Help, help me!" I cried.

Mother put an arm around me. "It's okay. You're safe."

"Why is Auntie here?" My voice wobbled.

"She was worried about you, and I asked her to come do khawv koob for you, so you can recover faster," Mother said. "Her khawv koob is what awakened you sooner than expected."

I recalled Der and Father's visit. "Der and Father visited me before I was awake. I asked to go with them, but they refused, saying I have duties to finish."

Mother's chin quivered. "I'm so relieved you didn't go with them. I believe the khawv koob and my prayer stopped Der and your father from taking you with them."

Maybe the khawv koob had saved me. But I felt certain Peter's prayers had helped, as well.

"I'm sorry for my inability to help you," Auntie said. "Will you forgive me?"

I lowered my gaze. I wouldn't forgive her.

"My son and I wanted you in our lives so much that we made big mistakes."

I shook my head, eyes on the white sheet covering my legs. "You could have helped me when I begged you."

"I thought you loved him. He said you accepted his watch and ring as promised gifts. I saw you wear the watch and thought he was telling the truth." Her voice trailed off. "Also, he threatened to leave me if I helped you. Who would take care of me if he left?"

I understood how she relied on Xa like Mother relied on me, but she hadn't done a thing to help me.

"Xa lied," I said. "In America, when we say we don't like someone, we mean it." I paused to catch my breath. "I begged you for help, but you did nothing."

"I now understand you were serious."

I still refused to look at her. My eyes suddenly felt heavy as led and I yawned.

"You need to rest," Mother said. "Nhia, tell everyone to go. Nou must rest."

I nodded as exhaustion lowered my eyes lids and my little nephew ordered everyone to leave.

38

I woke at seven-twenty a.m. Nhia lay curled beside me on the bed. I gently kissed his forehead, then looked around the dimly lit room. Mother and Auntie slept on a folding cot. Peter wasn't there. I tried to sit up but fell back on the bed, too weak to try again. Nhia rubbed his eyes, turned over, and went back to sleep.

Mother got up. Her eyes were still red and puffy. Strands of hair fell on her eyes and the hair clip hung from a few strands of hair against her neck. With only one hand, it was difficult for her to gather all the hair together and tie it.

"Mother," I said. "Come here. I'll fix your hair."

She sat on the edge of the bed with her back to me and I combed her hair with my fingers. I gathered the hair together, twisted it and tied it to the back of her head with the barrette clip.

She turned to me, tears in her eyes. "How would I have gone on if you hadn't come back?"

I wiped her tears with my fingers. "But I came back."

She smiled. "I love you so much."

"I love you and Nhia too. How many hours did you sleep?"

She felt my forehead. "Maybe an hour or two. Auntie and I stayed up while you slept."

"Who brought Auntie here?" I asked.

"Uncle." Mother looked at the clock. "They came around three."

The cot creaked as Auntie sat up. She rubbed her eyes. Like Mother, her hair was unkempt, but she smoothed her hair to the back of her head and clipped it with a barrette.

A few minutes later, Amanda entered the room. "Hi, Nou. How are you doing?"

"I'm doing better."

"Good. An officer would like to speak with you." She shifted her gaze to Mother and Auntie. "Can they wait in the waiting room?"

"Mother, a policeman wants to talk to me and wants you and Auntie to wait in the waiting room," I said.

"There are people in the waiting room. I don't feel comfortable there," Mother said. "I want to stay with you."

Auntie's face turned ashen. "Nou, I beg you not to tell the police what happened. If Xa goes to jail, who will take care of me? We thought it was okay to marry the traditional way and didn't know we were breaking the law until the police arrested Xa."

"You should have listened when I begged you," I said.

"I'm sorry. Please don't tell him."

Mother's expression softened. "You're safe now. You can do Auntie this favor."

I looked at the nurse. "My mother and auntie want to stay with me. They don't understand English and won't know anything."

The nurse nodded. "I'll tell the police officer. Two more things. Breakfast will be at eight o'clock and Dr. Nelson will look in on you around nine o'clock. If you need anything else, let me know."

"Okay."

She left and a minute later, a tall, uniformed officer entered the room.

"Hi, Nou, I'm Sergeant Ross. How are you doing?"

"All right."

He eyed Mother and Auntie. "Are they your mother and aunt?"

"Yes. They are afraid to stay in the waiting room and want to stay here."

He looked at me. "We talked to Mr. Thao and heard his side of the story. We want to know your side. Tell me what happened."

Auntie's eyes remained on me. A shadow crossed her features as she shook her head slightly. I faced a difficult decision. I hated to lie, but Auntie needed her son to take care of her as much as my family needed me.

"I went to his house. We had an argument," I said.

Sgt. Ross took notes on a sheet clipped to a clipboard. "What was the argument about?"

I picked at my nails as nervousness kicked in. It was difficult to tell lies. "I didn't want to go to bed with him. He got mad. I got scared and ran away."

"Did he hurt you?"

"No."

"Did he threaten to kill you?"

I shook my head. "No." At least this part wasn't a lie.

"Explain the bruises on your wrists and ankles."

I glanced at Auntie. Her eyebrows drew together, and her eyes shone with unshed tears. I gazed at the purple welts on my wrists. I remembered a game Nhia and I played in which we would eat chips with our mouths with our hands behind our backs.

"My nephew and me tie our hands and feet eating chips with our mouths. I got bruise from the game."

His eyebrows arched. "Why did you tie your hands and feet?"

I lowered my gaze. "To see who eat the most chips without hands. For fun."

Sergeant Ross's mouth thinned, and guilt spread through me. "Thank you." He gave me a card. "If you have any questions or need to talk, call me."

I nodded. "Thank you."

He left. A minute later, Amanda walked in with a tray of food and placed it on the cart.

"Enjoy your breakfast," she said. "Let me know if you need anything."

As soon as the door closed behind Amanda, Auntie asked, "What did you tell the police?"

"I said we had an argument, and I ran away."

Auntie sighed with relief. "Thank you so much."

"Auntie, I appreciate everything you have done for my family. At your request to save Xa from going to jail for kidnapping me, I lied to the police in return for your kindness." I paused to decide whether to stop or continue telling her how I felt. I was still angry at her for not helping me. "Our debt to you is now paid."

Mother gave me a disapproving look, but she didn't know what I had been through. Auntie had looked me straight in the face and ignored my pleas for help. I understood that no one helped her when her husband kidnapped her, but that didn't give her a reason not to help me or tell her son to stop.

Auntie nodded. "I understand."

I gently shook Nhia's shoulder. "Wake up. Breakfast is here."

He stretched his arms and opened his eyes. He sat up and we shared the scrambled eggs, links, and biscuit.

Peter arrived, looking like he'd slept in his clothes.

I swallowed my food, and asked, "Where have you been?"

"I took a nap in the waiting room," he said.

"You were up the whole night with my mother?"

He nodded. "Yes. I've been here since driving your mother and Nhia here last night."

I relaxed against the pillow. "Can you tell me more about what happened?"

"Emily called the police to report you were missing and when the hospital notified the police, they called your house and I talked to them."

"Peter was with grandma and me and he was sad Xa took you," Nhia said.

Peter ruffled Nhia's hair. "This kid has been an amazing translator."

Nhia giggled.

"When he saw you unconscious on the bed, he cried so hard, I had to take him for a walk in the corridors. Your mother was alone and frightened and was crying when we returned." Peter shook his head. "You're important to them." His expression turned tender. "You're important to me."

Tears filled my eyes. When I first met Peter, he was a stranger and I prayed he'd be compassionate. Now he was like a family.

He sat on the edge of the bed.

"Thank you for taking care of my family," I said.

He scooted closer. "You frightened all of us." He grasped Nhia's hand. "While you were unconscious, this kid sat on your bed just like now and tried to wake you up often. He's young but he knew you were in bad condition." He gave me a gentle smile. "We're so lucky to have you back."

My heart burst with gratitude and I hugged him. His arms tightened around me. I looked at Mother. Her eyes shone with joy. Auntie, however, glared. I averted my eyes, so as not to cause conflict, but I didn't care. Peter comforted me and eased the pain buried deep in me. We pulled away as Nhia climbed from the bed and went to sit by Mother.

A middle-aged man in a white coat with a stethoscope on his neck entered the room. He shook my hand. "Hello, Nou. I'm Dr. Nelson. How are you doing?"

"Better."

"Good. I understand this is your first winter. So, you probably don't know how important it is to stay inside when the temperature is below zero. You can get hypothermia in minutes, which is what happened. You didn't have your coat, mittens, or hat, young lady. You're lucky someone found you and warmed you up before the ambulance arrived."

"They saved me. Dr. Nelson, thank you for saving me too," I said.

"You're very welcome." He checked my feet, hands, and mouth, and listened to my heart with his stethoscope. "The injury on your wrists and ankles are minor. You're ready to go home." Dr. Nelson turned to Peter who stood on one side of the bed. "Are you taking her home?"

"Yes," he replied.

"I'll give you written instructions on how to care for her. You can review them together." The doctor looked at me. "Do you have any questions?"

"No. Thank you for helping me."

He smiled and said, "You're welcome," then left.

When I was discharged, Peter pushed me in a wheelchair to his car. I sat in the front seat with him while Mother, Nhia, and Auntie sat in the back. I wanted to tell Peter about what happened with Xa, but Nhia understood English, so my story would have to wait. Exhaustion had begun to take its toll, so we remained silent.

Peter parked the car, then got out and hurried around the hood to open my door. He lifted me off the seat. I wrapped my arms around his neck as he followed Mother up the stairs with Nhia and Auntie in the rear. We both smelled like sweat but I didn't care. It felt wonderful to be in his arms. Mother opened the door and Peter took me directly to my bed.

"Thank you, Peter," I said, as he pulled the blanket up over my chest. "You look tired. You go home and sleep."

He hesitated, then kissed me on the forehead. "Okay. Call me if you have pain or aren't feeling well."

"I will."

He kissed me again. "I'll come tomorrow. Rest."

"Bye," I said.

"Bye." He walked out and closed the door.

I woke to Mother calling me, "Nou. Nou."

I blinked up at her.

"The uncles are here to speak with us," she said.

"Why are they here?" I asked.

"I think they want to discuss Xa. They're in the living room. Come, I'll help you to the couch."

She helped me up and I leaned heavily on her until we reached the couch.

Xa's father Uncle Shoua Nu Thao, a stout man, and Uncle Cher Thai Vang, a tall, lean man, sat on chairs next to each other in front of the couch. Auntie sat on the couch. The youngest of the three men with long black hair introduced himself as Uncle Chong Ma Lee. Their stares and tight expression sent a wave of panic through me.

"*Niam tij*," Cher Thai called Mother. "I heard you have no family members here." He looked from Mother to me. "As a member of the Vang clan, I can be your representative. We're here because Xa was arrested last night. Someone called the police on him."

I swallowed a laugh. Emily did kick Xa's butt for me.

Cher Thai continued. "We're trying to get the authorities to release him. Bride kidnapping is illegal in America, but we've practiced the tradition for generations. Shoua Nu said Xa almost died during the war. Since then, he has good and bad days. Xa thought it was okay to marry the traditional way." He threw me a sharp look. "You know the trauma we all went through in our country. There are only eight Hmong families in the area, including your family. We are all a family. Xa being in jail hurts us all."

I sympathized with Xa's service in the war and understood how well trauma could drive people mad, but I wouldn't forgive him. By giving me the promised gifts then lying in saying I had accepted them, that proved he knew he was breaking the law.

"If word gets out that a Hmong man was arrested for kidnapping a girl, it will bring shame to us all," Chong Ma said. "Mai Lee said that early this morning, news reporters were at the police station wanting to know about last night. Mai told them that the issue was a lack of communication that will be dealt with in the Hmong community."

"We're a small community," Cher Thai said. "We don't want to be shamed for practicing our traditions. For the sake of our people, we're asking you to tell the police that you and Xa had a dispute, and you ran away."

The Hmong community was willing to cover up a man's crime to save face. I hated that girls had no value in our community. My pain didn't matter. Heat roiled in my belly. If the men were too ashamed to have Xa in jail for practicing a tradition that was against the law, they had better give him a consequence.

"I would like to speak," Mother said.

Cher Thai nodded.

"My daughter is too polite to say this, but I will. For Auntie's sake, she told the police that she and Xa had a dispute, and she ran away."

Pride filled me at my mother's bravery. I wanted to add that they should be happy I lied to cover up Xa's crime, but bit back the retort. Without a father or a brother, I couldn't anger them. If they disowned us, we would have no one to turn to for traditional rituals. The old traditions rendered me powerless as a girl, and my dependence on others made me worthless.

"Thank you," Shoua Nu said. "I appreciate it very much. I was worried that Nou may not agree to get Xa out and had asked Cher Thai and Chong Ma to come along for support."

"Without any relatives, we rely on all of you and will do what is best for our Hmong community," Mother said. "But I almost lost my daughter. She's a good daughter who considers everyone above herself. She lied to the police to save Xa. I'm asking you to provide a pig and two chickens to do a hu plig for her."

Shoua Nu nodded. "I'll take care of the hu plig on behalf of my son." He stood.

"Uncle, I need Xa to leave me alone," I said.

"I'll talk to him," he replied.

The other Uncles and Auntie stood. Mother said goodbye to them, and they left. I went back to bed with a throbbing headache.

I slept until lunch, then ate and watched TV with Nhia. A knock sounded at the door. Mother opened it and greeted Mai. A moment later, they entered the living room.

"Hi, Mai," I said.

"Hi, Nou. How are you?"

"Okay."

Mother sat on one side of the sofa beside me.

Mai sat on the other side and hugged me. "Sorry, I was busy talking to the police this morning and didn't have time to visit you at the hospital."

"It's all right."

"I was shocked Xa tried to force you to marry him and I'm sorry you got hypothermia." She smoothed my hair. "I'm happy you're okay now."

"It's a blessing to have her back," Mother said.

"Yes," Mai agreed. "Xa has been released, but he goes to court on January third. You have to be there too. I'll pick you up from school."

I scowled. "Why do I have to go?"

"You need to testify."

"The judge wants the truth," I murmured. "This means the Americans are trying to help me."

Nhia grabbed my hand. "Auntie, I need to go to the bathroom."

Mother stood and led Nhia to the bathroom.

Mai leaned close. "Nou, bride kidnapping is wrong, but you must understand that adjusting to this new country is difficult for our people. Some of us have depression, and we're ashamed to seek help."

I nodded. "Mother refuses to see a doctor for her health, even when I beg her."

"I think the shortage of Hmong girls made Xa bride kidnap. Your cooperation will help the Hmong in this case," she said.

My temples throbbed. Usually, respect kept me from speaking my mind, but Mai was a woman. She had to understand.

"So, it's Hmong versus Americans? I hate Xa for creating this problem. I might be the only age-appropriate girl for courtship in the area, but there must be girls in other states. I don't want any trouble for my family or anyone else." I shook my head. "Now I have to pick a side and choose between telling the truth or saving face. Mai, lying to a judge is a disgrace."

"I understand," she said. "I'm sorry you're being forced to choose. I pray you make the right decision."

By, *the right decision*, she meant lie to the judge to save Xa.

"More Hmong refugees will be arriving," I said. "We need to help them adjust and educate them about American laws and how to be good citizens. We should also help those already here."

She patted my hand. "I'm glad you brought this up. The Refugee Migration Services needs a Hmong to work for them and asked me, but I was pregnant and sick, so I refused the job. I can't work until my baby is older, so if you're interested, I'll let them know. I think your English is good enough."

A job helping Hmong?

"What exactly is the job?"

"Helping Hmong refugees resettle and providing them resources. Sometimes, translate for them. You have school, but you can work after school or on weekends."

I couldn't contain my excitement. "I'd love that! Please give me their phone number."

"They know me, so I'll talk to them and have them call you."

I smiled. "I believe that if I can help my people understand their new country and educate the community about the Hmong's existence, there will be peace for everyone."

"Absolutely." She stood. "My baby is probably hungry. I'd better get going. Call me if you want to talk or need anything."

"I will. Bye."

"Bye." She went to the kitchen and the door creaked open and closed.

When Mother and Nhia returned from the bathroom, Mother said, "Mai left already?"

I nodded and she sat with me on the sofa.

"Mother," I said, "I'm sorry for not telling you that I took Xa's watch and ring. He tricked me into taking them. I never loved him."

"I know. I was surprised when the messengers said you liked Xa and accepted his promised gifts."

"The ring is in the ring box on top of the dresser. I put it there after I came back from the hospital. You can give it to Auntie or Uncle when you see them. I left the watch on Xa's bed."

"I'll give the ring to Auntie when I see her." Mother went to the bedroom.

I lay on the sofa, my mind on the job at the Refugee Migration Services. I had an opportunity to help my people, so they wouldn't suffer as I had.

39

Abanging of pots in the kitchen brought my attention to the clock. The short hand pointed to five. Mother must be cooking dinner. I should help now that I felt stronger. I was glad it was Friday. The weekend would give me time to recover and attend school on Monday.

I rose from the sofa and slowly walked to the kitchen. Mother was cleaning the rice pot to cook rice.

She looked at me. "Nou, go back to the living room. You need to rest."

"I'm better. I can help," I said.

She put the pot on the counter, took my hand, and turned me back to the living room. A knock at the door startled us. We looked at each other and Mother walked to the door. I hoped it wasn't the uncles again.

She opened the door and Peter entered, carrying a bowl of food. Emily followed, then Mary and Tom. But I only had eyes for Peter and hurried to meet him. He handed the bowl to Mother.

Peter hugged me. "Are you strong enough to walk?"

"I should try. I plan to go to school on Monday."

He lifted me into his arms and carried me the few steps to the kitchen table. I laughed heartily. Mother put the bowl on the table and watched, but I was no longer ashamed.

"Yay!" Emily cheered.

Peter seated me on a chair by the table. "I'll serve you, my princess."

Again, I laughed.

Peter smiled. "Got you to laugh."

"Nice work, Peter," Emily said.

I held my stomach to calm down. "Hello, Emily."

Tom and Mary set the large plastic wrapped covered bowls and bags they carried on the table.

"Hi, Tom. Hi, Mary," I said.

"Hi, Nou," Mary replied. "Glad to see you laughing." She bent and hugged me. "How are you feeling?"

"All right."

She straightened. "We were worried about you."

"Thank you."

Mary hugged Mother and asked how she was doing. Mother didn't understand, so she just nodded.

Emily pulled a chair up next to me and set her bowl on the table. "Peter said you like pasta Alfredo." She pulled the plastic wrap off the bowl to reveal the fettuccine in alfredo sauce.

I gasped. "It is my favorite. Thank you."

"The food was Peter's idea," Tom said.

"One less meal you have to worry about," Mary said. "You have so much on your plate."

Tears pricked my eyes. Is this what it would be like to be part of Mary's family?

Mary uncovered the food. Besides the pasta, they had brought grilled brats, hamburger patties, and salad. She pulled bags of chips, buns, and canned soda from the bags, along with paper plastic plates and disposable utensils.

"Let's eat, then we can talk," Mary said.

Mother went to the living room to get Nhia.

Nhia took one look at the table and broke into a huge grin. "Soda!"

Laughing, Peter opened a can and handed it to him. Nhia and Mother took their plates to the living room. The rest of us ate at the kitchen table.

"Emily, it's delicious," I said.

She smiled and the corners of her eyes crinkled.

I looked around the table, grateful for these people who had done so much for my family. "Thank you for the food, everyone."

"You're welcome." Mary took a bite of her brat.

"Emily, thank you for calling the police," I said.

"I freaked out when your nephew told us that Xa took you to be his wife," she said around a mouthful of chips. "I knew you didn't like him."

"You did the right thing."

She laughed and gave me a high five.

"When the police came, I explained what I knew," she continued. "I found Peter's phone number in your notebook by the TV and called him. He came over, and we stayed with your mom and nephew. I had to leave when my mom picked me up, but Peter stayed with your family."

"Can you tell us what happened?" Mary asked.

"Xa picked me up from school, saying my mother wanted us to buy juice. He took me to his house and forced me to marry him. I begged him to send me home, but he refused. At night, I managed to get away. I didn't have my coat and shoes and got hypothermia."

Mary's brow furrowed. "Your mother needs to press charges. Kidnapping is against the law."

Peter clenched his jaw. "Did he hurt you?"

I knew what Peter meant and shook my head. "I escaped."

"I'll help you handle the legalities," he said.

"I go to court in January," I said.

He nodded slowly. "Good."

"Nou," Tom said, "as your sponsors, it's our job to protect you. We're concerned about your safety and wellbeing. Is there anything we can do to help?"

My father would have said something like that to me. I missed him. I wanted the Johnsons' protection, but only if it didn't create problems for the Hmong community.

"Very nice of everyone for helping my family. I'll ask if I need help."

We talked about school. Our conversation warmed the house and reminded me of my brother and sister-in-law. I wished they would come to America so we could be a family again. Life would be easier if my brother was here to deal with Xa. With him, Mother and I would be able to hold our heads high and express our anger more openly, and the uncles would be forced to respect us.

Still, the social support the Johnson family and Emily provided filled my heart with hope. In Hmong society, extended family was the center of support. Mother, Nhia, and I didn't have blood family, but we did have people who cared about us.

After dinner, Mary and Peter cleaned up and put the leftovers in the refrigerator. Peter carried me to the living room, then he and his family left. The house suddenly felt empty. I missed Peter. I wouldn't see him until next weekend. I went to the window and stared outside.

Mother joined me and stroked my hair. "Peter is a great man. I like him."

I looked at her. "Do you like him as much as Pheng?"

She looked out the window. "They're both good men. The problem with Peter is that I can't communicate with him, and I don't want to go to church. If you marry him, I don't know if he'll be comfortable with me staying with you. You're my only child. I want to live with you until it's my time."

"Of course you'll live with me."

She smiled gently. "Only if Peter agrees. "

40

For our breakfast, Mother reheated the leftover food from yesterday. She had brats with rice and Nhia and I had pasta Alfredo. The phone rang, interrupting our breakfast. Mother picked up the phone, said a few words, thanked the caller, then returned to the table.

"Mai is bringing us some steamed fish."

"How wonderful!" I cried. "We haven't eaten steamed fish since the refugee camp."

Mother nodded. "We won't have to cook lunch."

Ten minutes later, Mai arrived and set the container of fish on the counter.

She hugged me. "How are you doing, Nou?"

The phone rang again, and Mother answered it. She pulled the long cord into the hallway, and I wondered who she was talking to.

I returned my attention to Mai, who stared at me expectedly. I smiled. "I'm doing better. Thank you for the fish."

"You're welcome. I thought I could help with food."

"Very thoughtful of you. I appreciate it. We love fish."

Mai smiled. "I'm glad. I have to get going for my breakfast."

We said goodbye and Mai closed the door behind her.

Mother returned. "The uncles are coming to talk to us about you and Xa."

"Again?" I blurted.

The uncles arrived twenty minutes later. As Mother opened the door for them, I took Nhia to the bedroom and told him to play with his toys until the men left. My stomach turned over when I entered the living room to find Xa sitting between his father and two uncles. I kept my gaze down as I sat next to Mother on the sofa.

"Nou," Cher Thai said, "Xa wants to marry you and asked us to talk to you again. He loves you very much. As a Vang clan representative, I want you to marry him. It's best for you to have a husband to take care of you and your family."

I stared at the carpet. "Uncle, I'm sorry I can't marry him. I don't want to get married now."

"You don't have an extended family or a brother to look after you. Anything can happen to a girl. You should consider it."

"My answer is no."

"You don't want to marry me because the white man is better?" Xa said in a tight voice.

I snapped my head up. Of course, Peter was better than him, but I couldn't say that in front of the uncles.

"He's our sponsor's son. He's just doing the job of a sponsor," I managed in a cool voice.

"If he weren't around, you would marry me," Xa snarled.

My cheeks burned with indignation. "I'm not going to marry anyone anytime soon."

He smirked. "But you accepted my watch and ring."

Shoua Nu cleared his throat. "You accepted my son's watch and ring. You must marry him, as custom dictates."

My stomach roiled. "I didn't accept them willingly. He tricked me into taking them." I straightened my shoulders. "We live in America now. We don't have to follow the Hmong traditions. I put the watch on Xa's bed. He can have the ring back."

"My daughter has never liked Xa. He tricked her into taking the gifts." Mother fished in her pants pocket and retrieved the ring. She handed it to Cher Thai, who examined the ring carefully.

"It's an expensive ring," he said. "Nou, you accepted it. Your acceptance was your agreement. You must marry him." His eyes shifted to Mother. "Niam tij, you know our tradition. You must reinforce it."

"Xa told me they weren't promised gifts." I gave Xa the evil eye stare. "Tell them the truth!"

A sly smile spread across his face. "Nou, you loved me and accepted the gifts, but you changed your mind because of the white man."

Everyone's eyes fixed on me. The air in the room grew thick. My throat burned, and dizziness hit me in waves.

"You're lying." I shifted my gaze to Cher Thai. "We live in America. You can't force me to marry Xa."

I suddenly wished I already had the job at the Refugee Migration Services. Having a job title would give me authority and force them to take me more seriously.

Cher Thai shook his head. "The white man may be handsome and tall, but he doesn't know our ways. He might like you now, but not in ten years. Divorce is shameful. The Americans have a high divorce rate."

I had to bite my tongue to keep from reminding him that Xa's father had divorced Xa's mother to marry a younger woman.

"Don't take any chances," Cher Thai continued. "You'll be better off marrying Xa."

I straightened. "I won't marry him."

"Xa, is it true that she didn't take your gifts willingly?" Chong Ma asked.

"She accepted them willingly."

"Liar!" This was too much. He made it impossible for me to act like a proper girl. "I don't like liars! I need an honest husband." I hardly recognized the strength in my voice.

"We're not here to argue," Shoua Nu said in a high-pitched voice. "Let me ask you one more time. Did you take his watch and ring?"

"He tricked me." Tears streamed down my cheeks. "He even went so far as to threaten to take his own life if I didn't accept the ring."

Uncle Shoua Nu acted as if I hadn't spoken, and said, "If you had accepted only one item, perhaps an exception could be made. But to accept two items is a definite yes. You agreed to marry Xa."

I longed for my father and brother. If they were here, the men would show me some respect. I drew in a deep breath. "Uncle, I respect you and all the uncles. Please don't force me. We have a court date in January. I can still tell the judge the truth."

The room froze in a moment of complete stillness.

"Who are your witnesses?" Xa sneered.

I hated him so much I couldn't look at him. Xa's mother witnessed how much I had fought when he kidnapped me but, even if she would testify against him, the uncles would never listen. It never crossed my mind that people could be this evil. I should have told the police the truth. What an ignorant and inexperienced girl I was!

"Your family was the witness. They may choose to lie, but God saw everything. You will be punished."

Xa snickered. "I'm not afraid."

"Enough," Chong Ma said. "We're in America now. We can't force her."

I sagged with relief. Thank God he understood.

"You're right." Cher Thai sighed. "We did our best, but we can't force Nou to marry against her will. We're in America."

Xa's expression darkened. He fell to his knees before Mother.

"Auntie, I beg you. Please make Nou marry me."

"Get up," Mother said in a cold voice. "I respect my daughter's decision. If she doesn't want to marry you, I won't force her."

"Xa, in Laos, we could make her marry you, but in America,

we don't have the authority to make those decisions," Chong Ma said. "We must follow the law. You can find another girl who loves you."

"There are no girls in this area." Xa rose and huffed. "I'll wait for Nou until she's ready to take me as her husband."

His eyes glimmered with tears. He went to the kitchen and the door creaked open. I hoped he'd find a wife from another city or state soon.

"Marriage is off." Cher Thai handed the ring to Shoua Nu.

I swiped away a tear. "Thank you, Uncle Cher Thai."

He nodded. "Take good care of your mother and nephew."

"I will."

As the uncles rose to leave, Shoua Nu stepped closer to me. "We can't make you marry my son, but don't put him in jail." He turned and followed the others out.

I went to the bedroom to get Nhia.

"The men are gone?" he asked.

"Yes. You can watch TV now."

He frowned and jumped to his feet. "Did you cry?"

I blinked. "Yes. The men weren't nice."

"Auntie, I can yell at them. I'll protect you."

I could no longer hold back the flood of tears. I squatted and hugged him tight. "It's so nice of you."

He kissed me on the forehead. "I love you."

"I love you too."

Nhia made me feel like myself again. My heart burst with pride. He had spoken out when Emily came looking for me. This little boy had saved me. He would grow up and be our man.

41

After Mee and I took our seats in English class the following Monday, she asked why I hadn't come to school last Thursday and Friday. I was no longer ashamed to disclose the truth, so I told her everything.

Her eyes widened in disbelief. "What a fool! Xa shamed our Thao clan. I can't believe it."

Sharing the same clan, Xa was like a brother to Mee, so I understood her embarrassment. When a member of the clan did something awful, it brought shame to everyone.

"I didn't think it could happen, but it did, so you must be careful," I said.

She nodded. "Thanks for telling me. I'm sorry Xa bride kidnapped you."

The bell rang.

"It's a lesson learned," I said, and faced the chalkboard.

Mrs. Bell said, "For our grammar lessons, we'll do a quick review on adjectives and adverbs before studying prepositions. Who can tell me the difference between an adjective and adverb?"

A few students raised their hands.

I didn't understand adjectives and adverbs or the pronouns

lesson prior to my absence, so how could I catch up? I imagined the mountain of missed work in all my classes. My head felt heavy and tight like a blood pressure cuff being inflated on my head.

During lunch, Emily, Mee, and I sat in our usual spot between the bleachers and took out our lunches.

Thud!

I sprang from my seat, heart pounding. My lunch bag fell on the floor.

Emily grasped my hand. "Sit down."

I looked around. Everyone was eating and socializing. "What was that noise?"

"Someone threw a basketball from the bleacher to the floor. Are you ok?"

I picked up my lunch bag and sat down, heart still pounding. "Yes. Just a little jumpy."

"I know. I can't imagine what you went through," Emily said. "Hey, I have some news that might cheer you up."

"Awesome," I managed in a steadier voice than I felt.

"I learned that Jacob Shine has a sister named Kate. She graduated with Peter. She had a crush on him, but he was dating Susan. When Susan broke up with him, Kate thought she had a chance with him. Then you came along."

So that confirmed my suspicion. Kate liked Peter, and Jacob was her brother.

"Thanks," I said. "I need to find out if she told Jacob to bully me."

Mee nudged me. "The Jacob in our English class bullied you?"

I smiled at Mee. She had understood the conversation. Her English was getting better. "Yes. If he bullies you, you let me know," I said in English.

"You let me know too," Emily said.

"Okay," Mee replied in English.

During recess, I watched Jacob for an opportunity to talk with him, but he stayed with his friends.

The next day, I hurried to English class, put my materials on my desk, then waited outside the door. I saw Jacob walking my way, so I walked toward him. He smiled when I reached him.

"Hi, Jacob. Can we talk quick?"

He stopped. "What's up?"

"Is Kate your sister?"

He hesitated. "Yeah. Why?"

I tried my best English with him. "She likes Peter Johnson, right?"

His expression turned wary. "Yeah."

"You know, Peter is my sponsor. He helps my family because I can't drive. Kate can't be mad at me. Did she tell you to bully me?"

He hesitated again, then shook his head. "It was all my idea. When you showed up, she became depressed. It made me mad that you stole the guy she likes." He started toward class, and I matched his pace.

"Thank you for telling me. I understand now."

I was envious of Kate for having a brother who deeply loved her, but a brother who caused trouble for innocent people was disgraceful.

We reached the classroom and took our seats.

I thought back to Peter's graduation when I'd met Kate. Jacob had been there. He'd stared at me. She must have told him about me then. Did Peter know Kate had a crush on him?

After school, I called Peter, despite the expensive phone bill I'd have to pay.

"Nou, is everything all right?" he demanded.

"No. Peter, do you know Kate Shine?"

"Yes. Why do you ask?"

I exhaled. "The bully Jacob is Kate's brother. He bullied me because you love me. I learned that Kate loves you. Do you love her?"

"She calls me a lot, but I consider her a friend. Kate and I aren't dating. She suffers from depression, and I try to help her."

So, they had been talking. My chest tightened.

"Nou, are you there?"

"Why didn't you tell me?" I demanded.

"I'm sorry. I didn't know it mattered, and I didn't know her brother was the kid bullying you. But you've got to believe me, Kate and I are just friends."

I released a heavy breath. "I understand. Talk to you later. Bye."

He paused, then said, "Okay. Good night."

I hung up the phone and started slowly toward the living room. For Jacob to call me a sponger and throw eggs at me, Peter must have told Kate where I lived and that we received money from the AFDC program. I wasn't mad at Peter. He couldn't have known that he was at the center of my bullying problem. I couldn't undo the past, but what I learned would better prepare me for the future.

Around six o'clock that evening, as I read to Nhia on the sofa, someone knocked on the door. My heart sped up. Mother was in the bathroom and wouldn't hear the knock. I looked out the window. The streetlight cast a dim light on the darkened walk below and I didn't recognize the car parked at the curb.

I turned on the kitchen light and went to the door. "Who is it?"

"It's me, Peter."

I opened the door and blurted, "What are you doing here?"

"I got worried." He stepped inside and closed the door. He embraced me, then pulled back. "I talked to Kate. She didn't know anything about her brother bullying you, and I didn't know he was the bully. If I'd known, I would have taken care of the situation right away. I'm really sorry."

I couldn't believe it. He had talked to Kate, then drove all the way here to explain. "It's okay," I said. "It's good now."

"Kate and I are friends from high school," he went on. "She asked me out, but I don't have feelings for her. I love you."

My heart soared. "I love you too."

He leaned in for a kiss.

"We kiss outside," I whispered.

Peter opened the door, and we stepped outside. The cold air gave me goosebumps. He unbuttoned his coat and pulled me against his warm chest. His heart pounded. I closed my eyes. Then his lips touched mine. Heat rushed through me from head to toe. The door cracked open, and we jumped apart.

"Nou, are out here?" Mother asked.

Our warm breaths curled in the cold air. Thank goodness it was dark.

"I'm coming in. Just getting some fresh air."

"Nhia wondered where you were," Mother said.

She left the door open, and I waited until her footsteps faded, then said, "I don't think my mother knows you're here. She won't be happy if she knows I'm kissing you in the dark."

I glimpsed his grin in the dim light filtering out from the kitchen.

"Okay," he said. "I should get going. Seeing you made me feel better."

He pulled me close and kissed me again. He released me and I wished he would stay forever.

"I love you, Peter."

"I love you too," he whispered. "Good night."

"Good night."

I watched until he reached the bottom of the stairs, then disappeared around the house. I closed the door. The tingling in my body lingered, and I put my feelings aside. I read to Nhia, then worked on my homework, the work that promised a bright future. Hopefully, with Peter.

42

December arrived. I couldn't wait for the frigid winter to be over. The freezing wind froze me to the bone as I stood at the corner of the school's entrance. I caught sight of Mee on the sidewalk and waved as I did every morning. Mee lived two blocks away and walked to school. She smiled and hurried toward me.

"Hi," I said, as she reached me.

"Hi." Mee put her backpack on the step and unzipped it. "I'm done drawing the story cloth for you." She pulled out a clear plastic bag that contained the cloth and a variety of colorful threads from the backpack and handed it to me. "My mother provided the different threads. If you run out, let me know. I'll give you more."

"Mee!" I cried. "Thank you so much." I hugged her. "You and your mother made it easy for me. I was worried about where I would find threads."

"My mother brought the threads from Thailand," she said. "We don't know where to find them here, either."

"How much do I owe you? Please, I want to pay you."

She shrugged. "None. I'll need your help someday, so it'll even out."

I knew it was rude to accept money from friends or family members in our tradition. I retrieved my only ten-dollar bill from my wallet and pressed the bill into her palm.

"No!" she cried. "Don't do this!"

Nearby students turned and stared. We both smiled.

"Keep it," I ordered. "Can't let them think we're crazy."

"All right." She put the money in her backpack.

Mee was the oldest of six children. Her younger siblings attended elementary school. The Good Shepherd Lutheran Church sponsored her family, and I knew they needed the money.

The bell rang. We went to her locker near the door. She removed her coat and grabbed her English materials, then we walked to my locker. Three girls, one with a brown hair, one with curly hair and one with blonde hair, walked just ahead of us, giggling.

"That Oriental girl is a weirdo," the blonde-haired girl said.

"Let's follow the girls," I said to Mee in Hmong.

She nodded and we stuck close to them.

"Look at the gook's clothes," the brown-haired girl laughed. "An ugly brown sweater with dress pants and sneakers."

"Who dresses like that?" added the curly-haired girl.

"Are the girls talking about us?" Mee asked in Hmong.

"Yes. I'll explain later."

Mee headed to her homeroom around the corner, and I followed the girls on the way to my homeroom. They continued to make fun of Mee. Mee often dressed in mismatched colors and styles. Because we were poor, Mee and I received our clothes from the church and the clothes closet.

Peter and Mary had helped me pick my clothes and told me what looked normal. I should have known better and taught Mee. I had heard the word *gook* a few times and looked it up in my dictionary, but I didn't understand its meaning. I kept forgetting to ask Peter to explain it.

The girls stopped by a locker and the curly-haired girl said, "Yesterday, our history teacher asked her a question and her face turned bright red. She almost cried."

The girls laughed. I clenched my jaw. These ignorant girls had no idea how difficult it was to go from a small village in a rural area to a modern city, from thatch huts to houses, from manual labor to school. Everything was new to us, and we didn't know better.

When Mee and I met in English class later, I asked her if people were mean to her. She said people made comments she sensed were rude and laughed at her, but she didn't know what they were talking about.

"Have you heard people say *gook* to you?" I asked.

She nodded. "Yes. Often. The first few times I heard the word, I thought it was *good*. As I listened carefully, I realized that it was a different word. Do you know its meaning?"

"I think it's a bad word," I said. "A few kids called me *gook* too."

Mee bit her bottom lip.

"I'll ask Mrs. Bell later."

During reading time, I stood and walked to where Mrs. Bell sat at her desk.

She looked up and smiled. "What can I do for you, Nou?"

"Mrs. Bell, students call Mee and me *gook*. What does it mean?"

Her eyes widened. "They called you that?"

"Yes. Today, three girls called Mee that. Mee heard the word many times. I heard it a few times. I don't know the meaning."

Her mouth thinned. "It's not a word students should use."

"The students laugh about Mee's clothes," I said. "We're new here. We don't know how to dress. We don't have money for nice clothes."

"Do you know the three girls' names?" she asked gently.

"No. I think they're seventh graders."

"I'm so sorry students are being cruel to you and Mee. It's not okay to call people names and make fun of their clothes, or to be mean. I'll talk with Mr. Sherman, and he'll address this issue. Thanks for telling me. And Nou, if any students are mean to you again, you tell me. Ok?"

I nodded and returned to my desk. The more I learned, the more I felt like an outsider, unworthy of respect. Sadness weighed heavy on my heart. Maybe it was better not to know so much.

At lunch, Emily, Mee, and I sat in our usual place. We had all packed sandwiches. Emily had a thick slice of meat in her sandwich. Mee and I didn't have much meat in ours.

"Emily, why were you absent yesterday?" I asked.

"My grandma is sick. My dad and I went to see her at the nursing home in Milwaukee."

"What is a nursing home?"

She stared. "Geez, you don't know?"

"I don't know." I bit into my sandwich.

"It's a home where old people live, and nurses take care of them."

I frowned. "Your grandmother has your father. Why is she not living with him?"

She chewed her food. "My dad works and doesn't have time to take care of her. It's better for her to be in the nursing home."

"And she's okay with that?"

Emily shrugged. "Yeah."

"Why is your grandmother in Milwaukee and not in Appleton?"

Emily stopped eating. "Geez, you ask too many questions."

"I'm curious."

"My aunt lives there. She works, too, and can't take care of my grandma, but she can visit a lot."

I couldn't believe it. Americans put their elderly parents in nursing homes? My mother would be terrified and depressed if she lived away from us. A nursing home would be appropriate only for elders who didn't have children to care for them. I would never send my mother away. When I arrived home, Mother told me that Mai called to inform me to expect a phone call from the Refugee Migration Services. Excitement churned in my stomach, as Nhia and I played with his toys in the living room. I kept glancing toward the hallway leading to the kitchen, as if I could make the phone ring. At four o'clock, the phone rang. I hurried to the kitchen and picked up the receiver.

"Hello, this is Nou," I said.

"Hi, Nou. I'm Sara Goodfriend from the Refugee Migration Services. How are you?"

"I'm good."

"Mai told me that you're interested in the Hmong resettlement job."

"Yes. I am. I can work after school and weekends and full time in the summer."

"Good. I have a Hmong man from Wausau who is also interested in the job. The only day he can come for an interview is Wednesday, December 27, which is three and a half weeks from today. I'd like to interview the two of you the same day. Are you available that day at two-thirty p.m.?"

I placed a hand over my heart. "Yes."

"Good. Mai will stop by the office to pick up an application for you. Since you can't drive, you can complete the application and bring it the day of the interview."

"All right. Thank you."

"I'll see you then," she said.

"See you soon. Bye." I hung up and leaned my forehead against the phone.

This was too good to be true. This job would give me the opportunity to help my people. This job would also enable me to buy a car. I was one step closer to my dreams. I straightened. But what chance did I have of competing against a man who could drive and work full-time?

43

Since today was Wednesday, and I had no tutoring session with Emily, I played with Nhia and read to him before doing my homework. At eight o'clock, I finished my history assignment and marked it complete in my student planner. Looking at the calendar, I realized Xa's court date was a month away, the first week of January. I had to decide what to tell the judge. My decision would affect people's lives. My heart started to beat fast. What was the right thing to do?

A knock came at the door. I looked up in surprise. Who would be here so late and without calling? Peter? My heart soared. Mother entered the kitchen as I stood.

"Who is it?" she asked.

"I think Peter." I hurried to the door and opened it to find Susan standing on the landing.

Mother stepped up beside me. "Do you know her?"

"Hello," I said to Susan, still in shock, then said to my mother in Hmong, "This is Susan, a friend of Peter's."

"Hi, Nou," Susan said. "Do you remember me? I'm Peter's friend. We met at the library."

I nodded. I remembered. I had given her my number because I

hadn't wanted to be rude, but I hadn't expected her to call me, much less come to my house. How did she know my address? Who gave it to her? Could it be Peter?

"I'm sorry to come by without calling," she said. "But I need to talk to you. I hope you don't mind."

Something told me I should mind, but I said, "I don't mind. Please, come in."

She smiled, and Mother and I stepped back as she entered.

"I see you're doing homework," she said.

"Yes." I shoved my papers in the history book and set them aside. "Please, sit down."

She glanced at Mother and hesitated before sitting in the chair nearest where I stood.

"What does she want?" Mother asked.

"I don't know," I said without inflection. I didn't want Susan to know we were talking about her or that I was nervous. "Why don't you watch Nhia? I will see what she wants," I told Mother.

Mother nodded, though I could tell she was worried about leaving me with this girl she didn't know, and she went into the living room.

"Would you like something to drink?" I asked Susan.

"No, thank you," she replied. "I went to the library yesterday, but you weren't there. Do you still go there?"

I sat in my chair. "Yes. Emily and I go on Monday and Wednesday."

"Oh, I'll remember that. You know, Peter speaks really highly of you." She leaned toward me. "Can I share something about Peter and me?"

My insides quivered. "Sure."

"Before graduation, Peter and I were very much in love. But we had a problem. No matter how much we tried, his parents and I couldn't convince him to go to college. So, I broke up with him in hopes that would induce him to go to college. You know, just a threat. I didn't mean to end our relationship."

My head began to swim.

"Then you showed up. You motivated Peter. You're the reason he's in school. I want to thank you for that."

Her words were nice, but I wasn't sure she was truly thanking me. "Is that all?" I asked but knew she had more to say.

She didn't answer right away, and I hoped I was wrong, that she really had only wanted to thank me for helping her friend. Then she said, "I love Peter and can't move on."

My legs went weak as rubber. What was I supposed to say? I expelled a shuddering breath. "What do you want from me?"

Silence filled the room.

Finally, she said, "Nou, you seem like a great person. I admire your courage in coming to a foreign country."

I waited.

She straightened and met my gaze. "You haven't known Peter long. I've known him for years. I've loved him for years. I'm sorry, but you need to walk away."

My heart stopped. I wanted to tell her that I loved Peter, too, but said, instead, "Does Peter know you're here?"

Dear Father, please say Peter didn't send her to break up with me.

She gave a slow nod. "You're a smart girl. I know you understand what I'm saying."

Did this mean Peter didn't know she was here? Did that matter?

"Does Peter still love you?" I asked.

"Yes."

Was Peter's heart divided? Maybe he had never loved me but had used me to make Susan jealous. Would she have the courage to come here and face me if he didn't love her? I loved him. What should I do? I needed time to think. I couldn't make a good decision when I was hurt and overwhelmed.

"Can I have your phone number?" I asked.

She gave me the number and I wrote it in my notebook.

Susan stood and I walked with her to the door.

She opened the door, then turned and looked at me. "Peter and I are made for each other. We're alike. You know in your heart that he and you are too different."

Before I could think of a reply, she left. I sat back down in my chair and stared at her number. Susan wanted Peter back. She said Peter still loved her. Had they stayed in contact?

Uncle's words popped up in my head. *He might like you now but might not in ten years. Divorce is shameful.*

The vice around my heart tightened. I stood and filled a cup with water. Tears slid down my cheeks. I hated my life. The obstacles were a weight I feared would break me. I gulped the water, then breathed deep until my head cleared a little. Mother came in. I quickly wiped my tears away, then splashed water on my face.

"Nou, you don't look well. Are you all right? What did she say to you?"

"Nothing important," I said. "I have a headache. I'm going to bed."

She stroked my hair. "Okay. I'll stay with Nhia until his bedtime. You rest." She turned and headed down the hallway.

I glanced at the closed math book and wondered how I'd get the assignments done with a pounding head and broken heart. I started to cry again and rushed outside. I sat on the stairs in pajamas and slippered feet and cried until I was shivering. How foolish. Staying outside in so little clothes could give me hypothermia again.

I went inside to bed and snuggled under my blanket. As my body heat returned, I tried to process the new information. Three women loved Peter. Was Susan right? Were Peter and I too different? I was a minority with a different religion and culture, and of a low-class status with little education. Did that make me unfit for Peter?

Mother and Nhia came to bed at ten. Once their even breathing told me they were asleep, I got up and called Peter.

He picked up the phone on the third ring. "Hello."

"Peter. It's Nou. Sorry to call you this late."

"It's okay. You sound like you have a sore throat. Are you ok?"

I steadied my voice. "Yes and no. I have questions for you."

"Okay. Give me easy questions," he said in his calm, husky voice.

"You told me your grandmother lives in Florida. Does she live in her home or a nursing home?"

He chuckled. "Why do you want to know? I thought you call to tell me how much you miss me."

"I'm curious."

"All right. She's in a nursing home."

I couldn't believe it. "Why?"

"Well, she doesn't like Wisconsin's cold weather and my uncle works, so it's better for her to be in the nursing home."

Work was the excuse Americans used to put their elderly parents in nursing homes? "When your parents get old, will you send them to a nursing home?"

"Hmm. Maybe," he said.

I closed my eyes to suppress the pain that unfurled in my heart.

"Do you still love Susan?" I asked in a low voice.

"Whoa! Nou, where's this coming from?"

"I want to know."

"Okay," he replied slowly. "She calls me sometimes. She says she can't move on." He paused. "I do have feelings for her—I've known her a long time. But I love you."

"Okay," I whispered. "Thank you. That's all I need to know. Have a good night."

"Aren't you going to say you miss me?"

"I miss you and will always love you," I said from the bottom of my heart.

He released a heavy sigh. "I love you. Good night."

I placed the receiver back on the hook.

In bed, while Mother and Nhia slept, my thoughts swirled

around Peter. He was an alluring, kind, and caring man. The man of my dreams. I liked the American culture and could easily assimilate.

In the dream I'd had when in the hospital, Father told me not to disappoint Mother. I was my mother's only hope and I had promised to be a son to her. A good son cared for his mother until the day she died. I could never abandon her in a nursing home.

Would Peter divorce me if I refused to send her away?

44

On Wednesday, I arrived at my locker to find Liz and Ava standing at the locker beside mine.

"Hey, Nou," Liz said.

"Hi," I replied, my voice barely a whisper.

They had laughed at me in the past and I suspected they didn't like me. I hoped they didn't intend to cause me trouble.

"Do you know that Peter loves my cousin, Susan?" Liz said. "He told Susan that you're cute and kind of interesting, but you two are so different. Don't you think it's better for you to break up with him?"

Had Susan asked Liz to tell me this?

"Did you tell other students I date Peter?" I asked.

Liz's mouth tightened. "Of course not."

I didn't believe her.

"Excuse me, I can't be late for class." I pushed past them to my locker.

I pulled out the books I needed and hung my backpack in my locker. Tears slipped past my resolve. I swiped at my eyes with the back of my hand. Were they right? Were Peter and I too different? Could love overcome the differences? If Peter truly loved me, would he talk to Susan about me? Had he been talking to her of our differences?

I tried to focus in my classes, but I hardly comprehend a word the teachers said. My thoughts kept drifting to Peter and how he'd been shocked when my mother blew her nose into the grass. Maybe Peter's love for me blinded him to our differences, but how long would it be before my mother's ways embarrassed him so much that he insisted we send her away? How much conflict would arise between us when she insisted on performing Hmong rituals in the house Peter and I shared?

During lunch, Mee was absent, leaving Emily and I by ourselves. Today was the first day I wished I was eating alone.

"Nou, are you okay?" Emily bit into her sandwich.

"No."

She swallowed her food. "What's wrong?"

I stared at my sandwich. "Peter and Susan still love each other."

"Oh. I'm so sorry." She put her sandwich on the bag and hugged me.

I wrapped my arms around her, glad for the comfort. I pulled back. Emily ate her sandwich and listened in silence as I told her about Susan's visit to my house and Liz's conversation.

"If you love Peter, fight for him," she said. "If he's not worth the fight, then let him go."

My eyes shifted to her. "I love him and will fight for him. But...."

"But what?"

"We're so different."

She pressed her lips in thought. "Maybe. I'm not trying to be mean. You two are very different."

I didn't believe Xa, Susan, or Liz, but if my friend agreed that Peter and I were different, then maybe we really were *too* different.

Two days later, on Friday, I started cooking pasta Alfredo for dinner as soon as I got home. I wanted to make sure the food was ready when Peter arrived. Mother didn't care for pasta, so I boiled chicken with herbs for her.

When the food was ready, Mother and Nhia ate. While I cleaned their dishes, a knock came at the door. My heart picked up speed as I wiped my hands on a cheap towel I had recently purchased. I hurried to the door and opened it. Peter smiled at me.

"Hi," we both said simultaneously.

Peter stepped inside and we embraced. He glanced at the hallway, no doubt looking for Mother, then kissed me. My heart nearly broke. This would be the last time I kissed him.

We pulled apart and I nodded to the table. "I cooked pasta Alfredo for you."

He smiled broadly. "Let's eat."

He sat at the table. I served him a plate of fettuccine Alfredo and a cup of water. Then, I served myself and sat opposite him. He ate a mouthful of pasta and looked at me.

"Aren't you going to eat?" Peter asked.

"I don't feel like eating."

"Don't waste food." He forked pasta into his mouth.

I picked at my food, but the hollow feeling in my belly refused to take anything. I studied Peter's profile. I adored his blue eyes and full pink lips. I nervously tapped the cold, vinyl floor with my foot.

Peter frowned. "Are you ok?"

"Yes," I whispered.

He set his fork on the plate. "You look nervous. Is something wrong?"

"Eat. I'll tell you after." My voice wobbled.

"I'm finished." He pulled his chair close to me and grasped my hands.

"What's going on?"

I hugged him. Why was this so difficult? I should have called him and told him over the phone. I pulled away, then gathered my courage and met his gaze.

"Peter, Susan came to see me."

He frowned. "What?"

I stared at the table. "Did she tell you that she broke up with you to make you go to college?"

He hesitated, then said, "Yes."

I looked at him. "I've been thinking about you and me."

"Does this have something to do with your asking about my grandmother?"

I sucked in a deep breath. "I love you with all my heart. But I don't want to ruin your life. I know you still love Susan, and she loves you. She's a much better fit for you than me. You two will make a perfect cou—"

"Stop," he cut in. "*You're* perfect for me."

"I have my mother and Nhia," I said gently. "My mother won't attend church, and she will never live in a nursing home. Peter, I could never—I don't want to—put her in a nursing home. It is my job to take care of her. Can you imagine her living with us until she dies?"

Surprise flared in his eyes.

I nodded sadly. "Nhia's father may not be able to come to America for years. I will continue to raise him until he's an adult, if necessary. Are you prepared to help me raise him and care for my mother as she ages?"

Peter opened his mouth to reply, but I quickly added, "I know you love me. That isn't a question. But you cannot deny that my family will burden our relationship." I took a deep breath. "It's better for you and Susan to get back together. I don't want you to lose her. You take a chance with her, the woman you loved before."

His mouth thinned. "Did Susan convince you to break up with me?"

I lifted my chin. "No. My love for you is too strong to allow her to interfere. This is my decision."

A cloud passed across his face. He stood and ran a hand through his light brown hair.

I stood and grasped his shoulders, so that he was forced to meet my eyes. "Peter, I am sorry. You know how hard this is for me. But God has a plan for you. He's giving Susan back to you. She's the perfect woman for you."

He turned away. I hated myself for hurting him. Indecision unexpectedly gripped me. I loved Peter. Was I being stupid?

The silence stretched out.

Finally, his gaze met mine. "She broke my heart, but God directed me to you, and you healed the wound. Now, when I'm whole and happy, she wants me back. But I love you."

I had to be strong. "I know. But it's not enough. Give her another chance. I will always love you. I hope you don't hate me."

His mouth parted in shock. "Hate you. No. I—"

"Peter—"

He shook his head and left without saying goodbye.

I dropped onto the nearest kitchen chair and cried.

45

That following Sunday, I wasn't sure if Peter would take us grocery shopping and to the laundromat. If he or Mary didn't come, I would take the city bus to the store and do laundry.

To my surprise, Peter came after church. I was happy to see him, and I could tell he was glad to see me too, but the tension between us nearly broke my heart again. Memories of our kisses surfaced, but I reminded myself to be strong.

"I thought you wouldn't come anymore," I said.

"It's my duty to take care of your family until you're self-sufficient. Your breaking up with me doesn't mean I won't help you anymore. I don't hate you."

"Thank you for understanding."

We sat at the table.

"Christmas is approaching," he said. "I want you to write a wish list of what you, Nhia, and your mother want. The list is for Santa Claus."

"Is Santa Claus real?" I asked.

"What do you think?"

"I don't know. In the TV, he is real, but I think it's only in movie."

"I'll let you decide whether he's real or not."

How was I supposed to know?

I talked to Mother and Nhia about what they wanted. The first thing on Mother's wish list was to find out if her three daughters from her first marriage were still alive and to reunite with them. The second one was to have a garden in the summer, and the rest of her wishes were for clothes. Nhia wanted toys.

I had one thing on my wish list. I wrote a letter to Santa Claus. Peter edited the letter.

Dear Honorable Santa Claus,

Thank you for your love and caring for children and unfortunate adults. My family are refugees from the war-torn country of Laos. My sixty-five-year old mother, an amputee, my four-year-old nephew, and I, seventeen, are the only survivors from my family who made to America. We have no family members or relatives here and have been relying heavily on our sponsor to drive us around. We are a burden on the people who know us. I want my family to be self-sufficient. My family has been saving every penny but without a job, I don't know when we'll save enough for a car. My wish for Christmas is to have a car. An old car that still works would be great. I hope you can grant me my wish.

Thank you.
  Sincerely,

Nou Vang, the Dreamer

Peter put the wish list papers in his coat pocket. He took us grocery shopping and to the laundromat.

On Monday, at the beginning of English class, Mrs. Bell asked me if I would consider doing an all-school presentation in the auditorium. The teachers had discussed the name calling at their staff meeting, and the staff felt that it was important to educate the students about the Hmong, where we came from, and why we came to Appleton.

I hesitated, uncertain if I could do a presentation for the entire school.

A tinge of concern crossed Mrs. Bell's face. "The speech you did in class was excellent. Your story touched us. We'd love you to do it for the whole school."

"All right," I said slowly. "When do I present?"

"The last day before Christmas break, which is Friday, the 22nd."

That gave me two weeks to practice.

Lunch was the best part of the day because I could relax and spend time with my two friends. First, I told Emily about the presentation. She hooted. Then I told Mee. Her eyes widened in fear.

I nudged her. "I've done a class presentation before. The kids liked it."

Mee gave an uncertain smile. "I'm worried the students will make fun of you, but if you can do it, then do it."

"I'll be okay. Don't worry." I turned to Emily. "Emily, I have a question."

"What?" She chewed her food.

"Is Santa Claus real?" I unbagged my peanut butter sandwich.

"Geez, you don't know? Silly girl." She laughed.

My ears heated with embarrassment. "This is my first Christmas."

A lock of Emily's auburn hair fell on her eye, and she tucked it behind her ear. "Oh yeah, I forgot. Santa Claus isn't real."

I frowned. "Then who gives you presents?"

"Parents, grandparents, and relatives."

Mee tapped me on the arm. "Did Emily say Santa Claus isn't real?" she asked in Hmong.

"Yes. Did you know?"

She shook her head.

I returned my attention to Emily. "Gosh, I am brainless. I think Santa is real, and I wrote him a letter for a car."

Emily nodded slowly. "Hmm. That's a smart idea."

"No. I don't have family members to buy me a car."

"Who did you send the letter to?"

"I gave it to Peter. He asked for a wish list."

"Maybe Peter's family or his church will grant you your wish. You know, needy families get presents from rich people."

I didn't want Peter's family to buy me a car. They had done so much for us already.

When I got home, Mother told me that Auntie had called and said the soul calling for me would be in the summer when the weather was nice. Auntie hoped that I was feeling better and that I would make the right decision when testifying against Xa in January.

I had the presentation and job interview to worry about, and I planned to finish the story cloth for Peter before Christmas. With schoolwork, I had too many things on my mind. Once Christmas was over, I would think about Xa, and how I would testify.

46

Friday night, I embroidered the story cloth in the living room with the TV to keep me company.

The phone rang. I hurried to the kitchen and picked up the receiver.

"Nou?" replied a deep male voice.

"Yes. Who are you?"

"Pheng Yang," he said. "My family arrived in Minnesota today."

I squealed. "Pheng! You're in America!"

"Yes!" he cried. "How's everyone?"

My breath caught in my throat. "We are doing good. We miss you. Come to visit."

Mother entered the kitchen as Pheng said, "We're coming tomorrow morning. Can't wait to see you all."

I met Mother's gaze and squealed again. "Tomorrow! Who's bringing you?"

"My cousin. He said the drive would take about five or six hours. I'm so excited, I don't think I can sleep tonight."

I smiled from ear to ear. "Try to sleep, so you're not cranky with puffy eyes tomorrow."

"I'll try. Are you still at the same address from the letters?"

"Yes."

"All right. We plan to leave early, so see you tomorrow morning!"

"Bye."

"Pheng's in America?" Mother said as I hung up the phone.

I grinned. "Yes!"

A smile bloomed on Mother's face.

"No Xa, no Auntie, no worry. Pheng is here." I thrust a fist into the air. "He'll help us take care of Nhia and help with the traditional rituals."

A tear trickled down Mother's cheek.

Pheng was her dream son-in-law, but Der was dead. In the refugee camp, he visited us every day and proposed to me, but I refused because I wanted to come to America. His presence would warm her heart.

I scooped Nhia up from the sofa. "Your daddy is coming to see you."

"Daddy?" He grimaced.

"Yes. Do you remember him?"

He shook his head.

"You have a daddy. You'll see him tomorrow." I kissed his forehead, put him down, and returned to my embroidery.

When the phone rang an hour later, I looked at Mother. She shrugged and I hurried to the kitchen.

I picked up the receiver and said, "Hello."

"Nou?"

Peter's voice caught me off guard and my heart leapt.

"Hi, Peter," I said.

"I, uh, wanted to see how you're doing," he said.

I closed my eyes in an effort to hold back tears. He was such a kind man.

"I'm ok," I said.

He remained quiet for a long moment. "Ok, I was just checking. I guess I'll talk to you later."

"Peter," I said.

"Yes?" he replied so quickly that it made my heart ache. Was he still hopeful that I would reconcile?

"I...." How could I ask him for the favor I needed?

"Yes," he said in a low voice.

"Never mind."

"Nou, please. What is it?"

I hesitated. "My teacher asked me to give the speech you helped me with to the whole assembly."

A beat of silence passed, then he said, "I'm not surprised. It's very powerful."

"Thank you. I am going to make some changes. I wondered...." I couldn't say the words.

"Of course I'll help you," he said without hesitation.

"You're too kind," was all I could say.

"I love you," he said. Before I could reply, he added, "I'll come next Sunday, as usual?"

"That would be great," I managed, and wondered how I would manage to keep from crying when I saw him.

By midnight, my fingers ached from the embroidery, and exhaustion made it difficult to keep my eyes open. I wanted to give the story cloth to Peter as a Christmas gift, but I might not have it done on time. I had to get some sleep.

Mother and I rose early the following morning. I cooked rice, pork stir-fry with cabbage and broiled chicken wings. When I finished cooking, I joined Mother at the living room window and watched while Nhia watched TV. The snow stood about a foot high on the sides of the road, but the clear roads meant Pheng's journey would be safe.

At eight-forty a.m., a gray car pulled up and parked on the street. Two people got out. I recognized Pheng.

I turned to Nhia. "Your daddy's here."

I picked him up and the three of us went outside and waited at the top of the stairs. Without our coats on, we were all shivering by the time Pheng reached us.

A huge smile creased Pheng's face. "Nhia!"

"Your daddy," I said to Nhia.

Nhia hid his face on my shoulder. Pheng's bright almond shaped eyes locked on mine and his smile showed perfect white teeth. He was still the same handsome man.

"Come inside," I told them, and they followed us into the kitchen.

I turned to face Pheng, and he said, "I missed you all. Nou, you're beautiful."

My cheeks heated in embarrassment. Mother liked Pheng and wouldn't care he showed affection, but I didn't know his cousin who was staring at me. Pheng looked at Nhia.

"Turn to your daddy," I said to Nhia. "He loves you."

He turned slightly to peek at Pheng then twisted back to hide his face in my shoulder. Mother greeted Pheng and hugged him.

Then she said to the man behind Pheng, "Who are you?"

"I'm Teng Yang." The strap of a black briefcase hung on his shoulder.

"Nice meeting you, Teng," I said.

"Nice meeting you, too, Nou. Pheng told me a lot about you."

I looked at Pheng.

He grinned. "All good things."

"You two must be tired and hungry," Mother said.

I put Nhia down and Mother held his hand and led the men to the living room while I put food on the table. A minute later, Pheng returned to the kitchen. I set two cups of water on the table.

He beamed. "I can't believe I'm here with you and my son.

This is a dream come true." At twenty-two, he seemed as young as Peter, who was nineteen.

I gave him my biggest smile. "I can't believe it either. We missed you. Life has been hard, and we often wished you were here."

He sighed. "Thank God, my ancestors, and Heaven, your mother, and my son are well."

"God?" I blurted. "When did you learn about God?"

"In the camp. I prayed to Him and Der to protect our son."

I fought tears at the mention of my sister. Nhia had been born out of wedlock, but if Der hadn't been shot, she and Pheng would have married, and Nhia would know his father. I prayed she was proud of Nhia and happy that Pheng was finally here.

I grabbed two plates, spoons, and forks from the dish drainer, then set them on the table. "Have a seat."

Pheng sat. I went to the living room. Mother and Teng stopped talking as I approached.

"Teng, go eat with Pheng." I sat on the sofa beside Mother.

He stood. "Come, we all eat together. In Laos, the men eat first but in America, we all eat at the same table." He motioned for Mother and me to go with him.

Mother stood and I followed.

"Nhia, time to eat," I said.

Playing with his toys by the corner of the room, he shook his head. "I eat in here."

"Come eat with your father."

"No."

I hesitated, unsure if I should force him to eat with us, then decided he needed a little time to get to know his father. I went to the kitchen, got Nhia a plate of food and returned to eat with the men.

After we filled our plates with food, Pheng said, "Auntie and Nou, thank you for cooking us breakfast."

Mother's eyes shimmered with moisture. "You're welcome. I

have looked forward to this time when we would eat together like we used to in the camp. I'm so happy you're here. Let's eat."

Pheng's expression brightened. "Thank you, Auntie."

We ate, and Mother asked Pheng questions about his parents and siblings and asked Teng about Minnesota. Lively conservation filled the room and Mother beamed. Her happiness warmed my heart.

After our meal, we sat in the living room.

Pheng pulled a white envelope from Teng's briefcase and handed it to me. "Your brother Toua sent this letter."

I opened it and took out a picture and a letter. The picture showed Toua, his wife, and their child with another couple and five children. I gave the picture to Mother.

"Do you know the couple in this picture?" I asked her.

Mother studied it for a moment, then gasped.

"Who are they?" I demanded.

"My daughter, Youa," she said through tears.

"She's alive?" I said in awe. "Thank you, my ancestors, God, Father, and Der for bringing my sister to Thailand. Mother, you have two daughters now."

For the first time since Der's death, my heart felt full.

I read the letter aloud.

December 11, 1978

Dear Nou and Mother,

I hope you are all doing great. My family is doing fine. I performed the soul release for Der and Father.

I have good news to share. Mother, your daughter Youa and her family found me. They arrived in the camp recently and I have enclosed a picture of us together. Youa convinced me to come to

America with her family. My family and hers want you to be our sponsor. Our hope is to reunite with you within a year.

Both our families are low on food. If you have money, please send us some.

Goodbye,

Toua Vang

I couldn't believe it. I turned to Pheng. "Have you met my sister?"

"No. But Toua told me her family is healthy and doing fine."

I had saved a hundred and ten dollars from picking strawberries. We intended to use the money for a car, but my brother and sister needed money. I would send them eighty dollars. I prayed I would get the job at the Refugee Migration Services to send them more money and to save for a car.

47

Teng took us to Shopko that afternoon. Once inside, Pheng stared down each aisle in awe.

"It's a huge store," he said, as we followed Nhia to the toy section.

Along the way, Mother and Teng went off in another direction.

"Is this the first store you've been to in America?" I asked.

"Yes. I just arrived yesterday."

Approaching the toy aisle, Pheng said, "Wow! Lots to choose from." He looked around both sides of the aisle. "Nhia, pick a toy you like. Daddy will buy you one."

As Nhia browsed, Pheng edged closer to me. "Nou, you have been a wonderful mother for my son."

He paused and my heart began to beat fast.

"I believe Der would approve of you continuing as with his mother. I...I miss Der, but I know we must move on. Would you consider me as a husband?"

I blinked in surprise.

"My son needs a loving mother. Someone like you. I know this is soon," he continued in a low voice. "I only ask that you consider the possibility."

My heart ached. How I had longed to hear similar words from Peter. I looked at Nhia and couldn't help a small laugh. He pressed several toys against his chest while still looking for more. Peter had never given me even the tiniest indication that he would accept Nhia as his son. I loved the little boy with all my heart and wouldn't be able to part with him and I knew it would be the same for him.

I looked at Pheng. "I love Nhia, but I also have dreams."

His brow furrowed in confusion, then cleared, and he said with a soft smile, "I will support you as best I can."

I gave a small nod. "I'll consider the possibility."

He smiled. "Thank you."

"Auntie Nou," Nhia said, his arms filled with toys.

I squatted to his level. "You have too many toys. Pick one that you like the best."

He looked down at the bundle of toys, then handed me a Magna Doodle drawing board.

"Put the rest back," I gently urged.

I stood and when he had put the other toys away, I said, "Say thank you to your daddy."

Nhia held my leg and said, "Thank you."

"You've taught him well," Pheng said.

We walked to the candy section.

"What does Nhia like to eat?" Pheng asked.

"M&M's and chocolate bars."

Pheng grabbed one of each and put them in our cart. We went to the boy's clothes section, and Pheng picked out a shirt and pair of pants. We joined Mother and Teng by the checkout area. Pheng paid for Nhia's items. I wondered how he got the money.

In midafternoon, after our errands and chores were completed, I made Pheng play with Nhia and me. I gave Pheng the Superman action figure and Nhia the Spiderman action figure. I had the T-Rex toy. Nhia and I played with his toys often, and we knew how to play our games. Pheng didn't, so I whispered in his ear. The T-Rex chased Spiderman, bit his leg, and wouldn't let go.

"Help!" Nhia cried.

Pheng, playing the part of the Superman toy, flew over and yelled, "Daddy's coming!" Superman pulled off the T-Rex and saved Spiderman.

"Daddy is powerful!" Pheng shouted.

Nhia laughed. We laughed with him. We played again with different acts and different toys. After that, Nhia read from the picture books. His smooth reading brought tears to Pheng's eyes.

"Nhia has been translating for Mother," I told Pheng. "He can be your translator too."

Pheng's mouth fell open. "How did he learn to read and speak English when he's not in school?"

"We read every night, and he learns from TV."

"I...I owe you so much," Pheng whispered. "I have no words. You're everything to this child."

I laughed. "I try."

"Thank you for everything."

"You're welcome. It's my duty to my sister."

He smiled. "My son will be my teacher and translator." Pheng turned to Mother. "Auntie, we plan to leave at ten tomorrow morning, and I'm wondering if we can stay here overnight. I need more time with Nhia."

"Please make this your home. You stay where your son is. We're a family. If Der were here, you'd be my son-in-law," Mother's voice cracked. "We have a bed for you and Teng."

"Thank you."

That evening, Pheng helped me cook dinner. Unlike Xa, he was the oldest child in his family, so was accustomed to helping his parents and siblings. He was thoughtful and skillful. I understood why my sister had loved him.

As we ate dinner, Pheng said, "You have a nice house and good food. God has truly blessed you."

I swallowed my rice and said, "We have wonderful sponsors. If not for them, we would still be in the refugee camp."

"I hope to meet them someday," Pheng said. "I have to thank them for taking such good care of my family."

I froze in taking a bite of chicken.

Pheng frowned. "Is something wrong?"

I stared at him, unable to find my voice. Mother stared down at her food and Pheng exchanged a confused look with Teng.

"Peter!" Nhia cried.

Pheng looked from his son to me.

I took the bite of chicken and forced myself to maintain eye contact with Pheng. "Peter is our sponsor's son. He tutored me."

Pheng's brow furrowed, then he nodded slowly. "I can understand that. Any man would be lucky to tutor you."

I couldn't believe it. Xa had become crazy with jealousy at the mere mention of Peter. But Pheng seemed to recognize that I had a right to a life and...maybe he was also saying that I was an attractive woman? He smiled gently and, once again, I understood why my sister had fallen in love with him.

After dinner, Pheng refused to sit and stood at the sink with me, rinsing the dishes while I washed them.

"Cleaning dishes is a woman's chore. You don't have to help me," I said.

"Teng said we men need to help women do chores in America. He helps his wife. I want to get in the habit."

Nhia came into the room and stopped next to me. "Auntie Nou, my hand is sticky."

I lifted him to the sink. Pheng moved the faucet to my side of the sink. I washed Nhia's small hands, then turned off the faucet. He avoided Pheng's eyes.

I kissed Nhia's cheek. "Turn to your daddy."

He turned slightly.

"This man is your daddy. He loves you as much as Auntie Nou and Grandma. I want you to call him Daddy. Can you do that?"

He smiled, his dimples deep, but remained mute. Nhia had Der's dimples, his father's almond eyes, and a high, long nose.

"We met him in Thailand, and he brought you candies every day," I said. "Say 'Daddy'."

Pheng learned in Thailand not to touch Nhia because he was a traumatized child, so waited patiently for Nhia to be ready.

Nhia rested his head on my shoulder and whispered, "Daddy."

Pheng's eyes glistened with unshed tears.

"Come on. Look at your daddy," I urged.

He peeked at Pheng. "Daddy."

Pheng burst into tears.

"Your daddy cries because he's happy," I said. "Please hug him. If you hug him, he'll stop crying. It's magic."

Pheng extended his arms for his son. Nhia leaned over and allowed Pheng to pull him close. Pheng stroked Nhia's hair and kissed him on the cheek. I forced back tears. This was the first time Pheng had held his son. In Thailand, Nhia wouldn't relax around Pheng or any man. Maybe he learned to trust men after having Peter and Xa around. My heart constricted. Yet one more thing I had Peter to thank for—maybe even a little thanks belonged to Xa.

"Take him to the living room and play with him," I told Pheng. "I'll finish the dishes."

Pheng lifted Nhia up above his head and Nhia laughed all the way to the living room.

By the time I finished the dishes, swept the floor, and prepared food for the next day, it was eight-thirty. I joined everyone in the living room and noticed Nhia asleep on Pheng's shoulder as Pheng cuddled him close on the sofa. This time, I couldn't hold back the tears. Nhia needed his father's love and affection. The war had denied him his parents' love and affection. I wiped my tears with my hand quickly. Mother and Teng sat on chairs beside the sofa and their conversation about fleeing the Secret War echoed in the room.

I sat next to Nhia, unable to take my eyes off him, his cheek pressed against his father's shoulder. Der would be so happy. Her wish for Nhia to be with his father had come true. Nhia almost died from starvation during the trek through the jungle. My father, ancestors, and God had given me the courage to bring him to safety to start a life with his father. Their lives together stretched out in my mind's eye. They would be so happy. More tears filled my eyes. I had never been so grateful.

"Take Nhia to bed," I whispered.

Pheng stood, cradling Nhia, and I walked them to the bedroom. There, I pointed to the middle pillow of three and he lay Nhia down and tucked him in.

"I can't believe he still sleeps with you and Auntie," Pheng said.

"My mother doesn't want to sleep in the other room alone, and Nhia is also still afraid. So, we sleep together."

Pheng slipped his hand into mine and we watched Nhia sleep.

The following morning. I boiled a whole chicken and cooked rice for Pheng and Teng's lunch. Our tradition was to pack lunch for guests who traveled a long distance.

The men were to leave at ten, but Pheng delayed their departure because Nhia was in the bedroom teaching Pheng words from our picture books. Nhia said the word, and Pheng repeated it, just as Peter taught me and I taught Nhia.

The phone rang, and I yanked my attention from wrapping the chicken to the phone. Could Peter be calling? He was coming over this afternoon to help me with my speech. Pheng had been very sweet about my "tutor", but I didn't want to cause any unnecessary conflict. The phone rang again.

I hurried to the phone and picked up the receiver. "Hello."

"Hello, Nou, this is Auntie Shoua Nu."

I started at hearing her voice.

"I just wanted to see how you and your family are doing," she said.

I pursed my lips. More likely, she wanted to see if I had reached a decision about Xa.

"We're fine, Auntie. Thank you." I didn't want to be rude, but I didn't want to talk to her either.

Two seconds of silence passed, and I opened my mouth to say goodbye, but she said, "Nou, Xa is very sorry for bride kidnapping you. He now understands that the laws and traditions in America are different than ours."

I prayed she was right. I could almost have forgiven Xa acting upon our traditions, but.... "He lied about me to you and the uncles," I said in a low voice. "That is *not* part of our tradition."

"I know," she quickly replied. "And the uncles have warned him never to do such a thing again."

Most likely they warned him to save face for themselves and not to save some other poor girl from being bride kidnapped.

Mother came into the kitchen and gave me a questioning look.

"Auntie, we have guests," I said into the phone. "I'm sorry, but I have to go."

"Oh, of course. I-please say hello to your mother for me."

"I will," I said, and hung up the phone.

"Who was that?" Mother asked.

"Auntie Shoua Nu." I turned to the counter where I had been preparing the food.

"She wanted to know your decision about Xa?"

"Who's Xa?"

Mother and I whirled to face Pheng and Nhia.

My heart began to pound. "I—"

"Xa hurt Auntie," Nhia hurried to me and hugged my leg.

Oh, heaven, this child was too smart. I picked him up and he wrapped his arms around my neck and laid his head on my shoulder.

Teng entered the room. "We need to get going, Pheng."

"Just a minute," he said, his eyes locked on me. "What happened?"

"Nothing of importance." As a little girl, I had told white lies, but never had I told a serious untruth like this. But I couldn't let Pheng know what had happened. Only God knew what he would do if he learned what Xa had done.

Pheng looked at Mother. "What is this decision you're talking about, Auntie?"

Mother blinked, then looked at me, panic in her eyes.

"Xa asked me to marry him, but I said no," I said. This wasn't a lie.

Pheng frowned, then shifted his gaze to his son. "Nhia, how did Xa hurt Auntie?"

"Pheng," I cut in sharply. He looked at me in surprise. I took advantage of his sudden confusion, and said in a firm voice, "Don't talk to Nhia as if I'm not here. I'm an adult. I can speak for myself, and I am telling you, it is nothing of importance."

He hesitated, then said, "If it's nothing important, why won't you tell me what happened."

I lifted my chin. "Because it's none of your business."

He studied me for a moment, and my pulse skipped a beat when I recognized the intelligent, strong man Pheng had become.

"If something is wrong, you would tell me?" he said in a quiet, but firm voice.

I gave him a tremulous smile. "I would. As you can see, we're all right."

It was clear, he wasn't completely satisfied, but he said to Nhia, "Daddy has to leave. Daddy will be back to play with you soon."

"No. Don't leave, Daddy." Nhia extended his little arms toward Pheng, and Pheng pulled him close.

"Daddy doesn't want to leave you, but he has paperwork to

finish." Eyes on Nhia, he said to Teng, "You head out to the car. I'll be right there."

Mother grabbed her coat and followed Teng outside.

I extended my arms to Nhia. "Come to Auntie. Your dad has to go now."

I took him from Pheng. Pheng wrapped his arms around us, kissed Nhia on the cheek then pressed a kiss to my forehead.

"I'll be back to take care of all of you," he whispered.

A tremor rippled through my stomach. "Bye," I said.

Nhia and I followed him outside. We joined Mother at the top of the stairs and watched Pheng walk down the stairs and to the curb where the car sat. As they pulled away, Pheng waved to us, and we waved back.

Once back inside, I forced myself to work on my speech, but my thoughts kept returning to Pheng's words *"I'll be back to take care of all of you."*

I still loved Peter very much and worried about how I would handle seeing him today. So, why did I suddenly feel strange about Pheng? I couldn't deny my relief at the prospect of having a man to help me with caring for Nhia and Mother—and there was no doubt that Pheng would help care for Mother. She was his son's grandmother. We needed Pheng.

How foolish I was. Heroes weren't supposed to need anyone.

When a knock sounded at the door an hour later, my heart skipped a beat.

Peter.

Memory of the pain I had caused him muddled my brain and I sat frozen until a second knock sounded. I hurried to open the door. He stood there, tall and handsome as always.

"Hi, Peter."

"Hey." He walked in but didn't hug me or try to steal a kiss as he usually did.

Sadness tinged his expression. How I wanted his eyes to sparkle as they always had.

As we had done so many times in the past, Peter and I sat at the table. He read and edited the speech. Then I practiced speaking, enunciating every word slowly and clearly. He was still the same Peter, complimenting, praising, and encouraging me.

"I'm so glad you don't hate me," I blurted.

He frowned. "I couldn't hate you. You did what you thought was best."

"Yes." I dropped onto the chair opposite him. "I'm so lucky to know you."

A sad smile touched a corner of his mouth. "I'm the lucky one." He paused. "I'm considering being a teacher."

"What?" I said in surprise.

He gave a slow nod. "You taught me how much I love teaching."

I covered his hand with mine and gently squeezed. "Thank you for everything you have done for us."

He squeezed my hand back, then I pulled away.

"You'll do great on your presentation," he said. "I don't think you need more practice."

I put my speech paper in my folder. "Peter...would you and your parents come to the presentation?"

He nodded slowly. "Ok, I can come. I'll see if they're free."

He rose to leave and, this time, I hugged him goodbye.

48

On Monday, Mrs. Bell confirmed that I had twenty minutes for my presentation. A few students would perform in a talent show and the band would play afterward. Knowing that I wouldn't be the only person on stage lessened my anxiety a bit.

Emily and Mee encouraged me each day at lunch, and I practiced my speech every night before a mirror. Peter called me twice during the week to check on me and give me support. He said that Santa Claus loved hardworking, caring, kind, and ambitious girls. If I did well, there was a good chance I'd get what I wanted for Christmas. I scolded him for not telling me the truth that Santa wasn't real.

Thought of the whole school watching me on stage kept my stomach in knots, but I reminded myself how much my speech would help the students understand me and my family, as well as other Hmong like Mee.

On the morning of the presentation, I dressed in my necktie, a long-sleeved, cream blouse, and black jeans. I applied a little foundation makeup to my face, enhanced my eyes with charcoal eyeliner, and added some copper glow eye shadow to my eyes.

Some pink lipstick gave my lips a wet, glossy look. I tucked my long hair behind my ears. My new look boosted my confidence. I felt it made me look smarter.

The whole school assembled in the auditorium at eight-fifteen. Waves of anxiety washed over me. I spotted Peter, Mary, and Tom in the back of the auditorium. My heart swelled with gratitude, and I wondered if it might burst. My mother and Nhia hadn't come because Nhia would be unable to stay quiet around so many people.

I picked my way over to Mary, Tom, and Peter. "Thank you for coming."

Mary smiled. "We're happy to be here." We embraced, then she looked me over. "Look how beautiful you are."

I blushed. "Thank you."

Peter hugged me. "You'll do fine. Good luck."

I hugged Tom.

"Good luck," Tom said.

"Thank you."

I walked to the front of the auditorium and placed my folder of pictures next to the projector on the cart. Mrs. Bell would show each picture through the overhead projector when I gave her the signal. I had borrowed the pictures from Mai because visuals would help the students understand my message better. In addition, Mee had drawn a picture of my family before the war—my whole family.

In the front row, I sat in the first seat. My heart thumped so hard that I thought the student sitting next to me could hear it. On the stage, Mr. Sherman quieted the audience, welcomed everyone, and introduced me. He told the audience how quickly I had learned English, how I advocated for myself, and how brave I was to do a presentation in front of the whole school. He called me to the stage. I sucked in several deep breaths as I climbed the stairs to the stage. The audience welcomed me with applause.

I took the microphone from Mr. Sherman. "My name is Nou

Vang. I'm in ninth grade. I am a dreamer. My father had some education. He taught me that communication is the key to understanding others. I want to thank Mr. Sherman and all the teachers for giving me this opportunity to tell you why we, the Hmong people, came to America."

I paused and gave the signal. Mrs. Bell put the picture of Mother, Nhia, and me on the overhead projector.

"This is me, my mother, and my nephew. My mother's arm was amputated due to a gunshot wound during our journey through the jungle to safety in Thailand. My sister died during the trek, leaving her son for my mother and me to care for. I promised her I would help raise her son. Raising him in America was my dream. I have big dreams for him and I."

Mrs. Bell replaced the picture of us with one of General Vang Pao.

"This is General Vang Pao, our Hmong leader. CIA agent James W. Lair met with Vang Pao, and they initiated the covert military operations in Laos against the Communists. The Americans promised Vang Pao land if they won the war and a place to live if they lost the war. Vang Pao recruited his people to help the Americans stop Communism from spreading in Southeast Asia. This was how we got involved in the war known as the Secret War."

I paused. "This war was called the Secret War because American citizens didn't know about it. While the Vietnam War was going on in Vietnam, the Secret War was going on in my country, Laos. My father was a soldier and he fought in the war. He was shot in the leg."

The next picture was of a burnt village.

"I was always a curious child," I said with a laugh. "I loved stories and had two books in English, but I couldn't read them. I waited for the war to end so I could go to school to learn to read. Then the Americans withdrew from the war. The enemy burned my village, destroyed my books, and killed many people. My family fled from several villages, each time in fear for our lives. Finally, we fled to the refugee camp in Thailand."

Mee's drawing of my family before the war appeared on the overhead projector. I pointed to the drawing of my parents, older half-brother, older sister, younger twin brothers, and my grandmother.

"By the time we reached Thailand, only my mother, half-brother, and I had survived. My nephew was born just before we escaped through the jungle. My father and sister were killed, and my two younger brothers died of a mysterious disease."

My chest ached with so many sad memories. I took a deep breath. "My brother still lives in the Thai refugee camp with his wife and child. I brought my mother and nephew to America for a better life. I want my nephew to love school and someday become a doctor. He loves stories as much as I do because I read to him every day." I cleared my throat. "My duties to my mother and nephew are to care for them and make sure my nephew is successful in life."

I looked at the Johnson family sitting in the back. "I would like Peter, Mary, and Tom to come to the stage."

They stood, and the audience watched as they made their way to the stage. Peter stood next to me, and Mary and Tom stood beside him. Peter gave me a puzzled look. I hadn't told him about this part of the presentation which Mrs. Bell helped me write.

"This is the Johnson family, Tom, Mary, and Peter. They are our sponsors. They are the reason we came to Appleton. A sponsor has a lot of responsibilities, and they were willing to take care of us." I smiled at Peter. "Peter is my best friend and an excellent teacher. He taught me to read, write, and speak English. He started tutoring me in English the second week after we came to Appleton. We met two times a week for about two hours each, until he started college in the fall. Besides teaching me, he also drove us to stores and the laundromat every week. He still does."

My chest tightened as tears slid down my cheeks. I looked at

Peter, and our eyes met. "You are my go-to person, a shining light for me. You have always been there for me and my family. Thank you for everything." I looked at his parents. "Mary and Tom, thank you so much for taking us in. You are the most wonderful people in the world."

I faced the audience. "Without the Johnson family, I wouldn't be standing here now." I turned to the Johnson family. "Thank you."

The audience clapped.

Peter took the microphone from me. "I'd like to thank Mr. Sherman and the staff for giving Nou this opportunity to tell her story. She's an amazing girl. I was lucky to have the opportunity to teach her and get to know her and her family. She's the reason I decided to go to college to be a teacher. If not for her, I'd be doing an assembly job in a factory. This girl has a lot on her plate, caring for her family and going to school." He paused. "Some of us are ignorant and hurt her family. In one incident, a kid threw eggs at her."

The audience gasped.

"Another kid told her family to go back to their country. Words hurt. I hope you won't do that to her. Thank you."

More applause from the audience.

I took the microphone. "My family are refugees who came to America for a better life, not to cause trouble. I just want to have friends and go to school like any teenager. Thank you for listening to my story."

The audience clapped and I handed the microphone to Mr. Sherman.

He waited for the applause to end, and everyone sat down, then said, "Nou, thank you for sharing with us. I hope everyone learned as much as I did."

I left the stage and sat in the front row as Mr. Sherman continued to talk about bullying, name calling, and being mean to others in general. When he was done and the talent show started, Peter, Mary, Tom, and I went into the hall.

Mary hugged me. "That was nice of you to thank us in front of the whole school. You didn't have to do that."

"I want people to know about your kindness."

"Well, thank you. And thank you for turning my good son into a great man. He cares for us more than ever before."

"Yes." Tom hugged me. "He calls to check on us far more often than he used to."

Peter smiled. "Congratulations, Nou! You did a phenomenal job."

We said our goodbyes and Peter gave me one final smile before he and his family left.

When the students were dismissed from the auditorium, Mee found me in the hall.

She grinned. "Good job. You looked so brave up there."

"Thank you."

"I hope to be like you someday."

I clapped her shoulder. "You will. Probably better."

"Nou."

I turned to face Emily. She pushed through the crowd toward us.

Reaching us, she said, "Awesome presentation." Emily gave me a high five. "You did it."

"Thank you."

Students I didn't know complimented me and called me by name. Throughout the morning, students greeted me in the hallway between classes and stopped to ask questions. Teachers I didn't know praised me.

Things felt different. Maybe that was because today was a half-day of school and the last day before Christmas break. Maybe it was because I finally felt welcomed.

49

All day Saturday, I worked on the paj ntaub, the story cloth. Carefully, I embroidered each person, their face, eyes, mouth, clothes, and hat. In the story, the Hmong men wore traditional black clothes with red sashes and black hats. The women wore traditional clothes with black shirts and colorful, pleated skirts. Mee sketched me with long hair and pants instead of a skirt, and I embroidered my clothes with blue thread so Peter would know it was me. At the bottom of the cloth, the United States portion, she drew Peter and Mary waiting at the airport.

As I worked, I finally allowed myself to consider Xa's upcoming court date. My respect and sympathy for Auntie had made me disclose only a snippet of information to the officer, which ended up hurting me but avoided shaming others. Xa had left me alone and the uncles hadn't tried to enforce an illegal marriage, so I wanted to save face. Still, I didn't want to lie to a judge.

By Sunday noon, when Peter usually came over after church, I was only three fourths done with the story cloth. I'd have to give him a late present. When the hands of the clock reached two and Peter hadn't come, I started to worry. Usually, he called if he was going to be late. Since we were on Christmas break, maybe he would come on Monday. Or maybe he decided he just didn't want to see me anymore.

At three o'clock, there came a tap at the door. I opened it quickly to find Mary, Tom, Peter, *and* Susan standing outside, their arms full of presents. Mary walked in and handed me a fruit basket covered in plastic wrap. Tom set a clear plastic bag of wrapped boxes on the floor. Peter and Susan each carried a wrapped box and set them on the table. I put the fruit basket on the table and hugged Mary and Tom.

"Hello, Susan," I said.

She smiled. "Nou, thank you for everything. I owe you my life."

I smiled, then turned to the gifts and studied them in awe. "Thank you all for the presents. I learned that Santa Claus isn't real, but the people who give are."

Peter laughed softly. "Now you know."

I narrowed my eyes. "Thanks for not telling me before."

"Some of the gifts are from the families at our church," Mary said.

"Please thank them for me," I said.

"We will."

Mother came into the kitchen, and Mary hugged her.

"Keep the presents hidden so Nhia doesn't know we brought them here," Peter said. "He needs to believe that Santa Claus is real. Christmas is more interesting for kids that way."

I quickly put the presents in the bedroom closet then returned.

"Let's go outside," Mary said.

I frowned. "You're leaving already?"

"No. We're all going outside," Peter said. "Bring Nhia and your mother."

My pulse sped up. Did they bring me a car? No. Who could give such a costly present? I got Nhia from the living room, then we all went outside.

A battered green car sat parked on the street. Peter opened the door to reveal a sign that read, *Merry Christmas* on the passenger front seat.

He pressed a set of two keys into my right palm. "It's your car."

A lump rose in my throat. "Thank you so much."

"Are they giving us the car?" Mother asked in Hmong.

I nodded.

She looked at them and said in English, "Thank you."

Nhia squeezed my hand.

I swiped at a tear that I couldn't hold back and squatted eye level with him. "This is our car. I can take you to the store every day, and we can go to the park in the summer. Say thank you to Peter, Susan, Mary, and Tom."

He looked at them. "Thank you."

"Good boy," I said, and stood.

"You can thank the rich man who bought you this car," Peter said.

"Who is he?"

"A member of our church," Mary said. "He's a businessman. After reading your letter, he decided to adopt you for Christmas."

"Give me his name and address. I'll write to thank him," I said.

"He wants to remain anonymous," Peter said.

"What's that?"

"Keep his name secret."

I shook my head. "I don't understand."

"Just be thankful that you have a car from a generous man. He is your real Santa Claus," Peter said.

Why wouldn't he want me to know him? Having a car was like having legs. I wanted to thank him for giving my family legs. I must not let this person down. Someday I hoped to pay forward the gift we had received.

My first dream of attending school had come true. Now my second dream had come true. I had registered for the driver education class at West High School for the third quarter. I would get my driver's license before school ended. I couldn't believe my luck. Bad things happened, but good things happened, too.

The cold weather forced everyone back inside, leaving Peter and me. We got into the car, and he explained its interior. He inserted the key into the ignition and started the car. He drove it to park in our section of the driveway. Peter said he'd take me for driving practice once I got my permit.

That night after Nhia went to bed, I put the presents by the TV.

I woke Nhia at six a.m. the following morning and carried him to the living room where Mother waited. He squealed at sight of the presents, and I told him that Santa Claus brought him gifts for Christmas because he was a good boy.

We opened Nhia's presents first. He received Batman Action Figures and toys, Tonka Trucks, books, and clothes. Mother received clothes and slippers. Mary gave me two books, *Roll of Thunder, Hear My Cry* by Mildred D. Taylor, and *The Last of the Really Great Whangdoodles* by Julie Andrews Edwards. The text in the books was difficult, but I aimed to be able to read them by summer. I received clothes too.

After all the troubles I had been through, Christmas brightened my spirit and brought hope. I hope I would get the job at the Refugee Migration Services. Having a job title would give me the power to connect and bring my people together and help organize a Hmong New Year celebration for us in this area. In Laos, around this time, we would celebrate our New Year, where the youth would play ball tossing games while the adults socialized and watched the youth sing traditional songs. It saddened me that there was no New Year celebration this year due to lack of funding and leadership in my small community.

I prayed, "Father, my ancestors and God, may the people at the Refugee Migration Services hire me."

50

The day of my job interview arrived. I completed the application with Peter's help and carried the folded document in my purse. I paced the living room carpet, as I waited for Peter.

The job was my chance to help my community and to shine. A job would enable me to financially support my brother and sister's families in Thailand. A job would give me a head start to my dream jobs as a doctor and writer. I would never have to work in the fields again. I would be off the AFDC program, and I no one could call me a sponger.

I watched out the window for Peter's car. At two o'clock, his blue car turned onto our street, and he parked behind my green car in the driveway. My heart swelled as it always did every time I looked out the window and saw *our* car.

"Mother, I'm going to the interview," I called. "Be back later."

I hurried outside to where Peter stood at the open front passenger door. He still opened the door for me even though we were no longer courting.

"Thank you," I said.

"I'm excited for you."

Along the way, I asked Peter about the type of questions employers ask during an interview. He gave me a few tips, and I practiced the answers in my head.

When we arrived, a new wave of anxiety rushed through me. I was worried about my accent. People who knew me understood me. Would others understand me?

The building was small and built of white stone. We were early and waited in the car in the parking lot. A middle-aged Hmong man walked out of the building and went to his car. He must be the other interviewee.

"I think they are done with the person before me," I said. "We should go in."

Peter nodded and we got out of the car.

In the foyer, chairs lined a wall across from a large window. A young, brown-haired woman sat behind a desk opposite the door.

"Hi. Can I help you?" she asked.

"I'm Nou Vang. I am here to see Sara Goodfriend," I said.

"Have a seat. I'll let her know you're here."

Peter and I sat. I rubbed my thumb and index fingers nonstop.

Peter laid his large, warm hand over my hands and gently squeezed. "You'll do fine."

I drew in a deep breath. A door to the left opened and an older woman with short, wavy, blonde hair emerged from inside and approached us. She looked friendly.

I stood as she reached us.

"Hi, I'm Sara Goodfriend." She extended her hand, and I shook hands with her. "Come on into my office."

I followed her into the room. She told me to sit in a chair in front of the desk, and she sat behind the desk. I handed her my application.

She read it, then looked up. "How do you say your name?"

"Nou."

"Nou, Mai has been helpful when we need her to translate, but she has a baby and can't help much. We're looking for someone who speaks Hmong and English and has a passion for helping refugees resettle. Mai told me that you are a good fit for the job. I want to hear a bit about you."

I took a deep breath, then told her about my struggles with learning English, adjusting, and understanding the American culture. I explained the troubles I experienced and what I learned from them, and how I'd use my experiences to help refugees so they wouldn't face the same struggles my family had. I told her that my goal was to help refugees become self-sufficient and successfully integrate into the community while continuing to practice Hmong traditions. I wanted the community to be supportive and culturally sensitive.

"Very impressive, Nou," Sara said. "I like the goals you've set about creating understanding among refugees and the community. How are you going to do that?"

I exhaled. "Not understanding each other's culture creates problems with religion, rituals, laws, and other issues. I gave a presentation for the students at my school about why the Hmong people came to America, and it helped them understand us. If I get the job, I can give presentations for the community. I want to teach the refugees English and help them understand the laws in America."

Sara studied me. "How long have you been in America?"

"Seven months."

"Wow! Your English is quite good."

"Thank you." I relaxed a little.

"It was very brave of you to do an all-school presentation."

"Thank you. I tried my best, and it went well."

"You told me on the phone that you can work after school, on the weekends, and full-time in the summer. Are you still able to do that?"

"Yes."

"We're fortunate to have a young person like yourself who's passionate and wants to make a difference," she said. "I know you'll do great on the job. You're hired."

I blinked. "You're hiring me?"

She nodded.

"Thank you so much," I stammered past the excitement that jumbled in my stomach. I couldn't believe she had chosen me over the Hmong man.

"The starting pay is $2.25 per hour," she said. "Mai told me that you won't get your license until summer, which is fine. We'll have someone drive you until then. In the summer, you'll work full-time. You will help all the refugees in Fox Valley, Oshkosh, and Green Bay. You'll travel, but you'll be paid for that." She took a business card from a card holder on her desk and handed it to me. "Call me if you have any questions. I'll call and talk to you more in the next few days."

"Thank you."

Sara leaned on the back of her chair. "Do you have any questions?"

I hesitated. "Yes. What is the job title?"

"Good question. Your job title is Hmong Support Specialist."

"Thank you. I don't have any more questions."

She stood and I followed suit. "Thank you for coming," she said. "I look forward to working with you."

"Thank you for the job. Very nice meeting you."

She walked me back to the lobby and shook hands with me, then returned to her office. I hurried to Peter as he stood.

As soon as we were outside, I squealed, "I got the job!"

"Already?" He grinned. "Wow! Congratulations!" He gave me a high five.

I bounced as I walked. "No more picking strawberries, tomatoes, and corn."

"You deserve this. You see, hard work pays off."

"Thank you so much for teaching me. You made a difference in my life."

We got in his car.

On the way home, Peter stopped by Dairy Queen and bought us ice cream cones. Dating or not, it didn't matter. He still celebrated my achievement, and that made him my hero.

51

Peter parked his car on the street and came inside as I requested. In the living room, Peter sat in a chair, and I sat with Nhia and Mother on the sofa and told them the news.

Nhia hugged me. "Auntie, you'll have money to buy us ice cream now."

"I don't get paid until I work, but yes, you can get ice cream."

"Yay!"

"Good job, my daughter." Mother beamed and hugged me. "You've always tried your best, and I'm proud of you."

Mother went to the TV and picked up an envelope laying there, then handed it to me. I started at seeing the letter was front the courthouse. I opened the mail and tried to read but the big unfamiliar words flew over my head. I gave the letter to Peter. He read it with his brows knitted together.

He looked up at me. "Xa's case has been dismissed. I can't believe it."

"What does that mean?" My heart pounded.

"The court doesn't need you and Xa to testify. The letter

explains that based on what you and Xa told the police officers, the judge decided it was a miscommunication between you two."

Disappointment stabbed, but I had to admit that I was relieved. I didn't want to lie to a judge.

"It's best the case is dismissed," I said. "Bride kidnapping is wrong, but Auntie needs Xa. I don't want him to go to jail."

Peter's mouth thinned. "Okay. If you're okay with it."

Whether I liked it or not, I had to forget about Xa and move on. With my job, I would prove to the community that a girl with no family had value, and that her feelings and place in society mattered.

Now, I wanted to give Peter his gift. I had made the story cloth the best possible. I sewed blue borders on four sides. The layers between the blue borders and story cloth consisted of white and gray strips along with blue and gray triangles. I had framed it in a 30x40 inch picture frame and set it against the wall by the sofa with the story cloth facing the wall.

"We'll put this letter away." I took the letter from Peter and set it on the table. "Stand here," I told him. He gave me a quizzical look, but I grabbed the frame, turned it around, and presented it to him. "This is my gift for you. I made it just for you."

"It's beautiful," he breathed. Peter traced a finger from top to bottom. "This cloth is about your journey to America." He pointed to the brown-haired man and woman dressed in American clothes. "Are these two my mom and me?"

"Yes. You and Mary were at the airport receiving us." I pointed to the girl in blue. "This is me."

"That's you trying to cross the river." He touched the girl on the raft. "The scene is beautifully drawn and stitched. Did you draw this?"

I laughed. "I can't draw. My friend Mee Thao drew the story cloth. This will help you remember the struggle of my people."

He looked at me. "You're the reason I'll never forget."

"Maybe someday you'll show the story cloth to your students about how we came to America."

He smiled. "Perhaps."

"Peter, you have done a lot for my family. We have nothing for you. We feel bad. I wanted to give you this at Christmas, but it wasn't finished. Please know that my family appreciates all your help."

"I'll always be here for you."

"Thank you."

He opened his arms, and we embraced. He hugged Mother and Nhia, as well, then left.

We watched from the window as he walked toward his car. When I first saw Peter at the airport, I had prayed that he would be compassionate. He turned out to be the most caring, kind, and big-hearted man I've ever known. He had always been there for me and my family, and remained a shining light that led me through the dark tunnel to my dreams. He accepted our breakup without hatred, repayment, or curse. He continued to be himself. He was a good role model and my hero.

He reached the car parked at the curb, turned, and looked up at our window. Our eyes met and he gave me a gentle smile that made my pulse skip a beat, then he got into his car. I stared until he disappeared around the corner.

These last seven months in America, I had felt like the meat in a sandwich, crushed by the pressures of two cultures.

The New Year would bring a new beginning. I would get my driver's license and become self-sufficient. We might even be reunited with my brother and sister and their families. But most important, this year would be better because we had Pheng.

Funny, I had thought that heroes didn't need anyone. I couldn't have been more wrong.

Everyone needs others. Especially heroes.

THE YOUNG GUARDIAN

The Illiterate Daughter
The Dreamer's Dream

To keep up on all the Scarsdale Publishing authors, join our
NEWSLETTER